drift child

Rivers Inlet

•Bear Creek Landing

Queen
Charlotte
Strait

Scarlett Point•

•Cabin

Port Hardy•   Malcolm
                     Island

Shinglewood•

Vancouver Island

Campbell River•

PACIFIC OCEAN

a novel

drift child

Rosella M. Leslie

NeWest Press

Copyright © Rosella M. Leslie 2010

Library and Archives Canada Cataloguing in Publication

Leslie, Rosella M., 1948 –
    Drift child / Rosella Leslie.

ISBN 978-1-897126-71-4

    I. Title.

PS8623.E849D75 2010   C813'.6   C2010-903640-9

Editor: Elaine Morin
Cover and interior design: Natalie Olsen, Kisscut Design
Author photo: Betty C. Keller
Proofreading: Michael Hingston

NeWest Press acknowledges the support of the Canada Council
for the Arts, the Alberta Foundation for the Arts, and the Edmonton Arts Council for our publishing program. We acknowledge
the financial support of the Government of Canada through the
Canada Book Fund for our publishing activities.

#201, 8540 – 109 Street
Edmonton, Alberta T6G 1E6
780.432.9427

NeWest Press   www.newestpress.com

No bison were harmed in the making of this book.

printed and bound in Canada   1 2 3 4 5 13 12 11 10

This book is dedicated to my husband, lover, friend, and constant supporter, John O. Alvarez.

My endless thanks to Betty Keller, Maureen Foss, Gwen Southin, and Dorothy Fraser of the Quintessential Writers Group for their critiques, insights, and encouragement.

Thanks also to the many people who so generously provided me with pictures, maps, and background information.

PROLOGUE

The father sat on the boat's only seat, his broad shoulders bent to the task of rowing. The girl fixed her eyes on the back of his red plaid shirt as he reached and pulled, reached and pulled. *My daddy.* She wore his denim jacket beneath her plastic poncho and life jacket, and she wriggled so that she could feel the fabric of the sleeves, as if his arms were holding her, keeping her safe. So long as he was there, she was not alone. Not a drift child.

Whenever the zodiac rocked wildly in the trough of the giant grey waves, she gripped the ropes fastened to the starboard pontoon and braced the heels of her runners against a plastic floorboard. The bow leapt high in the air and smashed back into the trough, pitching the girl against her two siblings. She pulled herself free, leaving them clinging to each other and the blanket they shared.

"Those two have each other," her aunt had once told a neighbour, "but this one is alone. A *drift child.*"

A gust of wind blew rain into the girl's face. *I can't see! I can't see!* She blinked and blinked, but every time she raised her head, her face was drowned anew. She couldn't breathe. *I can't see!* Bending forward, she swiped her face against the plastic covering her knee, then, looking up, squinted until she found the red plaid of his back again. Strong. Purposeful. Working the oars. *My daddy!* The words screamed inside her head.

ONE

Sunshine streamed through the skylight and fell on the mushroom-shaped mound of spinning clay. Emma Phillips compressed the mound into a solid bell shape. On the floor beside the potting wheel a large calico cat rolled playfully onto its back, tummy exposed and paws clawing the air.

"Forget it, Purkins," Emma said, pursing her lips in concentration. She was using more clay than she had ever worked with before and it was proving much harder to centre. Gently pressing downward, she formed a hollow in the top of the mound and began widening it into a bowl, oblivious to everything except the sound of the wheel and the rhythmic hum of the motor.

I'm getting it! Scarcely daring to breathe, she pulled up the sides, then took her hands away and studied the bowl. There was still a lot of clay at the bottom. *One more pull.* Smoothly applying pressure, she began working the clay upward.

Suddenly the telephone rang, and Emma's hand jerked outward. Her right foot dropped to the flywheel, braking it slowly to a stop, but the damage was already done, and as she lifted her hands away from the clay, she stared in disgust at the misshapen bowl. She cursed herself for bringing the phone into the studio, then cursed the phone because it continued ringing. Finally, without bothering to wipe the clay from her hand, she answered the damned thing.

"What?"

Taking his cue from her greeting, Sam Gabriel said, "I'm sorry to trouble you on a Sunday, Emma...."

"Uh-huh...." Her lawyer-boss was famous for turning a simple acknowledgement into such an unequivocal yes that the Supreme Court of Canada would have a hard time dismissing it.

"Kazinski called me this morning," he continued carefully. "He's probating a will and one of the beneficiaries lives in Bear Creek Landing, near Rivers Inlet. Apparently his secretary mailed the cheque to the woman before arranging to get the release signed."

Emma put the phone between her ear and shoulder and reached for her clean-up rag. John Kazinski had recently been made a partner in the Toronto law firm where Sam had worked before semi-retiring to British Columbia five years earlier. "Why doesn't he fax it to her?" she asked, wiping clay from between her fingers. "They do have fax machines in Toronto, you know."

"Well," Sam said, "for one, this Mary Dahl — she's the beneficiary — could flat-out refuse to sign it, since she's already cashed the cheque. For another, it seems she lives out on a ranch in the middle of no place. She doesn't have a phone or access to a fax machine. And for a third, the estate's executor is complaining because it's taking so long to probate the will."

Emma tossed the rag aside and took the receiver in her hand once more. "Rivers Inlet is a long way from Shinglewood, Sam. How do you plan on getting there?"

"Kazinski will pay for a charter there and back. The thing is, I'm delivering the keynote address at that conference in Vancouver this week. So it has to be you." Resorting to his usual authoritarian manner, he added, "He's emailing me the release, and the plane will be at the dock at eleven. That will get you to Bear Creek Landing by noon, and you're booked on the regular flight back tomorrow morning."

Emma glanced at the clock. "Sam! It's already ten now. You can't expect me to pack, stop at the office for the release, and be down at the dock by eleven!"

"It's the only time I could get," he said. When she didn't respond, he added, "This could mean that Kazinski will give us more work in the future."

"Right," Emma said. "Never mind that you're sending me out into the middle of God-knows-where, just so long as we maybe get some more work out of these Toronto guys — which you don't have time to do anyway!" She looked at her collapsed bowl and her voice hardened.

"I can't do it, Sam."

The line between them was silent.

"I'll pay you extra."

Emma pictured moths flying from Sam's wallet. "Five hundred bucks," she said finally. "Over and above my salary. You can add it to Kazinski's bill."

She hit the off button, ending Sam's sputtered protest, and turned back to her table as the outside door opened and a scruffy, wheat-coloured Norfolk Terrier bounded across the room. Purkins sprang onto Emma's shoulder, knocking her off balance as he leaped for the safety of a nearby shelf. Emma grabbed the potting wheel to save herself and plowed her right hand through the bowl.

"Damn it, Twill Lafferty!" she yelled, shaking a clay-covered fist at the tall, bearded man who had followed the dog into the studio. "I told you to keep Rugrat out of here!"

"And how the bejaizus am I supposed to be doin' that when he's slippin' through my legs faster than a cadfish with a seal bitin' his arse?" her friend and neighbour said as he made a grab for the dog, who sensibly abandoned the cat and skittered back outside. "I'll be bound now if you think you're ridin' back with me!" Twill shouted after the dog.

Emma waved at her ruined creation. "Like that's going to help," she scoffed, unimpressed by the Newfoundland dialect that Twill slipped into when his emotions ran high.

Skeptically eyeing the mess, he ran calloused fingers through his grey-streaked hair, taking care not to dislodge the transmitter coil of his speech processor. "Didn't seem like you was havin' much luck with that jar anyways," he said. Noting Emma's glare as she scraped what was left of the bowl into a slippery ball, he added, "Though it was clear as day you was workin' hard to fix it."

"Your damned dog ruined my bowl!" Emma got up from the wheel. "What are you doing here, anyway? I thought you were going to Campbell River."

"Just gettin' back," he said, visibly relieved by the change of topic. "I picked up an Oscar Peterson LP." Twill was the only person Emma knew who still bought vinyl records. He played them on an old-fashioned cabinet-style stereo that he and his wife had received as a wedding gift. Listening to the music they had shared was the only thing that sustained him after her death.

"Which one?" she asked, certain that he already had every recording the pianist had ever made. She threw the ball of clay into a plastic bag and began cleaning up the tray attached to her potting wheel.

"*Tracks*, recorded in 1974. I thought maybe you'd like to have a listen tonight over dinner. Fresh hatchery trout and some of Leonard's huckleberry hooch." He ogled her. "No tellin' where *that* might take us."

Emma grimaced. Leonard Smythe was the assistant manager at the fish hatchery Twill managed. The last time she'd tried his homemade wine, she was ill for a week. "I'll bring the wine, and we'll see about the rest," she said. "But it'll have to wait a few days. I've got to fly up to some place called Bear Creek Landing in about forty minutes."

Twill's right brow rose.

As she sponged out the splash pan, Emma explained what Sam wanted her to do. "He figures I'll be back tomorrow afternoon, but this woman lives out in the middle of nowhere, so it could take me an extra day or two. I'll leave food out for Purkins, but if I'm not back tomorrow, I'd be grateful if you'd drop by and give him some more."

Twill leaned against the door and watched as she carried her tools to the sink, washing them at the same time as her hands. "I'd a lot rather be fetchin' that signature for you," he said. "I could use a few days away from the hatchery."

"And I'd be happy to let you," Emma responded, as she whipped a worn towel from its hook on the wall and dried her hands, "but the bonus Sam's going to pay me will help buy my new roof."

"So you're finally taking my advice about that...." Twill began, then wisely muttered something about finding his dog and made a hasty exit from the studio.

Emma had no patience with men, not even with Twill, whom she had known since she was fourteen and came to live with her grandparents in Windrush. He had been a big brother to her then, and it wasn't until many years later, after his wife had died and Emma's marriage to Tommy had ended, that they had drifted into a closer relationship: friends with benefits.

It took only a few minutes for her to change and throw an extra pair of slacks and a sweater into a wheeled suitcase, and less than that again to set out food and water for Purkins. He had disappeared through the cat flap in the boot room and didn't return even when Emma went outside to call him. She looked anxiously over the tangled garden that skirted the rear of the two-storey grey clapboard house. Two robins were fighting noisily over a piece of string while a Stellar's Jay screamed at them from the lowest branch of a nearby cedar. Far below them, the Stuart River ambled eastward through marshy second-growth forest. But there was no sign of her cat and finally, with a last regretful look at the river, she turned away.

"He'll be fine," she told herself. Gathering her gear, she headed for the truck.

On the way to the Shinglewood harbour, where she was to catch her flight, Emma stopped at the Rusty Anchor Coffee and Gift Shop to deliver a box of bowls to Sam's wife Kate.

"I brought you all that's left from my last firing," Emma said, setting the box on the counter.

The redheaded proprietor opened the cover. "Same old, same old," Kate said with disappointment. "I was hoping you might branch out into something more... creative. Like those pieces in your basement."

A few years earlier, while searching for items to include in a rummage sale for the hatchery, Kate pulled out a box of hand-built stuff: horses with goddess heads and serpent manes flowing behind them, bearded muscle-men rising from grotesque tree stumps — the kind of fancy Emma had indulged in before her marriage. At the time she'd refused to include them in the sale, and now she deliberately misunderstood her friend's request.

"I *was* trying to build a bigger bowl, but between your husband and Twill, I smashed the damned thing," she said. "And now Sam's sending me halfway up the coast on my day off." She watched Kate set the box aside. "Anyway, the tourists buy them, and that's what counts."

"Tourists. What do they know about art?" Kate leaned her elbows on the counter. "I bet Sam that you wouldn't go."

"He didn't give me a chance to refuse," Emma said, "but he's going to pay dearly for it."

"Well, as far as I'm concerned, you could do with a little

adventure. Anything to get you away from that mausoleum of yours."

"I had my fill of adventures crewing on fish boats for nine years," Emma said stiffly. "And Windrush may be old, but I'd hardly call it a mausoleum."

Kate sniffed. "It looks like one. All those trees, and more moss on the roof than shingles." She jabbed the air with her index finger. "You think it's a safe place, Emma, but one day you're gonna wake up dead and realize you've never lived."

"Yeah, well, if I miss that plane, I won't have to worry about living because Sam will kill me." She headed for the door. "And who knows? Maybe I'll see something on the trip that will inspire me beyond bowls."

TWO

The aroma of drying mussels permeated the air as the morning sun warmed the pilings of the government wharf at Port Hardy. Overhead, seagulls flashed white wings and screamed for attention as they circled the fishing boats moored to the dock. From the water came the ragged *putt-putta-putt-putt* of an engine badly in need of service, and a moment later a large yellow zodiac rounded the end float. The lone occupant of the boat cut the motor as the boat glided alongside the only open berth. After securing the stern line to a metal cleat, he climbed onto the wharf and tied the bowline to a second cleat. Buttoning his denim jacket halfway to cover the oil stains on his plaid logger's shirt, he rubbed a hand over his unshaven face, then got to his feet and stomped toward the ramp. He had just reached the top when a car turned onto the pier, its tires *thump-thumping* softly on the uneven surface. As it came to a stop in front of him, the doors opened and three young children bounded out. "Daddy!" They screamed in unison as they ran towards the man.

The eldest, a ten-year-old brunette whose limbs were much longer than the clothes covering them, reached him first and wrapped her arms around his waist. "I knew you'd come, Daddy!"

"Hey, Julie-girl!" he said, hugging her with one arm. With his free hand he grabbed the youngest child, a towheaded six-year-old boy who had the same wiry build as his father, and swung him up under his arm.

"Caden, come on up here!"

"Let me go!" The boy shrieked, kicking until the man let him down.

The third child, an eight-year-old girl with honey-blonde hair and fierce blue eyes, hung back. Still, there was an eagerness in her expression that she couldn't completely hide. The man reached for her.

"Come on, Skylar," he said. "You know you want a hug." His grin was infectious and reluctantly the girl allowed him to hug her, then quickly pulled away and pointed to a woman emerging from the driver's seat.

"Aunty Glenda says you gotta take us!"

The wraith-like woman wore a long batik dress in various shades of purple. Her hair was as blonde as Skylar's and there was an aura of peacefulness about her as she walked languidly toward the group — a serenity not shared by the children's father.

"What's this all about, Glenda? I thought we had an arrangement."

Glenda smiled. "I'm sorry, Dennis. This isn't working. You're going to have to take them."

He glared at her. "And how the hell am I supposed to do that? The camp's fifty clicks up the strait, remember?"

Her laugh tinkled, but it held no humour. "How could I forget, Dennis? It's where you've been hiding ever since my sister died. Six months without a card or a phone call. Not even on Caden's birthday." The rebuke startled the children, who clustered closer to their father as if to protect him.

Dennis' reaction was angry. "I'm a logger, for Christ's sake! What do you expect?"

She waved her hand. "You have to take them," she repeated.

"They're disturbing my energy field."

"Yeah, right," he said. "And how the hell are they doing that?"

Caden piped up, "Skylar scared the dead guy away!"

"I did not!" the blonde girl said, punching her brother's arm. "And anyway, he wasn't even real!"

Dennis grabbed Skylar's hand, preventing a second punch. "Knock it off, you two." He looked at Glenda. "A dead guy?"

"I was conducting a seance for a woman who recently lost her husband," she said, "and I had barely contacted his spirit when this one began howling like a banshee!"

Stepping closer to her father, Skylar scowled at her aunt. "I was just makin' it more spooky."

"You frightened his spirit," Glenda snapped. "Now it will take me weeks to coax him back!"

Dennis's lips twitched. "She didn't mean to upset you, Glenda. And she won't do it again, will you, Skylar?"

"No way," Skylar vowed. "That screaming old lady scared the shit out of me!"

As Dennis fought a sudden coughing spasm, Glenda closed her eyes and stretched her arms upward, lifting her hands towards the sky. Finally she lowered her arms and opened her eyes.

"I'm sorry," she said, her voice edged with anger. "I simply can't live with all that… that negative energy." She began walking toward the rear of her car. "I have their things in the trunk."

"What part of living in camp aren't you getting, Glenda?" he shouted after her.

She responded with another benign smile. "Andrea and I grew up in logging camps, Dennis. The children will be fine. Besides, I've asked Spirit to help them."

"*Spirit?*"

"My spiritual guide," she said as if that explained it. She extracted four large plastic garbage bags from the trunk of her car and put them on the pier. "I've included some blankets and their school things. You'll have to contact the correspondence branch about courses for them." She slammed the lid on the trunk, then pulled a bottle of pills from her pocket. "This is Skylar's Ritalin. Make sure she takes it."

As soon as he took the bottle from her hand, Glenda turned back to her car and climbed in behind the wheel. Dennis shoved the Ritalin into the pocket of his jeans. "Well, thanks for nothing!" he called out. Then he glared at the children. "Come on, grab yourselves a bag and follow me."

He walked several steps before he realized his middle child wasn't moving.

"Come on, Skylar. I haven't got all day."

Skylar tilted her chin. "We're hungry."

Her siblings nodded.

"Yeah! I'm starving," the boy insisted.

Julie said quietly, "We only had porridge for breakfast, Daddy."

Dennis stared at the three of them, then shook his head in defeat. It was almost a three-hour drive from Glenda's home in Campbell River to Port Hardy. They probably *were* starving. "All right! We'll stow your gear and then we'll go for hamburgers, okay?"

Without a word, Skylar hoisted her bag over her shoulder and half-dragged, half-carried it toward the ramp.

Three burger-and-milkshake combos later, and with the children wearing ill-fitting life jackets, Dennis steered the zodiac out of the harbour and headed across the strait.

THREE

The gravel logging road was pitted with potholes, their depths obscured by muddy water from the previous night's rain. By driving slowly, Emma could steer the Rent-a-Wreck around most of them, though occasionally she was forced to plunge the car into one and plow through it, rattling everything that wasn't securely bolted. Her hair slipped out of the elastic band securing it in a ponytail, and her limbs protested every bump.

She peered at the thick stands of hemlock and western red cedar trees that grew on either side of the road. From their dark upper branches hung ragged clumps of grey-green lichen. On the previous afternoon, the frightening wildness of the land had exhilarated her — until darkness had fallen and she was forced to accept that there was no damned way she was ever going to find the Trapper Creek Bridge, or the gravel turnoff "just north of it" that was supposed to lead her to the Black Fly Ranch.

A sensible person would have turned around and headed back to the comfortable room she had booked at Bear Creek Landing, but Emma was too determined to accomplish her mission to even consider that option. Instead she had pulled off the road and spent a long night cramped and shivering in the Toyota's back seat as she listened to the howl of wolves and a thousand other sounds that she was sure were coming from giant grizzlies, bent on tearing the little car and herself to pieces.

"Stubborn," her mother used to say. "Like your dad." As a teenager, Emma had treasured the comment as an intangible link to her father, who died when she was ten. Later she decided that "determination" was the quality that guided most of her decisions.

At first light she had retraced her route without finding the bridge or the turnoff. Now, although she knew Sam was going to be furious about failing Kazinski's client, she was forced to admit defeat because the Toyota's fuel gauge was wobbling dangerously close to the quarter-full mark. She had barely enough gas to return to the settlement.

As she turned the car around and headed west, she cast a brief glance at the clock on the dash. It was almost seven, and the plane that was going to take her away from this rain-drenched patch of the north central coast was leaving Bear Creek Landing at ten-thirty. She had already tried a dozen times to call and beg the airline to delay the flight, only to find that there was no cellphone reception in this area. She pressed on the accelerator. *No way am I staying four more days at the Landing waiting for the scheduled flight!* She glanced at the clock again. She glanced at the clock again. If her calculations were correct, she could make it back and still have time to stop at the bed and breakfast for a hot bath that might soak the stiffness from her legs.

The car bounced over a large rut into a hole, splashing mud over the windshield and momentarily obscuring her vision so that she didn't see the man who had stepped onto the road until she was almost upon him. "What the hell!" She swerved to the left and hit the brake, barely missing the man and coming to a stop on the edge of the ditch.

"Are you trying to get yourself killed?" she yelled as he sauntered across the road. He was dressed in mud-splattered gumboots, denims, and a torn grey sweater that Emma doubted had ever seen the inside of a washing machine. His gaunt face was covered with at least a three-day growth of salt-and-pepper whiskers, and strands of hair protruded at odd angles from under a grease-stained black bill cap with "Lazy Bones" emblazoned on the front. Seemingly unperturbed by his near brush with death, he opened the Toyota's passenger door.

"Figured I had a twenty-mile hike in front a' me," he said, settling uninvited into the front seat and giving Emma a toothless grin. He reeked of stale cigarette smoke and yesterday's wine, but he seemed harmless enough. Nevertheless, Emma wished she had kept the car doors locked.

"I could have killed you!" she snapped. For a nanosecond she toyed with the idea of kicking him out, then, realizing it was a physical impossibility, restarted the car. Slamming it into reverse, she backed away from the embankment, shifted into forward gear, and accelerated.

"Yer was driving crazy." He braced himself as the car bounced over a large mound of dirt.

"What do you expect? My windshield's covered with mud."

He leaned back against the seat. "Damned tie rod broke on my truck."

"Where at?" she asked. "I didn't see any vehicles."

"It was back a ways, in them woods." He peered at her. "You from the gov'ment?"

She negotiated the car over a series of ruts and asked, "What makes you think that?"

"Don't get city women up here. Least, not ones that are young and pretty."

Emma knew she was many things but pretty wasn't one of them. Except for a few grey strands that didn't show, her hair was a nondescript brown, her eyes wavered, depending on the light, between green and hazel, and her nose was too small.

What's more, her wrinkled, mud-stained blouse and slacks could not have identified her as a city woman. Suspecting that he was either deranged or plotting some nefarious act, she said, "Listen, mister, I'm thirty-five, I'm PMS-ing, sleep-deprived, hungry, and ready to kill for a cup of coffee. So don't try anything."

Startled, the man edged closer to the door, grabbing the handle for support as the Toyota bounced in and out of another hole. "Ooh... kay...."

She frowned as she negotiated a slippery corner. "I'm trying to find a woman named Mary Dahl. You wouldn't happen to know her, I suppose?"

He relaxed and leaned back into the seat. "From the Black Fly?"

"That's the one."

"What you want her for?"

"Jesus!" Emma slammed her fist on the steering wheel. "What's with you people? I've got a stupid document that I want a stupid woman to sign and all I get from anyone around here is either silence or nosy damned questions or directions that take me nowhere!"

The man's grip tightened on the door handle and he swivelled his head to stare out the window like a trapped animal appraising his chances for escape. Cautiously, he said, "Folks 'round here don't talk to strangers on account of the grow-op." He lowered his voice. "Mafia."

"Are you serious? I didn't think marijuana would grow this far north."

"Will if you have the right equipment." With a nervous jerk, he removed a cigarette package from his shirt pocket. As he did, she glimpsed a gold watch half-hidden by his sleeve.

Emma shook her head. "No smoking in my car."

He shoved the package back into his pocket. "The cops keep

trying to find out where it is, but it ain't worth nobody's life to talk to them. Last guy that did was found in pieces up near Cougar Bluff."

"So how come you're talking about it?"

"Aw, they need me too much to touch me."

"Oh, sure." From her experience as a legal assistant and her passion for crime novels, Emma knew that every person in the drug world was dispensable. There might be a few private grow-ops in the area, but she doubted that even those operators would trust someone as talkative as her passenger with information of any value. Still, he *was* wearing a gold watch.

"I need Mary Dahl to sign some documents," she said. "And they have nothing to do with grow-ops."

The man scratched his beard, then retrieved the cigarette package. "Tell you what. You give me twenty bucks and a ride to the Landing, and I'll show you the way to the ranch."

Emma frowned. Parting with twenty dollars seemed much easier than listening to Sam complain for the next month because she hadn't accomplished her mission. And she would get her bonus.

"How far is it?"

"Oh, 'bout twenty clicks back the way we come."

"And you didn't tell me? Jesus!" She glanced at the clock. *If I give up the bath, I should still be able to make it.* She studied the gas gauge, then shook her head. "I've only got enough gas to get back to the Landing."

He removed a cigarette and placed it, unlit, between his lips. "Mary'll have some we can borrow."

"Perfect." Emma hit the brakes and, since there were no turnoffs in sight, managed to edge the car around by shifting between reverse and drive. When she was finally headed east again, her companion removed the cigarette he'd been chewing and introduced himself as Captain Arnold Forgessen.

"Captain of what?"

"Forty-foot troller called the *Lazy Bones*."

Emma smiled. "I worked on a friend's troller after I got out of high school. The *Twillingate*. We were long-lining for halibut off the Queen Charlottes."

He snorted in disgust. "Well, that sure don't happen much now. No money to be made fishing aye-tall." He started ranting about the mismanaged fishery and the "goddamned enviro-freaks," a diatribe that somehow mutated into the telling of his life story, how he and his late brother had been born and raised in the north country and how both had married local women.

Forgie — as he suggested she call him — had been divorced for many years, his wife having objected to his "wayward ways."

"Now I'm living free as a bird on the *Lazy Bones*," he said, "and running her as a supply boat."

"And that's why the Mafia finds you so indispensable, right?" She meant it as a joke, but instead of responding with a laugh, Forgie frowned and fell silent. Emma wasn't sure if it was because she'd hit on the truth or because he thought she was mocking him. Either way, she welcomed the break from his implausible ramblings.

Although the turnoff to the Black Fly Ranch was mostly obscured by bushes, and the marker bearing the ranch's name was covered in mud, Emma berated herself for missing it twice. She wasn't accustomed to getting lost. Still, she had to admit, even if she'd seen the signs, she might not have braved the access road that just seemed to plunge down the muddy bank.

"Well, whatcha waitin' for?" Forgie asked when she stopped at the top of the incline.

"I don't want to get stuck."

"Aw," he patted the dash, "this thing'll climb in an' out of there no problem."

She studied the access road a moment longer, thought she

saw a way through the mud, and eased the car down onto a track that proved to be even more rugged and pot-holed than the main way. After fifteen minutes of driving they reached the ranch. Emma parked in front of a large log cabin. Beyond it was an even larger log barn and several small sheds. Two black-and-white goats grazed on a grassy mound near the barn while a host of multi-coloured chickens roamed the yard, several of them taking shelter beneath the rusting skeletons of two old trucks and an ancient tractor with a hay trailer attached.

Mary Dahl was a large woman with a welcoming smile. She stood in the doorway, a chubby baby on one hip and three youngsters clustered close to her like chicks following a hen. These she shooed outside. "Go open the gas shed for Forgie," she told the eldest, then added in an aside to Emma, "Won't hear anything with them about."

"They're beautiful children," Emma said, watching them cavort around Forgie, obviously familiar with him.

"You have any?" the woman asked as she led Emma into a roomy kitchen-cum-living room and motioned her to a seat at a wooden table.

Emma shook her head. "Tommy and I talked about having a baby. Fortunately, we divorced before it happened." She settled on a chair near the window and lifted her briefcase to the table.

Mary scrutinized her. "You're still young enough."

"Not going to happen," Emma said. "The relationship I have now is way too casual, and we're both too set in our ways for children."

"A woman needs kids," Mary said. "Makes her whole." She shifted the baby to a more comfortable position. "You want a coffee?"

"I'd die for one. I've been searching all over for you. No one would give me directions I could understand."

"In these parts, people learn to keep their mouths shut about their neighbours," she said, bringing a cup of black coffee to the table. "You never know when you're going to need a helping hand."

Emma glanced about the cozy room, noting a number of baskets on the mantel above the fireplace and on the wall. A smaller bottle-shaped basket on the windowsill held a faded bouquet of dried baby's breath and bachelor buttons. "That's an Iroquois cornhusk bottle, isn't it?"

The woman nodded. "Not many folks would know that."

"I was into baskets for a while. Now I pot." Emma studied the even weave and the pattern of colours. "Did you make it?"

"Yeah. Helps me earn a little extra cash." Mary settled into a chair on the opposite side of the table, the baby on her lap. "I sell them through a buyer in Vancouver."

Emma shook her head. "You must be great at time-management. I've got nobody but me and my cat to look after and I can barely keep up my garden, never mind my potting." Glancing at the clock on the mantel, she opened her briefcase and pulled out the waterproof pouch that Sam had entrusted to her. "My boss is a little over-cautious," she said, extracting a pen and two thick documents from the pouch. "I believe your late aunt's lawyers have already sent you a cheque?"

Mary nodded. "That's why my husband isn't home. He's in Prince George buying a new tractor."

"Yes, well, Kazinski & Company have engaged us to secure your signature on this document. It more or less says that you're releasing the executors from any future claims against the estate."

"Oh?" The woman took the paper and scanned the document.

Emma drank her coffee and looked out the window as she concocted a series of dire consequences that would befall the woman if she refused to sign. The baby gurgled and reached for the document, forcing Mary to hold it away from the child's hands. "What are you doing, you little scamp?" she chided, prompting a squeal of delight.

Emma glanced again at the clock, and the woman finally laid the document on the table and reached for the pen. "Seems okay to me," she said.

Hiding her relief, Emma witnessed the signature, put a copy of the document in her pouch, and secured the Ziploc flap.

"That's it, then," she said, getting to her feet.

Mary went to the stove and lifted the coffee pot. "You want some more?" she asked. "Don't get much company out here."

Emma shook her head. "I'd better not." Before leaving the table, she discreetly tucked a twenty-dollar bill under Mary's copy of the document. Somehow, she didn't believe that Forgie would ever return the gas they had borrowed.

It was only ten-twenty when Emma and Forgie pulled into the parking lot of the Bear Creek Landing General Store, but as she got out of the car Emma heard the unmistakable roar of a seaplane taking off. Leaving her luggage in the vehicle, she ran towards the dock, waving her arms.

"Stop!" she shouted, charging down the ramp. By the time she reached the float where the planes docked, the aircraft was already lifting off.

"Won't do you no good yelling," Forgie said. "He don't wait for nobody."

"Damn it! My boss paid $400 for that ride!" She pulled her cellphone from her pocket and checked the time. It was ten-forty-five. "That goddamned clock in that goddamned car was running slow!" She glared at Forgie. "You knew that, didn't you?"

Forgie rubbed his whiskers. "He'll be back on Thursday."

"I'm not sticking around here until Thursday!"

"Well, you kin always charter a plane. Or," he added, "I kin take you as far as Port Hardy. Fer a price."

Emma shoved the cellphone back into her pocket. "What about your truck?"

"It'll wait." He led the way along the dock to an old wooden troller with the name *Lazy Bones* painted on the starboard bow. Except for a railing that was held together with duct tape, the outer deck and cabin seemed in good repair.

"Does everything work?"

"What we need works," he said in a way that made her take a second look at the boat. Still unable to detect any major flaws, she asked, "How much?"

Forgie beamed. "A hundred bucks?"

From Port Hardy Emma knew she could catch a bus that would get her to Shinglewood in a couple of hours. More importantly, Sam would probably reimburse her for the expense. On the other hand, she knew practically nothing about this man except that he wore a gold watch and claimed to have connections with the Mafia. Who knew if the boat was even his?

"I don't think so," she said, turning away.

"Suit yerself," he said. "But if a storm comes in, yer could be stuck here a lot longer'n four days."

She stopped. He wasn't lying about that. She was familiar enough with the waters of the central coast to know that storms could blow up without warning and sometimes last for a solid week. She scanned the boat once again and, as before, found no major flaws. An image of Forgie playing with Mary Dahl's children flashed through her thoughts. If Mary trusted him, he couldn't be all that bad.

"It's a deal." She extended her hand. "I'll just pay for the rental and get my things from the bed and breakfast and we can be off."

He pumped her hand with such enthusiasm that she almost lost her balance. "Only I gotta have the money now," he said. She raised her eyebrows. "I gotta get some... supplies. Fer the boat."

"Nuh-uh. I'll give you half now," she said, wondering once again what the hell she was getting herself into. "The rest when we get to Port Hardy."

At the bed and breakfast, Emma indulged in a hot shower and a plate filled with eggs and bacon, as well as pancakes smothered in wild blueberry syrup and topped with thick cream. Half an hour later, she trundled her suitcase onto the pier, pausing a moment to observe the cluster of fish boats nestled against the floats below. They reminded her of the harbour back home in Shinglewood, where she had spent her teenage years hanging around the docks and begging Twill to let her help him on his troller. She picked out the *Lazy Bones* and took a quick picture of it with her cellphone, just so she could show Sam the sacrifice she'd made to save him a few dollars. It wasn't until she stepped off the ramp that she noticed Forgie arguing with a man who was standing next to the boat. The man was dressed in a suit and didn't look as if he belonged in the Landing. As Emma approached, he broke off in mid-sentence and stalked past her.

"Who was that?" she asked, handing her suitcase up and clambering aboard.

There was an edge to Forgie's voice. "Nobody."

She didn't believe him, but having committed herself to this journey, she was too anxious to get it over with to question him any further. As he dropped her luggage at her feet, she noticed that his right sleeve was pushed up and the gold watch was missing.

"We'd best be off," he said curtly. "Storm's s'posed to come up this afternoon."

Emma followed him into the cabin. Her suitcase banged against the stove as she squeezed through the narrow aisle that ran from the door through the small galley. "Should I be worried?" she asked.

He shook his head. "Nah. We'll be in Hardy before it hits."

She paused at the end of the aisle, where a covered hatch in the floor between the captain and mate's seats led to the engine room and sleeping quarters below.

"You kin stow your gear on one of them bunks," he said. "Take a nap if you want."

Emma pulled back the hatch and climbed down the steep steps, wrinkling her nose at the combined stench of diesel fumes, the mildewed bedding covering the bunks in the forward hold, and stale urine from the head separating the hold from the engine room.

"I think I'll go outside," she said. "Get a little sunshine and fresh air."

Forgie was focused on starting the engines. "Suit yerself. You kin cast off for me while yer out there."

As the *Lazy Bones* plowed westward along Rivers Inlet toward Smith Sound, Emma lay on the sun-warmed cover of the hatch, a box-like structure that rose two feet from the deck. It was almost as long as she was tall, and was situated midway between the cabin and the stern. Protected from the breeze by a surprisingly clean albeit oversized floater coat that she'd found in the hold, she was cozy and comfortable, her thoughts straying lazily from one subject to another: the spring garden tasks waiting her for at Windrush, the satisfaction she would have telling Kate about her daring adventure, and Twill's amusement when she recounted her difficulties in locating Mary Dahl. Twill would have liked Mary but not her brood of children. It wasn't just that he was set in his ways. After his wife died following a prolonged and painful battle with bone cancer, he'd become a dedicated bachelor who placed children and emotional commitments in the category of things to be avoided.

Not that I'm much better, Emma thought. Her knowledge of children was limited to a few babysitting jobs as a teenager.

Would children have made a difference to her marriage? Would it have kept Tommy from leaving her? She watched the wispy horsetail clouds drifting above her. Not that it mattered. The hurt she had felt over Tommy's desertion had faded so far into her past she could scarcely remember what he looked like.

She turned her attention to the hills forested in various shades of green on either side of the passage, their lowlands reaching out to the water like layers of odd-shaped fingers. The tide was out and she could see reddish-brown kelp and black mussels colouring the rocky shoreline, while the tree limbs above them were encased in moss so thick it made her think of giant green teddy bears. For a time she watched two eagles soaring high over the water until one of them swooped down to the surface, grabbed something, and flew off into the trees, the booty clutched tightly in its talons. As the eagles disappeared from view, her attention turned to a distant tugboat pulling a barge.

For two years Emma had travelled this passage as a deckhand on Twill's troller. Although the *Twillingate* had not been much bigger than the *Lazy Bones*, Twill had kept his boat painted, spotless, and in perfect running order.

"Way a man tends his boat says a lot about how he tends his life," he'd told her once. He'd changed after his wife's death. Sold his boat. Started drinking heavily and might have continued along that path if Emma hadn't taken him in hand, bullying him into accepting the job at the hatchery. One stormy night she had made him dinner and afterwards put on a record and coaxed him into dancing with her. She figured it was the wine that made him kiss her, and she told herself she was only comforting him when she let it go further. But he was a thorough lover, exploring every part of her body before possessing her, denying his own satisfaction until she was almost spent, then joining with her in a final, explosive climax. The next time it was she who initiated their love-making.

Emma smiled, remembering. Then she yawned, turned onto her stomach, and with her head resting on her arms, closed her eyes. Before long, the soft *chug-chug* of the engine had lulled her to sleep.

FOUR

The boy and his older sister sat near the bow of the zodiac and leaned against a plastic bag filled with blankets. It was the only one their father had been unable to fit into the cargo well, and he'd made it into a cushioned backrest for them instead. Their faces were tense as they watched him work on the outboard motor, removing this part and that, then replacing them, yanking on the starter cord and letting out a stream of obscenities when the pistons still didn't fire.

A short distance from the stern, Skylar sat on the zodiac's single bench, which created a bridge from port to starboard. The motor cover rested on the floorboards beside her, and in her lap she held an oiled canvas package of tools from which she extracted whichever item her father called for. Her face was also tense, but more from concentration than fear. She seemed unaware of the wind tangling her hair, or of the ever-increasing waves that were pushing the zodiac this way and that like an amusement park ride.

When another pull on the cord failed to start the motor, Dennis slammed the side of his fist against the housing. "Useless piece of shit!" He looked past the children to the horizon, where angry grey clouds darkened the sky. The wind was rising.

Giving up on the motor, he replaced the cover, wrapped the tools back into their canvas package, and shoved the whole thing into a compartment along the starboard float. From another compartment he retrieved a long length of rope.

"Okay, hoodlums, things might be getting a little rough here, so I'm going to make sure you don't fall overboard."

He crawled past Skylar to the bow and secured one end of the rope to the rigging on the zodiac, cut off a length of line, and secured that end to Julie's life jacket.

"What's wrong, Daddy?" she whispered.

Her brother was more blunt. "Are we gonna be drownded?"

"Good God, no! You don't think your daddy would let that happen, do you?" He secured a similar line to Caden's jacket. "It's just gonna get a little rough, that's all."

Skylar gazed from him to the waves then back to the rope he was fastening to her. She shivered.

"You're cold!" Dennis said.

"Am not!"

He pulled off his jacket and removed her life vest. "This should keep you nice and warm," he said as she slid her arms into the sleeves. The coat was much too big for her, but the worn denim still held his warmth, and she managed to push the sleeves far back enough to free her hands so she could do up the zipper and replace the vest.

"Hey, what about me?" her brother asked. "I'm cold too!"

"Jesus, Caden!" Dennis glared at the boy. "I don't have another jacket." He grabbed the seat for support as a gust of wind slammed against the zodiac. Julie put her arm around Caden, tugging him closer. "I'll keep you warm," she said.

"Jesus," Dennis muttered again as he rummaged through the contents of one storage compartment after another until he found a roll of plastic garbage bags. Pulling one free, he dug a pocket knife from his jeans, cut three holes into the bag, and wrestled it over Caden's life jacket. "That should do it," he said gruffly, adjusting the top opening to form a hood and helping the boy wriggle his arms through the side holes. The poncho rode up on either side of the tether, but it would have to do.

It had started to rain, so he made similar ponchos for the girls. From the bag that Caden and Julie were using as a backrest, he withdrew a blanket and draped it around the two of them.

Julie touched her free hand to her father's unshaven cheek. "Thanks, Daddy."

He kissed her forehead. "We're going to be okay, Julie-girl," he promised. He picked up a pair of oars. "Skylar, you scoot up there with Julie and Caden."

But when Dennis was seated and looking around for the passage leading to Silver Bay, all he could see were waves, rain, and black clouds. Nevertheless, he began hauling on the oars, steering the zodiac in what he hoped was a southwesterly direction.

FIVE

Raindrops splattered onto her uncovered head, pulling Emma from sleep. Assaulted by a sudden gust of wind, the *Lazy Bones* dipped hard to starboard, and she grasped the handle of the hatch cover, saving herself from sliding onto the deck. She stared in alarm at the wild water around the boat. The waves were steep and black and crested with white foam, the distant shoreline so blurred by rain that she could no longer identify any landmarks.

The vessel righted itself, and she staggered across the deck and into the cabin, closing the sliding door behind her.

Forgie was leaning out of his pilot's chair to peer through the windshield.

"Wow! That's some wind!" Emma said. She pulled her cellphone from her pocket and glanced at the time. It was almost five o'clock. They should be getting close to Port Hardy.

Forgie gripped the wheel with his left hand and lit the cigarette dangling from his lips with the other.

"Where are we?" Emma shouted, climbing onto the mate's seat. She stared out at the rain that was now pelting the wheelhouse windows. As the boat pitched forward and a huge wave crashed against the bow, she repeated her question.

Forgie sucked on his cigarette and the end turned bright orange. "Straits," he said, shoving the lighter back into his pocket.

"I figured that." They had to cross the Queen Charlotte Strait to reach Vancouver Island. "Have we passed Scarlett Point?" she asked. The Scarlett Point lighthouse was only ten miles northwest of Port Hardy, and although the currents around it were tricky and dangerous, a few miles to the south was a snug cove on Hurst Island that could provide them safe anchorage — if she was remembering it correctly. She braced her feet on the top rung of the chair and grasped its curved wooden arms as the boat lurched forward and aft. "We could shelter in God's Pocket," she suggested.

Intent on manoeuvring the boat through the next wave, Forgie said nothing. Moisture streamed down the windshield as the single wiper, with half of its blade missing, fluttered uselessly back and forth. But it wasn't the wiper that concerned Emma. Over the stench of cigarette smoke and the unwashed odour of the captain's clothes, she was sure she could smell cheap rye whiskey.

Without jarring the ash at the end of his cigarette, Forgie scratched nervously at his whiskers, then, confirming Emma's suspicion, reached for a half-empty bottle that was wedged between his chair and the bulkhead. Expertly removing the cap with one hand, he tilted the rim to his lips and swallowed deeply.

"You're drinking?" she yelled.

He flashed her a toothless grin and replaced the cap, tucking the bottle safely inside his jacket. "Courage," he said, slurring the final consonant so it sounded like "courash."

The *Lazy Bones'* bow dipped forward and a wave washed over the outside of the cabin, showering white foam and translucent green water over the windows. Emma braced herself once more, noting the moisture seeping through cracks around the panes and onto the sill, where a set of yellowed false teeth sat among crudely rolled marine charts and empty cigarette packages.

Outside, bits of rigging that were not properly fastened

banged against the cabin. Her head was beginning to ache from the noisy hum of the bilge pump that was clicking on and off at alarmingly frequent intervals, the constant *rat-a-tat-tat* of the engine, and the diesel exhaust that was now mingling with the other putrid odours invading the cabin.

She nodded towards a v H F radio mounted behind the captain's seat. The microphone had broken free of its holder and dangled below the set, bumping the wooden cupboard as the vessel was jolted this way and that. "Have you radioed our position?"

Forgie gave a shallow laugh. "Don' know our poshision." He bent even closer to the window to peer through the waterfall. "Radio's broke anyways."

"But you have a G P S, right?"

He shook his head. "In the shop."

"You said everything worked! Jesus, Forgie!" She glowered as another green wall of water cascaded over the windows. *Breathe, Emma. In and out, in and out. Slow deep breaths....*

She checked her cellphone. The black line slashing through the tiny image of a phone on her monitor indicated no reception.

"Damn!" The boat pitched forward and the windshield flooded, but when it cleared this time, Emma saw a flash of light in the distance. It flickered a second time, and she pointed. "The lighthouse!"

Instead of steering toward it, Forgie swore and spun the wheel, turning the vessel hard to port so abruptly that Emma was tossed off her chair and into the aisle. Her cellphone flew from her hand, landing beneath the galley table. She scrabbled for the phone, shoved it into the pocket of her coat, and returned to her seat. Looking out the window, she saw they were leaving the light behind and heading into the wind. "What are you doing?" she shouted. "That's got to be the entrance to Christie Passage!"

Forgie's hands trembled on the wheel. "Rocks," he hissed.

"You don't know that! We were too far away." She winced as a fresh wave washed over the bow.

"Rocks'll drown yer." Forgie said, staying the course.

"So will goddamned boats that are falling apart!"

They topped the next wave and crashed down, repeating the motion again and again. Emma had been in worse storms than this with Twill, but his equipment had worked — and his boat hadn't shuddered with each jolt as if it was about to break in half.

Suddenly she leaned forward and stared at the water off their starboard beam.

"What the hell?"

Dangerously close to the *Lazy Bones* was a yellow zodiac overflowing, it seemed, with children clinging to ropes that were strung along the pontoons. "Forgie! Oh my God! We're going to hit them!"

The old man gaped as the *Lazy Bones'* bow plunged almost on top of the inflatable, and he spun the wheel hard, achieving little more than a few inches' distance between the two vessels. Emma scrambled from her seat and grabbed a grease-stained coil of rope from the galley.

"Yer can't help them!" Forgie shouted.

"I can damned well try!" she yelled back. After tying the first few feet of rope around her waist, she headed for the door, kicking it hard to make it slide open. A blast of cold air entered the cabin, prompting a torrent of curses from Forgie. Emma ignored him. With fingers that haste turned into thumbs, she struggled to fasten the free end of the rope around a metal bar bolted to the outer wall of the cabin. Gripping the line, she inched her way across the slippery stern deck to the starboard railing.

Their boat was inching away from the zodiac. Still, it was close enough for Emma to see that there were three children aboard and a man crouched over the outboard motor in the stern. The man waved and shouted something that Emma couldn't hear over the roar of the wind and waves pounding the boat. Rain lashed her face as she motioned toward the rope. Clinging to the deck rail, she untied the length around her waist, coiled as much free line as possible, and tossed it toward the zodiac just as the *Lazy Bones* tilted sideways, knocking her off balance. She caught hold of the balustrade and the patched railing wobbled beneath her hands as the wind sent the rope flying uselessly behind her.

The deck levelled and she made another attempt, snaking the line to within a few feet of the zodiac, which had now slipped almost astern of the *Lazy Bones*. Emma hastily re-coiled the rope as the man motioned the children to the starboard side of the zodiac. As he leaned out toward the fishing vessel, she steadied herself and in the split second between wind gusts flung the coil towards him. The tip of the rope whipped past his head and dropped into the water. He grabbed for it, missed, and grabbed again, submerging his head and upper body beneath the surface. Emma held her breath, certain that the rest of him would follow, and she almost cried when he rose up, the yellow rope gripped tightly in his hand.

As soon as he secured the rope to the zodiac's bowline, and the inflatable was safely following behind, Emma staggered back across the slippery deck. But now, the *Lazy Bones* veered unexpectedly westward and an oncoming wave hit the port bow, plunging the starboard side toward the sea. Thrown back onto the rail, Emma watched in horror as the water rose close to her face. Miraculously, the rail held, and as the boat righted itself, she regained her balance, only to lose it again as the deck careened sharply to port.

What in the hell was Forgie doing?

Grasping the rope that now connected the zodiac to the metal bar, she pulled herself hand over hand to the open door. In the dimly lit cabin she could see Forgie's body crumpled in the aisle beside his chair. Above him, the wheel spun unchecked.

At first Emma thought that he'd simply passed out, but as she stumbled forward she saw a puddle of dark liquid on the floor. Forgie's forehead rested against the metal edge of the step, and when she turned him over she gasped at the blood covering his face and flooding eyes which stared blankly at the ceiling. Pressing her two middle fingers beneath his jaw and just below his right ear, she felt for a pulse. There was none.

Oh my God!

She tried to remember the resuscitation procedure she'd learned in a long-ago first aid class, but before she could initiate it, the *Lazy Bones* lurched violently to starboard, tossing her sideways.

"Jesus!"

They were still close to the rocks that Forgie had warned her about, and suddenly she was torn between saving the boat and saving him. Then she thought of the zodiac. If the *Lazy Bones* went down, so would it. She wished that she had never tied the zodiac to Forgie's fish boat. Instead of increasing their chance of survival, she had put the man and his children in greater danger.

The boat lurched again, and she grabbed the handle of a galley cupboard to keep from falling, then, stepping over the body, climbed onto the captain's chair. Taking hold of the wheel, she peered through the window and tried to focus on the water, but she couldn't connect what she was seeing with a corresponding action. Wave after wave broke over the bow, and her hands began shaking so violently that she could barely maintain her hold on the wheel. The sea had become her master and, as if to affirm its power, the most intense wave yet slammed against the hull, almost jarring her off her seat.

But the jolt knocked her panic aside, and, inexplicably, in its place came a deep calm. Fear disappeared along with her internal chatter. All that existed was the helm, the bow, and the waves. She knew that the breakers came at regular intervals and she began to time each one, rotating the wheel clockwise so the boat met the wave at an angle just before it broke. Holding fast as the bow surged forward and the wheel was almost wrenched from her hand, she kept a steady course into the wind.

Keep the angle, hard to starboard, now to port. Keep the angle. She repeated the mantra over and over, almost lulling herself into a sense of security until another massive wave splashed over the bow and onto the window, shocking her back to reality. As the window cleared, she leaned forward. Another light was flashing.

That can't be Scarlett Point! We passed that a long time ago. The light flashed again. *Could we have turned around?* She tried to picture how the waves were hitting the bow before she had gone out to rescue the zodiac. They were washing over the wheelhouse, she remembered, much as they were doing now. But had the wind changed direction? Her hands shook even more as she faced the possibility that they could be heading out to the open ocean, a prospect that was far more horrifying than any rocks.

"Rocks'll kill yer."

Emma glanced down at Forgie's body. "But so will heading blindly out into sea, and the rocks *won't* kill me if I know what I'm doing."

If this *was* Scarlett Point, Emma was certain that she could get through the passage into God's Pocket. She'd done it before. But just as she turned the *Lazy Bones* toward the beacon, the engine sputtered. She pushed the throttle forward and the sputtering stopped, but at that moment Emma realized she hadn't heard the click of the bilge pump since she'd taken over the wheel. She flicked the manual control on and off with no result.

I should go down to the engine room and check it, she thought, then shook her head. Even without Forgie's body blocking the

45

hatch, she didn't dare leave the wheel. The engine coughed again and she fed it more gas.

Barely skirting panic, and knowing that without the engine she would have almost no steerage, Emma entertained the notion that she might not make it out of this mess. *It only takes three minutes to drown,* she thought as she tried to block out images of sinking beneath the water. *But a whole lifetime of agony can be experienced in three minutes.*

She shuddered.

Underlying her fear was a deep sadness — a sense of a life lived pointlessly. What had she done to make her mark? Kate was right in saying that Emma put safety first. She'd run away from her mother to the safety of her grandparents, and she'd left *them* behind to fish with Twill, who knew everything about the sea and boats. Even marrying Tommy had been safe. He hadn't made demands on Emma, and he'd let her be the boss of both his boat and their home, which she'd managed with equal efficiency. She hadn't even accepted his name, maintaining that she'd been born Emma Phillips and that's how she intended to die.

He'd left her for a waitress from Port Hardy. "She needs me," he'd written in his farewell note.

Seems like I got my wish, Emma thought dourly, nudging the throttle ahead.

And now who, she wondered, besides Twill and her cat, would care that she'd died? Would anyone else even notice that she was gone? Sam would, of course. He hated change, and he'd probably be more annoyed than sorry. And Kate. With her own two children married and raising families in Toronto, she'd adopted Emma as a surrogate daughter. Kate would arrange a wake — a big party with lots of noise, the exact opposite of what Emma would want, although her friend would never believe that. She saw the world and all that was in it from a my-way-is-best perspective, a characteristic that Emma found both amusing and infuriating.

"I'll change!" she promised. "Get me out of this and I swear I'll make my life count for something!"

She looked pleadingly towards the horizon. Daylight was fast fading and within an hour she wouldn't even be able to see the waves. Meanwhile, the flashing light was growing brighter, and as the boat drew closer she discovered with a sickening feeling that the beacon didn't mark the entrance to Christie Passage. It marked the granite cliffs and boulders that loomed just ahead.

"Shit!" Too late, she spun the wheel hard to starboard, and the *Lazy Bones'* hull grated against something solid. The tiny cabin exploded with noise.

Throttling down, Emma thrust the engine into reverse. Inch by slow inch, she backed the boat away until she was sure it had cleared the danger area. Then she eased the throttle ahead. Now it was harder to turn the wheel, and the boat wasn't responding as it should. Even worse, the engine was coughing more frequently and even advancing the throttle didn't help anymore. With growing dread, she climbed off the chair and tugged at the captain's body, moving it back just enough to open the hatch to the lower deck. In the flickering light of the bare bulb she could see water sloshing over the bottom bunk.

Dropping the hatch cover into place, she returned to the wheel. The boat had left the cliffs behind, and as she peered through the rain to the shore, she thought she could see a small beach a long way off the port bow. *If I can make it there, maybe I can run it aground*, she told herself. But before she could put her plan into action, the engine cut out completely.

"No!" she yelled and jabbed frantically at the starter. There was no response.

She thought of the children and prayed that the man had already cut the zodiac free.

Knowing that within minutes the *Lazy Bones* would go down, she scrambled from the chair, leaped over Forgie's body, and stumbled sternward, grabbing the galley rail to keep from falling. By the time she staggered outside, the fish boat was listing steeply toward starboard. Almost knocked over by the force of the wind and rain, she grabbed the rope she'd tied to the cabin to steady herself. With a sickening feeling, she saw the zodiac still following off the starboard side, but the man was on his feet, leaning toward the *Lazy Bones*, unfastening his line from the one she'd thrown him.

"Be careful!" Emma shouted, but her words were lost in the wind.

As the rope came free, a wave swept the zodiac away from the fish boat. The man teetered, arms flailing, then toppled into the water. At the same time, the rope was jarred from Emma's hands and she half-slid, half-staggered across the deck, landing hard against the patched railing. With a crack it gave way beneath her. She screamed and grasped air in a futile attempt to stop herself from falling. Her rigid body hit the icy water, and she plunged beneath the waves.

She surfaced, coughing and sputtering, blinded by the breakers that kept washing over her. Pulled underwater once more by the current, she desperately clawed her way back up and this time she rode with the wave, rising high enough to see that she was less than a metre from the zodiac.

I'm going to make it! she vowed as she tackled one wave after another. While the bulky floater coat impeded her arm movements, it gave her the buoyancy she needed to be carried forward, inch by inch. At last she was able to grasp the rigging along the pontoon. Blinking water from her eyes, she looked around for the man. He was nowhere in sight.

Behind her the *Lazy Bones* gave a muffled groan and rolled onto its side, sending the mast crashing into the water, narrowly missing Emma's head. She held tight to the zodiac as it was swept forward. When it settled briefly into a trough, she tried to climb on board, but no matter how hard she pushed from below, her arms, already taxed by the strain of steering the fish boat, lacked the strength to lift her upper body onto the pontoon. Then someone tugged at the collar of her coat, and Emma felt a rush of relief. Somehow the man must have managed to get back on board.

The tugging gave her the momentum she needed to climb the rest of the way over the side. She rolled into the boat, landing on her back between a centre seat and the bow, her feet smacking the opposite pontoon. Looking up, she saw the frightened eyes of a young girl staring down at her and knew that her saviour was not the man. The girl was no bigger than a toothpick, as Twill would say.

Twisting onto her side, Emma crawled to her knees. Two children who appeared even younger leaned over the port pontoon, screaming.

"Get back!" Emma hollered as the girl moved to join them.

"Daddy can't swim!" she sobbed. "And neither can my brother!" She grabbed the smallest child in her arms and edged to the centre of the boat.

The third child continued to sprawl over the pontoon, ignoring the waves that splashed her face. "Da-a-a-ddy!" she screamed.

Emma grasped the bow rope that the man had been holding and pulled it toward her. There was no resistance. She looked around, ready to fling it out to him. *Where are you? Damn it!* She crawled to the other side and stared so hard at the water that her eyes burned. As the zodiac was swept farther and farther away from the *Lazy Bones*, she was forced to accept that he would never emerge from that grey, angry water.

Wiping the wetness from her eyes, she turned back to the

children. The tallest, her face contorted with fear, still huddled in the centre of the boat, one hand grasping the seat, her other arm around the boy, whose frantic wails could be heard even though the roar of the wind swept most of the sound away. The middle child continued to lean over the pontoon, refusing to give up her search. When the bow plunged, breaking her hold and tumbling her sideways, Emma grabbed her arm and forced her onto the floor.

"I've gotta find Daddy!" she shouted.

"He's gone," Emma shouted back. "There's nothing we can do!"

The child fought against her hold, but with less and less passion. Finally, she stopped struggling, and Emma released her. As the girl crouched beside her siblings, Emma saw a rope tied about her waist, securing her to the rigging that encircled the boat. A closer inspection revealed similar tethers around the two other children, and as the boat twisted and lunged about in the waves, she reconsidered her opinion of their father's competence. Without the ropes, they would most certainly have been tossed into the sea.

As if to emphasize this point, the boat rose steeply, sending everything loose sliding toward the stern, including a bulging plastic garbage bag that bumped against the seat. In the next instant, the zodiac crested the wave and slammed downwards, tossing the bag into the air and onto the edge of the pontoon. Emma grabbed for it and missed, and the bag slid over the side, disappearing beneath the waves.

Now clinging to the seat, clearly afraid that he too would be swept overboard, the boy was screaming hysterically. The girl holding him was crying. Although the middle child wasn't making any noise, Emma could see that she was also terrified.

"We'll be okay!" Emma shouted, and wished she could believe it. Trying to time her movements to those of the boat, she crawled awkwardly past the children and over the seat, positioning herself in front of the motor. The younger girl watched her squeeze the ball on the gas can and yank on the starter cord.

"It's broke," she yelled, her words garbled by the wind.

Emma tried a few more times before deciding the girl was right. The motor wasn't going to start, and there was nothing she could do in this sea to repair it.

"Are there any flares?" she shouted at the older girl.

Still crying, the girl shook her head.

Her sister yelled, "They fell in the water."

Emma swore under her breath as she picked up a small bucket that was tied to the transom. At least six inches of water was sloshing about the floor of the zodiac, and she emptied as much of it as she could. Next to the starboard pontoon was a pair of oars. Emma toyed with the idea of using one of them as makeshift rudder, then glanced at the waves and abandoned the notion. Even if she knew a direction to follow, she didn't have the strength to steer the boat through this kind of sea. Until it calmed, they were better off drifting, hopefully toward a friendly shore.

The boy had stopped screaming and was now slumped against his sister, a single, sodden blanket pulled around both of them. The middle child sat alone, shivering violently despite her plastic poncho and life vest. Now that the adrenaline rush from falling into the water was abating, Emma was also feeling the effects of the wind through her wet clothing. She crawled forward once more, and positioning herself near the cargo hold that bridged the bow of the boat, she motioned to the middle child. At first the young girl shook her head, but as another chilling gust of wind swept over them, she reluctantly crawled onto Emma's lap. Unzipping her floater coat, Emma wrapped the front of it around the girl's thin little body.

"It's going to be okay," Emma said. Refastening the zipper, she leaned back, supported by the cargo hold. They were following the waves, the boat rising and falling like a roller coaster. Wind blew spray into Emma's face, soaking her cheeks and eyes. She blinked. Was that dark mound off the starboard side the mainland, she wondered, or an island? Would there be more rocks? She looked beyond the stern. The *Lazy Bones* had completely disappeared. All she could see were rain and waves and even these were being rapidly obscured by the gathering darkness.

The child's shivering gradually gave way to the heavy limpness of sleep. As near as Emma could tell, the other two were also sleeping.

Where the hell are we?

Without disturbing the girl, she reached into her water-filled pocket and pulled out her cellphone. Its tiny monitor was blank and pressing the power button produced no response.

"Crap," she muttered.

She stared out at the darkness, mesmerized by the black waves rolling past the zodiac. Without being aware of hours or minutes passing, she gradually became conscious of a change in the storm. The rain had stopped.

Her eyes closed of their own accord, and she allowed herself to doze. Whenever her mind relaxed enough for deep sleep to happen, however, she saw Forgie lying on the floor, his stare vacant and his face red with blood. She would banish the image by opening her eyes, then dozing again, a pattern that repeated itself until a tingling in her feet finally brought her fully awake. Clumsily, she undid her coat and nestled the girl beside her siblings, pulling their damp blanket over her, too. "It's okay," she whispered. "It's okay."

As the girl settled back to sleep, Emma looked around. The wind had died and the sea had calmed to a light ripple, but a thin fog had rolled in. Although the mist occasionally lifted to reveal a sliver of moon, there was not enough light for her to identify the dark slopes that rose from either side of the channel they seemed to be drifting through. She couldn't even tell if it was an incoming or outgoing tide.

With stiff fingers she unfastened the ropes that secured a canvas tarp over the cargo hold. Inside was a collection of plastic garbage bags containing what felt like toys, books, and clothing. She was contemplating how the bags could be used to keep the children warm when she saw a flash of silver in the bottom of the hold. Squeezing her hand under the bags, she pulled out two thin packets bound with fluorescent silver tape — emergency survival wraps, identical to the one she kept in the glove compartment of her truck. Carefully unfolding the packets, she tucked the wraps around the children. Then she crawled to the centre seat and, after bailing the water that had accumulated on the floorboards, picked up the oars.

She began rowing slowly toward the nearest dark shape, which vaguely resembled an island. The zodiac slid smoothly over the water, and since she was moving with the tide, she made swift passage. Soon the dark shape became a cluster of cedar trees, one with a long branch that sprawled over the water like an arm reaching for freedom. Emma rowed closer. What lay beyond the trees was an impenetrable mystery, but since the bough appeared strong enough to keep the boat from drifting away, she set the oars aside, grabbed the bow line, and fastened it to the nearest limb, leaving enough slack in the line to compensate for a low tide. As an extra precaution, she lifted the motor out of the water, and, finally satisfied that the zodiac was safe for now, she wrapped herself in the tarp from the cargo hold and curled up beside the children. This time she slept without dreaming.

SIX

A child whimpered, and Emma felt a rocking motion accompanied by a thudding sensation. Rock and thud. Rock and thud. She woke shivering.

Where the hell am I?

She raised her head and was instantly overwhelmed with a nauseating dizziness. A dull pain throbbed behind her right eye. She moaned and closed her eyes until the dizziness stopped, then opened them to stare blearily at the sleeping lumps beside her.

Jesus!

The blanket had slipped away from the eldest child's head, revealing limp strands of dark hair and a deeply furrowed brow. Next to her were two blanket-covered mounds topped at one end by a sodden tangle of blonde curls. A slight rise and fall of the mounds assured Emma that the children were still alive.

She struggled to a sitting position and gripped the side of the zodiac to brace herself as the boat bumped against the rocks.

At least they're keeping each other warm, she thought as her own shivering increased. The grey dawn carried an extra chill that penetrated her floater coat, turning her clammy skin icy cold. She ran frigid fingers over her damp hair and grimaced. It was salt-stiff and heavy.

Where the hell are we? She pushed back the panic tightening her chest, and forced herself to study her surroundings.

Waves slapped the algae-covered rocks at the base of the tree she had fastened the zodiac to. The tide had receded, but she had left enough slack in the line to compensate for the difference. It was also preventing the boat from slamming too hard against the shore.

Beyond the small hooked cove that was sheltering them, the sea was having another tantrum, its wind-whipped waters specked with white foam. Still, it was not as rough as the strait had been during the storm, and the mists of the night had given way to a cloudless sky.

Gripping the side of the zodiac, she squinted at a granite face rising from the far side of the cove. There was something very familiar about the thousand shades of grey and ochre that coloured its sharply angled surface, so deeply scored that it reminded her of a jigsaw picture. She blinked and stared at it again.

We're in the bloody Broughtons!

A melange of mostly uninhabited islands and islets scattered between the mainland and Vancouver Island, the Broughton Archipelago lies between the south end of the Queen Charlotte Strait and the north end of the Johnstone Strait. If by some miracle they had indeed drifted into this area, they were no more than an hour's boat ride from Shinglewood. But a second look at the channel diminished her relief. Before they dared venture back into the strait, the sea had to calm, and she and the children needed to get warm. Unfortunately, the little cove offered no further hospitality. The trees lining it were too thick and the rocks too high for her to get ashore on her own, never mind with three small children.

She scanned the shoreline on either side of the boat. More than ten years had passed since Emma had last been in the archipelago, and she found it difficult to remember the exact location of the channels and coves where she had once fished. All the same, she was almost certain that at the end of a bay on the other side of this hook was a summer cabin. She glanced at the oars and instantly dismissed the idea of rowing. There was no way she could compete with the strong currents now ruling these waters. Somehow she had to get the damned motor running.

The children didn't stir as she quietly laid the tarp over them, then crawled over the seat to the stern. There she lifted the gas can, expecting it to be heavy with gas. Instead, it was almost weightless.

"Crap! What the hell was he doing out there with no gas?" She shook the can, and was encouraged by the splash of liquid inside. While it might not get them to Shinglewood, there was more than enough to get them to the cabin.

After lowering the leg of the motor into the water, she squeezed the ball pump on the gas line, sent a silent prayer to whatever gods or sea spirits might be on hand to listen, and yanked the motor's starter cord. When nothing happened, she yanked again, and again.

"I told you it don't work," the middle child said, tossing her covers aside. "Daddy says it's a piece of shit."

Emma raised her eyebrows. Her knowledge of children was limited, but she didn't think swearing was a natural part of their dialogue. "Did he also say if there were any tools on board?"

The girl pointed to a pocket on the port side of the zodiac. Its Velcro fastener made a loud ripping sound as Emma lifted the flap. Inside were several lengths of rope and a canvas roll containing a haphazard assortment of rusty tools.

The child crept closer and watched intently as Emma removed the cover from the black Yamaha 45.

"You got a name?" Emma asked, handing the cover to the girl before turning back to the motor. Nothing seemed out of place and both spark plugs were secure. *Probably need adjusting*, she concluded. She chose a spark plug wrench from the packet and managed, by placing one shivering hand over the other, to attach the tool to the first plug and twist until it was loose enough to remove with her fingers.

"Skylar." The word bubbled between the child's chattering teeth.

Emma cleaned the plug with an oily cloth that was wadded in with the tools and used the adjuster at the other end of the wrench to narrow the gap between the electrode and the ground strap. This was one of the first jobs Twill had taught her to do.

First thing you always check when your motor's bust is the plugs, he used to say. *Nine times outta ten, that'll be your problem.*

She screwed the plug back into the socket.

"My name's Emma," she said, as she removed the second plug. "Skylar. That's a nice name."

The girl made a face. "It's dumb."

"Yeah?"

"Daddy says...." She choked up suddenly, scowling back tears.

Emma frowned over the electrode as she wiped it clean. "What does your Dad say?"

Skylar looked down at the engine cover and mumbled, "He says it's a no-brainer. Like our mom."

"That doesn't sound very kind."

The girl shrugged. The cover wobbled in time to her shivers as she watched Emma insert the plug back into its holder and tighten it with the wrench.

"So where are you from, Skylar?"

"We used to live in Campbell River but Aunty Glenda says we gotta live with our Daddy now."

A strangled wail made them both turn. The boy was sitting up in the middle of the boat, his expression bewildered.

"Where's my Daddy?" There were dark hollows beneath his blue eyes and he seemed half-starved, his arms and wrists thin and bony. He, too, was shivering, and Emma saw that besides his life jacket, all he had on under his garbage-bag cape was a thin fleece jogging suit. "Where's my Daddy?" he repeated.

How do you tell a little kid that his father is dead? Emma floundered in a sea of grown-up rhetoric.

"He's drownded, Caden," Skylar said. "He fell in, remember?"

The boy studied her suspiciously then shook his older sister's shoulder. "Joooleee!"

She sat up and grabbed his hand. "Daddy's okay."

Caden shook his head. "Skylar...."

"I saw him," Julie said.

Skylar snorted. "Yeah, right, Julie. You did not!"

"I had a dream, like Aunty Glenda does." The older girl began to shiver as the warmth of the discarded covers evaporated. "Daddy swum to a big island and he said, 'Don't worry, Julie, you'll be okay.' And then he walked into the forest."

"What forest?"

Julie shrugged. "I think he was going to get someone to help us."

Pulling his hand free, Caden rubbed his stomach. "I'm hungry!"

Emma turned to Skylar. "Your dad pack any food?"

"Nope. Aunty Glenda did."

"That's all gone," Julie said, but she crawled to the port pontoon and began rummaging through a side pouch similar to the one that held the toolkit. From the depths of the pocket she extracted a scruffy brown teddy bear with a zippered belly and tattered ears.

"Bear-Bear!" Caden cried.

The girl held the stuffed toy out of his reach until she had rescued four foil-wrapped cereal bars from its belly pouch, then handed him Bear-Bear along with one of the bars.

"Packrat!" Skylar said accusingly.

"Don't call me that! Call me Julie." She glared at Skylar and held the other bars beyond her sister's reach.

Skylar made a face. "Okay, Joooleee." She grabbed two bars from her sister.

"Hey! One's for Daddy!" Julie protested.

Skylar handed one to Emma, driving her sister close to tears.

"You save it for him," Emma said, returning the bar to Julie.

"She'll hide it," Skylar said.

Emma frowned and turned her back on them. She had more important things to think about, like getting the hell out of here before they all succumbed to hypothermia. The way the boy was shivering, she knew they were dangerously close.

"You girls get back under the blankets and tarp with him," she ordered. At first Caden protested, but he finally joined Julie.

"I'm not cold," Skylar insisted, refusing to move.

"It doesn't matter. You need to keep your brother warm." Emma set the wrench aside, dabbed at the carburetor with the cloth, and after pumping the gas line again, grasped the starter cord and yanked hard. The motor didn't make a sound.

Damn.

The throbbing in her temples was getting worse, and her shivering was making it difficult to hold the wrench and remove the plugs. *Concentrate!* she thought, and held her forearms tight against her chest, steadying her hands and fingers enough to narrow the gap between the contacts of first one plug, then the other.

Having finished his bar, Caden began to fuss with the rope tied to his life jacket.

Julie pulled his hands away. "No, you have to leave it on."

He squirmed from her grasp. "I gotta pee," he insisted, and scrambled up onto the cargo hold where, with his back to the girls, he relieved himself, directing most of the flow over the pontoon. Then he turned and jumped back onto the floorboards, splashing water onto his sisters and rocking the boat so violently that Emma almost dropped the plug she was working on.

"Knock it off!" she yelled. Caden cringed beside his sister and clutched his teddy bear to his chest.

Skylar glared at Emma. "I gotta pee, too."

For a moment, Emma was stumped. She looked around helplessly until she spied the bailing bucket.

"Here." She kicked the bucket toward the girl. "You can use this."

An expression of horror flitted across Skylar's face. Clutching the motor cover tight against her chest, she shook her head. "I'll wait."

Emma replaced the plugs and yanked the starter cord. This time she was rewarded by a feeble explosion in the cylinders. Encouraged, she yanked even harder and the motor coughed to life.

Skylar glowered at the motor. "Piece of shit." She thrust the cover at Emma. "My daddy could'a fixed it."

"Can you untie the painter?" Emma asked Julie, pointing to the bowline that attached the zodiac to the cedar branch.

The girl looked nervously toward the white-capped waves beyond their shelter. "Can't we stay here?"

"We need to get warm," Emma said. She nodded at Caden, who was shaking with cold. "Especially your brother." Then she added, "Don't worry. I'll find us a safe place."

Skylar jumped to her feet, shouting, "I'll do it."

"No!" Julie stood and grabbed the line. "I will." Wobbling unsteadily, she pulled the branch close enough to unfasten the knot.

"You're gonna fall, Julie!" Skylar yelled.

But the rope came free, the limb swung back into place, and Julie dropped safely beside her sister.

As they left the cove, Emma turned southward, even though they were running against a flood tide and fighting a stiff north-easterly wind, which prevented them from making much head-way. Tight-faced, Julie grabbed her brother and pulled him onto the floor between the seat and the cargo hatch. Skylar crawled forward and leaned over the hatch, facing the wind head on. Assured that they were positioned safely, Emma advanced the throttle. As the bow rose, forcing water to the stern, she grabbed the bucket with her free hand and began bailing.

The bay that she had been so sure must be around the hook didn't materialize, and Emma found herself in another channel battling white-capped waves. She was just beginning to think she had made a mistake when she spotted another small cove and a weather-beaten dock just off the starboard bow. Although there was no other sign of human activity along the shore, she suspected a cabin or at least some type of shelter might be hidden beyond the trees.

"Where are we?" Skylar demanded a few minutes later, as Emma guided the zodiac alongside the wharf.

"The painter," she said as she cut the motor and grabbed one of the wooden cleats. Julie let go of Caden and handed Emma the bowline. Once the boat was secure, she studied the shore where the far end of the dock was grounded in mud that smelled strongly of sulphur. Leading to a bank above the beach was a steep, rickety ramp that was tilted to one side, but it would be hours before the tide rose high enough to level it. She glanced at the shivering children. Navigating the ramp, she decided, was most certainly a better option than remaining in the boat.

"Let's see what's here," she said, climbing onto the dock, where she helped Caden, who was caped with the wool blanket, and Julie over the pontoon. Skylar clambered out on her own.

Emma's legs began to shake as soon as she started walking and the boards beneath her seemed to move up and down, but she knew it was simply an illusion, the result of being on the water for so long. The children were evidently experiencing the same sensation.

"Hey! I'm drunk!" Skylar exaggerated her weaving gait. Dropping his blanket, Caden copied her actions and would have fallen into the water had Julie not grabbed a strap on his life jacket.

"Watch those broken boards," Emma cautioned, rescuing the blanket.

The ramp was even shabbier than the dock, and she had to show the children how to walk up it sideways, holding onto the railing. "Here, take my hand," she said. Caden grasped her fingers and maintained a stranglehold on them until they were on solid ground.

As soon as they left the ramp, Julie and Skylar disappeared behind a clump of salal to relieve themselves. Emma opted for her own bush. She emerged to find Julie staring at the solid thicket of salal and salmonberries that hedged the shore.

"There's nothing here," the girl said.

Emma looked past her to a faint trail through the underbrush. "There might be a cabin," she replied. She headed into the tangle. To her left, she could hear water rushing, and in places where the bushes were sparse she could see a small rocky stream. After a few minutes the trail opened into a clearing, where, a stone's throw away from the creek, stood a small, dilapidated cabin.

"Look!" Caden cried, pointing to sunbeams that were streaming through a break in the clouds and dancing among the swaying treetops above the cabin.

"It's a ghost house," Skylar said, and began making spook sounds.

"Don't!" Caden ordered, hiding behind Julie.

The cabin door was nailed shut, but nearby hung a rusting hammer, which Emma used to free the nails. Inside were a table and three chairs, two wooden bunks and an old-fashioned wood stove. The whole place had the sharp, sweet odour of mice. A scurrying beneath the lower bunk suggested that the creatures were firmly in residence, and not pleased with their unexpected guests.

Skylar wrinkled her nose. "Stinky ghosts."

Reddish-brown rust coated the stove. Emma prodded its surface and squeezed the similarly corroded pipes, but found no visible holes. She lifted the firebox lid and saw that nestled on the grating was a clear plastic bag containing some news-paper and bits of wood. She pulled it out, scattering black ash and rust.

"We need some matches," she said, picking through the contents of the bag.

Emma inspected the room's only cupboard, a free-standing box with cream-coloured paint peeling from its boards and a door that creaked when she opened it. Inside was a collection of canned food, an odd assortment of dishes and cutlery, two pots, and a frying pan. There were no matches.

"Daddy has a lighter," Skylar said.

"Yeah?" Emma pictured the lighter resting in the man's pocket as he sank below the waves. She shuddered.

"In the boat," the girl persisted. "With his stash."

"You know where it is?"

"Yup. Right by the tools. I'll get it for you!"

Emma thought about the ramp. "No. I'll get it. You stay here with your brother and sister."

"I'm a good climber," Skylar insisted.

"No! You stay here and gather up some wood." But as she started down the path, Caden followed.

"There's ghosts!" he said, his lower lip quivering.

Not to be outdone by her brother, Skylar announced that if Caden was going, she was damned well going, too. Julie, who was clearly weighing obedience against fear, finally gave in to the latter and trudged after her siblings.

"Just stay off the ramp," Emma advised.

On the boat she quickly located the lighter, then grabbed one of the bags from the cargo hold, thinking it might contain dry clothes. As she started back to shore, she saw Caden jump from the bank onto the beach, promptly sinking to his thighs. He bent forward, groping at the mud.

She peered at him from the safety of the ramp.

"What the hell do you think you're doing?"

"Skylar made me drop Bear-Bear!" Shivering even more than he had on the boat, he held up the teddy covered in muck.

Tossing the bag to Julie, Emma dropped to her stomach and grabbed Caden's free hand, but when she tried to pull him up, he yelled, "You're hurting me!" She grabbed the loop on his life jacket instead, this time hauling him onto the ramp.

"I didn't push you," Skylar said, glaring at her mud-splattered brother. "You tripped."

"Because you bumped him," Julie said.

Emma hoisted the bag over her shoulder. "Come on, let's get up to the cabin so you can change."

"He smells like shit!" Skylar said, backing away from Caden. "You do stink," Emma agreed, although it was Caden's shivering that worried her more than his smell. Back in the cabin, she grabbed a pan from the cupboard and handed it to Julie. "You girls get some water from the creek. As soon as it's warm enough in here, we'll scrub him up."

Refusing to stay with Emma in the cabin, Caden followed his sisters. During their absence she gathered some wood scraps and started the bundle in the stove burning. As soon as she put the cover over the opening, however, smoke began pouring from the cracks in the stove and chimney. She thumped the pipes hard and was rewarded with a whooshing sound, then opened the lid to find the dried mud remains of a bird's nest scattered over an unburned portion of the paper. Shaking the pile so the mud fell through the grating, she blew on the few sparks that remained, coaxing the flickering embers into flames. Gradually the wood started snapping and crackling. Satisfied that it would continue burning, she replaced the lid and stepped outside to gather more wood scraps.

The children returned from the stream with Caden in the lead.

"We got some berries," he announced and held out a grubby fistful of green salmonberries. "Skylar eated hers but I brunged mine for you."

He was now shivering so hard that the gift almost fell from his outstretched hand. Emma couldn't bring herself to tell him that the berries were not ripe. "Yum," she said, placing one in her mouth. It tasted bitter, and her throat constricted when she swallowed.

"They're green," Julie informed Emma. "Our Mom said green berries make you sick."

"I'm not sick," Skylar said, a hint of worry in her voice.

Emma shook her head. "A few won't hurt. Just don't eat any more." She went back into the cabin, pulled a chair close to the stove, and lifted Caden onto it. "You sit here with Bear-Bear," she said, "and I'll get you some dry clothes."

"Bear-Bear's drownded." Caden held up the stuffed animal, which was dripping water over the floor.

"Maybe not, Caden." Emma placed the pot of water on the stove and covered it with a lid from the cupboard. "We'll just give him a little squeeze." She stepped outside and wrung as much moisture from the teddy as she could. "When your bear gets warm and dry, he'll be as good as new," she said, placing the stuffed animal on top of the lid.

"He couldn't drown anyways," Skylar said. "He's a toy."

Changing the children's clothing was a complicated project.

After obliging Caden, who insisted that all three females exit the cabin before he would remove his clothes, she faced another argument from Skylar. Having removed her plastic cape and life jacket, she refused to take off the oversized denim jacket she wore underneath.

"It must be awful heavy," Emma said, feeling the sodden collar and sleeves.

Skylar jerked away from her. "No! It's mine!"

Lifting her hands, Emma backed away. "Okay, okay."

"It's not your coat, Skylar," Julie said. "It's Daddy's."

"Daddy's — "

"Just change your pants," Emma said swiftly, thrusting a pair of jeans at the younger girl. Skylar glared at the pants and then at her brother. "He's gotta turn around. And close his eyes!"

Julie changed her outfit without a fuss while Emma scrubbed some of the mud from Caden's face.

With the wet clothes draped over a cord that some previous occupant had strung above the stove, and the children using the bunks as a pirate ship, Emma slipped outside for more water.

On her return she used an ancient can opener with a rusty blade to remove the tops from three tins of pork and beans, and set the tins on the stove. As they heated, Julie located some cracked plates and empty plastic food containers, four spoons, two plastic glasses, and two mugs with broken handles, and carefully arranged them on the table so there were two place settings on each side.

"What're we gonna drink?" Skylar asked.

"Water," Emma said as she ladled lukewarm beans into the dishes. The children were far too hungry to wait for the meal to get any hotter.

Skylar attacked her meal with the fury of a general routing enemy forces, plunging her spoon into the fray, scooping her victims into her mouth, and chewing fiercely. Julie organized her beans into a tidy rectangle, carefully removing small spoonfuls from the edges, and rearranging the rectangle following each bite. Caden ate nothing.

"I thought you were hungry," Emma said.

Caden frowned and shook his head.

Skylar nodded at the heap of beans on her brother's plate. "They're touching," she said. "He doesn't eat things that touch."

Emma noted that the shirt and wool sweater he was now wearing hadn't stopped the boy's shivering.

"If you don't eat, Caden, you won't get warm."

He still made no move toward his food.

Now what the hell am I supposed to do? She tapped her index finger against the table.

"Here," Julie said. Pushing her own meal aside, she took Caden's plate and, one by one, separated some of his beans so they each stood alone. His brows knit as he speared one of the beans with his fork and tasted it. When he took another, Julie relaxed and went back to her own meal, pausing occasionally to separate more beans for him.

The meal partially alleviated Emma's hunger, but did nothing to ease her headache — for that she needed caffeine. In the cupboard she found a jar half-filled with instant coffee, and although it had hardened into a solid mass, she was able to break off pieces with a table knife and dump them into a cup. She removed Bear-Bear from his perch long enough to pour some of the heated water into the cup.

I might live after all, she thought as the caffeinated warmth soothed her throat.

Halfway through her second cup, she heard a loud droning above the cabin. Plates and coffee were abandoned as she and the children rushed outside and began waving frantically at a bright yellow floatplane that swept across the clearing.

"Daddy!" Julie cried. "Daddy!"

The plane flew steadily westward until it disappeared beyond the treetops, and the throbbing of the engines faded away.

"I guess they couldn't see us," Emma said, breaking the silence that followed. Despondent, she returned to the cabin. "Don't worry," she promised. "I can get you home. As soon as the waves die down."

Julie shrugged. "Daddy'll find us."

"That's dumb!" Skylar said. "Daddy drownded!"

"He did not!" There was an edge to Julie's voice. "He's on a island. I saw him!"

Emma stepped between them. "We can't be sure what happened, Skylar. What counts is that we're all safe. Right?"

Skylar's cheeks puffed into a scowl. She didn't respond, but she didn't argue further.

"Is somebody gonna be looking for you, Emma?" Julie asked.

"Not yet." Emma tried to think of when it would actually occur to someone that she was missing. Sam wasn't returning from his conference in Vancouver until this evening, and even Twill wouldn't start to worry for another day or two.

"What about your mom and dad?" Skylar asked.

"My dad died when I was ten," Emma said, "and I haven't seen my mom for about six years now."

Julie frowned. "How come?"

"It's a long story." Emma looked at Julie and braved the question she had to ask. "Where is your mom?"

"Dead as a doornail," Caden said.

Now Julie frowned at him. "That's not nice, Caden,"

"That's what Old Jim said." The boy imitated an adult voice: "'That dame's dead as a doornail.'"

"She was an attic," Skylar said, earning another glare from Julie.

"She was sick, Skylar."

Fearing that the conversation was headed in directions that

she was not qualified to deal with, Emma said, "Okay, I'm going to get some more wood. Julie, maybe you and Skylar could wash up these dishes with what's left of the water."

"What about me?" Caden demanded.

"You stay by the fire." Emma didn't really expect him to comply. "Otherwise you'll start shivering again."

Outside the trees were swaying in a wild, communal dance beneath a squadron of black rain clouds. Hoping to make it to the boat and back before the children noticed she was gone, Emma ran along the trail to the water. At the top of the ramp, she paused and stared at the rolling waves that were rocking the now-floating wharf. Across the water to the west the sun was shining on the hilly slopes, but below them she was sure she could see the metallic glint of a fish farm.

We can easily run that far with the gas that's left, she reasoned.

"I don't think Daddy wants us to go in the waves again."

Emma swung around. Julie stood at the edge of the trail.

"I told you to stay in the cabin," Emma said, annoyed to find herself privately agreeing with the child. Alone she could have made it. With three frightened youngsters, it wasn't worth the risk. She turned abruptly and started down the ramp. "We might as well haul up the rest of your things."

Fortunately, because the tide was in, the wooden incline had levelled a little, and although the boards shuddered and creaked beneath them, they were able to walk down without much difficulty. The swaying wharf was harder to navigate, and the zodiac was bucking against the restraint of the bow rope. Emma retied it, cinching the boat tight to the wharf, and once aboard she secured the stern with the rope the children's father had used as a tether. After tilting the motor leg out of the water, she gripped the pontoon to steady herself and moved forward.

"We'll need these," she said, holding out the tarp and emergency wraps.

As she took them, Julie said, "Our blankets were in the bag that went overboard."

Emma wrestled the two remaining plastic bags from the cargo hold and lifted them over the side and onto the dock. Back on the wharf, she hoisted the bags over her shoulders while Julie gathered up the tarps. Together they staggered up the ramp to the trail.

"What have you got in here — rocks?" Emma asked as they paused for breath.

"It's our stuff. It's all we got."

In the clearing, Skylar was using a low-hanging cedar branch as a swing.

"Where's Caden?" Emma asked, looking around.

"Making graves." Skylar pointed to the side of the cabin.

"Graves?" Emma dumped her load just inside the door and walked around the corner of the building to where Caden was busily making crosses out of sticks, laying them in rows on the ground. "What are you doing, Caden?"

"I'm making graves for the ghosts. So they don't stay in the house."

Still bewildered, Emma turned to Julie, who shrugged. "Caden's always making graves. Aunty Glenda says he used to be a gravedigger."

"Yeah," Skylar agreed, coming behind them. "She says he's a rim creeper."

"A what?"

"A grim reaper," Julie corrected.

It was all too weird for Emma. "Just save some wood for the fire," she said, and escaped to the front of the cabin. Breaking some small branches and windfalls into burnable pieces, she carried them inside and dumped them on the floor beside the stove. Then she investigated the wooden bunks, peering under the clear plastic sheet that the children had half-pulled from the top bed and pressing her hand down on the plywood frames. They both felt sturdy. A calendar from 2005 was tacked to the wall of the bottom bunk, and a mound of chewed paper, moss, and seeds was tucked into a corner of the bed. Mouse droppings scattered over the rest of the boards attested to the owners of the cache. She scooped up the mound with a shingle and was tossing it into the firebox when Julie came inside.

"I told Skylar we had to do the dishes, but she won't come in."

Emma closed the firebox. "No problem."

She turned around as Skylar burst into the cabin, slamming the door behind her. With a sleeve-covered hand, she pulled down the inside latch, then leaned her back against the door. She was out of breath and the cuffs of her sleeves brushed the floor when she moved.

"Let me in!" Caden yelled from outside.

Julie frowned at her sister. "Let him in, Skylar."

"No! He's gonna kill me!" Ignoring Caden's thumps against the door, Skylar went to the largest bag and began emptying the contents onto the floor.

"Skylar!" Julie yelled. "You're messing everything up!"

"So? It's a junky old place anyway." She withdrew a yellow plastic squirt gun from the pile of stuff on the floor, took it to the table and immersed it in Julie's dishwater. A noisy squabble ensued, which Emma tried her best to ignore as she finished arranging the top bunk. Outside, Caden continued to yell and kick the door, each blow threatening the fragile truce Emma was maintaining with her headache. "Let your brother in," she ordered, "before he breaks the door!"

She jumped as Caden banged noisily on the windowpane. He peered through the weathered glass. "I see you!"

Pushed beyond patience, Emma yelled, "Open the damned door, Skylar!"

It was Julie who released the latch and grabbed Caden when

he stormed in, holding him long enough for Skylar to escape outside. Seconds later Caden was after her, and the two squabblers disappeared behind the cabin.

Julie went back to her dishes, and Emma collapsed on the lower bunk. She massaged her temples. *This is why I never had kids. Jesus!*

For dinner she heated the last of the food from the cupboard, this time being careful to keep the creamed corn separate from the cocktail wieners.

"Where's your plate, Emma?" Julie asked, eyeing the three containers set out on the table.

"I'm not very hungry," Emma lied. "I'll just make myself more coffee."

Julie studied her for a moment, then went to one of the bags and rummaged through the contents.

"Here," she said, thrusting a box of macaroni and cheese at Emma. "Now you can eat."

"I told you she was a packrat," Skylar said as Emma dumped the noodles into the water heating on the stove. They were almost done when Julie jumped up from the table and ran to the bags once more, this time tossing their clothes and toys onto the floor.

"What're you looking for?" Emma asked.

"Skylar's pills!" Julie yanked another handful of clothes from the bag.

Skylar shook her head. "They're in Daddy's pocket."

Julie stared at her, horrified. "Aunty Glenda says you have to take them, Skylar!"

Imagining diabetes and other life-threatening diseases, Emma asked, "What kind of pills?"

Julie said, "If Skylar doesn't take those pills, she'll drive everybody crazy."

"Daddy says they make me stupid," Skylar said.

"What kind of pills?" Emma repeated.

Julie frowned in concentration. "I don't know, but Skylar has to take them so she stops fighting all the time."

"Well, she's not fighting now, so I guess she doesn't need them," Emma said. She drained the noodles outside, mixed in the cheese, and spooned a good helping onto each plate. Julie watched closely, refusing to touch her share until Emma dished a plate up for herself.

The rain began while they were clearing up the dishes, a mild sprinkling on the roof that quickly turned into a torrent. Water sizzled onto the stove and splattered over the table, chairs, and floor.

"Hey! Our toys are getting wet!" Skylar cried. She and Julie began stuffing their things into the bags.

"Put them on the bunks," Emma said. "It's getting dark anyway, so we might as well crawl in with them and go to bed."

"We can't," Skylar said, pointing to the upper bunk, where drips were falling on the bedding.

Emma grabbed some pots and was placing them under the drips when she spied a nail in the wall above the bunk. She yanked the clothes from the line over the stove and tossed them onto the bottom bunk, then unfastened one end of the cord. It was just long enough to reach the nail and after tying it in place, she draped the sheet of plastic over the line, creating a partial tent above the top bunk. Because of the angle, however, half of the bed was still exposed.

"A couple of pins would be useful," she said.

"There's one on the wall!" Skylar pulled out the tack holding the calendar and handed it to Emma. Balanced on a chair, she pinned one side of the plastic to the wall, a few inches below the ceiling. Now the drips plunked harmlessly on the plastic and rolled onto the floor.

Julie was already in the tent, spreading clothes from their bags over the thermo blanket. Emma tossed up two life jackets. "You can use these for extra covers," she said, then turned to the boy. "Up you go, Caden. Time for bed."

"No way!" he protested. "It's still light out!"

"It won't be for long," Emma assured him, "and there's no sense staying up and getting soaked."

Still, Caden didn't move from his chair by the stove. "I gotta go pee."

"So do I!" Skylar danced cross-legged around the kitchen and Caden giggled.

Emma groaned, but knew there was no point in fighting. Draped with plastic bags, and screaming as they were once again lashed by wind and rain, the children raced for the outhouse. Emma followed at a more sedate pace and waited outside as one by one each bladder was emptied before taking a turn herself. By the time they were back in the cabin, she was soaked and cranky.

"Now to bed," she said in a severe no-nonsense tone.

Julie scrambled to the top bunk. "Come on, Caden. It's like a cave in here."

He climbed up behind her. "Lemme see!" Before entering the cave, however, he stopped. His lower lip trembled as he looked down at Emma. "Where's Bear-Bear?"

"Right here, sweetie." She held up the damp bear and as soon as it was safely in his arms he disappeared into the tent.

"I'm coming up too!" Skylar said.

"No!" Julie poked her head out of the tent opening. "There's no room."

Emma pointed to the lower bunk. "You're sleeping down here, Skylar. "

"Nuh-uh!" Skylar said. "Not with you!"

"Then I guess you'll have to sleep on the floor."

"All right, I will." Skylar found a semi-dry spot on the floor near the stove and curled herself into such a tight ball that her father's jacket almost covered her whole body.

Emma added more wood to fire. She remembered a conversation between her grandparents during one of her own rebellions. *Give the kid a chance to paddle her own boat, Lenora,* her grandfather had advised, *and she'll eventually find her way back to the right dock.*

She busied herself straightening the table, occasionally glancing at the little girl. Drips splashed Skylar's face until she moved closer to the stove and covered her head with one sleeve. A moment later she turned onto her other side. Finally, she lay facing the ceiling. "Arggh!" she cried when a large drip landed on her eye. Crawling to her feet, she stomped to the lower bunk and flopped under the cover. Emma joined her a few minutes later.

Squeezing as close to the wall as was possible, Skylar yelled up at her brother who was thumping his heels against the plywood above her, "Stop it, Caden!" The kicking increased and she shifted her anger onto Emma. "I don't like you."

"That's fine by me," Emma said, turning away from her.

Gradually the thumping and muttering from the top bunk died away and the room grew dark and cold. After a long while Skylar edged closer to Emma, so their backs were almost touching.

"Emma?" Julie's voice drifted through the darkness.

"Yeah?"

"Can we stay with you? 'Til Daddy finds us?"

The simple request made Emma feel as if she had stepped into quicksand. It was the same sensation she got every time her mother phoned, an event that occurred every three or four years and was usually accompanied by a lengthy monologue about how Emma was breaking her heart by refusing to visit her and Emma's stepfather. Even worse was the occasional announcement that her mother was coming to Windrush, a two- or three-day marathon of polite dialogue that stayed far away from the reason for their estrangement.

"You'll be okay, Julie. Tomorrow we'll go to Shinglewood, where I live, and get in touch with your aunt."

In a small voice that sucked Emma deeper into the sand, Julie said, "Aunty Glenda doesn't want us."

"You should keep us," Skylar said.

Amused that the child could so quickly forget her earlier declaration, Emma asked, "And what would I do with three little hooligans?"

"We wouldn't be any bother," Julie said. "I can take care of Skylar and Caden real good."

"No!" Emma's voice was sharper than she intended. "My life isn't the kind that kids fit into."

Skylar retreated back against the wall. "You gotta look after us. Julie saved you."

"And I saved you," Emma said.

"That's why you have to keep us."

As the hours crept by, Emma listened to the rain and the wind and wished she could sleep as easily as the children seemed to be doing. Instead, her mind kept pestering her with questions about the accident. Why had Forgie fallen? Should she have tried to revive him? And what if she had left the zodiac alone? Sure, it looked like they were in trouble, but what if they weren't? After all, it didn't sink when she came aboard. Maybe if she hadn't thrown the rope to the man, he'd be alive, not her. And the children would have a father.

Stop it!

But the questions continued. In desperation, she began a silent recitation of Tennyson's "Ulysses." She had learned the words at school and they always gave her a sense of being strong and in charge.

77

It little profits that an idle king,
By this still hearth, among these barren crags,
Match'd with an aged wife, I mete and dole
Unequal laws unto a savage race,
That hoard, and sleep, and feed, and know not me....

Eventually the familiar words lulled her to sleep. At some point during the night, she dreamed of two mice scurrying over the blankets, searching for their cache of seeds.

SEVEN

Dawn was breaking when Emma crept out of the cabin. For a few sweet moments her mind was calm as she listened to the high-pitched *konk-la-ree, konk-la-ree* of blackbirds competing with the varied tones of tree sparrows and warblers. Above her the sky was clear, and the treetops were still. On the landing she found that even the water was calm, the ebbing tide having once again grounded the end of the float.

The recriminating questions nudged their way back into her thoughts as she checked out the boat — to counteract them, she busied herself with the motor. Lowering the leg, she yanked the starter cord and was rewarded with an enthusiastic roar. Nevertheless, she adjusted the spark plugs one more time before returning to the cabin.

The children were just waking as she banged open the door.

"Up and at 'em, kids. We're heading home!"

Skylar crawled out of the bunk. "We don't got a home," she said, "an' I'm staying here."

"What about the owners?" Emma asked. She was beginning to understand that, invariably, if someone said "left" to Skylar, the child was bound to respond "right."

Caden climbed from the upper bunk and turned his hands into an imaginary machine gun. "We'll shoot 'em."

"We have to go so Daddy can find us," Julie said from the

bunk. She handed down the bag into which she'd stuffed their makeshift bedding, then helped Emma pull the plastic back.

Skylar shot her a look. "Daddy...."

"We're leaving," Emma cut in, thwarting a renewal of the argument over their father, "and that's that."

"We don't have to go with you," Skylar declared, clamping fisted hands on her hips. "You can't make us."

"No, but I can send someone after you."

"Then we'll hide in the bush."

Julie climbed from the bunk. "Where are we going, Emma?"

"To a fish farm I saw yesterday from the dock," she replied. "We can get some gas there and head across to Shinglewood. It shouldn't take us more than an hour."

"Well, I'm not damn going!" Skylar stomped outside and disappeared around the back of the cabin. When Caden started to follow, Julie grabbed his arm.

"We've got to go with Emma, Caden. There's no food here."

Caden wrenched his arm away from her. "I'm staying with Skylar!" he roared. He ran through the open door then stopped. "Skylar! Where is you?"

Julie stood in the doorway and yelled, "Daddy's gonna be mad at you, Skylar!" When there was no response, she said with less certainty, "She'll come."

Caden continued to call for his sister while Emma and Julie stuffed the rest of their gear back into the garbage bags and cleaned up the cabin as best they could. Once everything the children owned was outside, Emma hammered the board securing the door back in place. As she and Julie hauled the bags to the wharf, Caden followed, carrying Bear-Bear.

"I'm hungry!"

Emma lifted him into the boat.

"Julie already told you there's nothing left to eat, Caden."

But as soon as Julie climbed into the boat, she opened a side pocket and extracted the cereal bar that she'd been saving for her father. "Here," she said, handing it to her brother. She looked shoreward, searching for her sister. "Maybe she's lost."

"I won't go without her," Emma promised, scanning the trail entrance.

Only Caden seemed unconcerned. "Leave her here," he said around a mouthful of cereal bar.

Julie glared at him. "Shut up, Caden."

As soon as she started the motor and unfastened the mooring ropes, Emma saw the yellow flash of Skylar's shorts as she raced down the trail and onto the wharf. Without a word, the girl jumped into the boat, took a position near the bow, and turned her back on everyone. Putting the motor into gear, Emma gave a thumbs-up signal to Julie, who was sitting on the floorboards between the seat and the bow, her fingers gripping the ropes that lined the starboard pontoon.

From a distance the fish farm appeared to be deserted, but as they drew closer Emma could see a blue canvas-topped speedboat tied to the main platform upon which stood a small house and shed. Somewhere inside the house a dog was barking, and through a window she could see what looked like a man seated at a table. As she guided the zodiac to a spot behind the speedboat, the door to the house opened and a black and white border collie charged out. Cutting the motor, Emma wrapped the painter around a beam. She drew back as the dog snapped at her fingers.

"Whoa, boy," she said, cautiously extending her hand for the dog to smell. "I'm not going to hurt you." Ignoring her hand, the dog kept barking and charging back and forth along the float. At last a thin, long-haired man wearing a stained purple t-shirt and torn jeans stepped out of the house. He glared at Emma and the children. "This is private property."

Something about the man disturbed Emma. She wasn't sure

if it was the naked women tattooed on his biceps, his reaction to their intrusion on his privacy, or the fact that although she was familiar with most of the fish farmers in the area, she'd never seen him around Shinglewood. Whatever the reason, she found herself on her guard.

"I need some gas," she said, managing a tight smile.

His expression showed how little he cared. "So?"

"So I thought maybe I could get some from you," she said, giving up on pleasantries. "Or," she added, nodding towards the cellphone clipped to his belt, "use your phone to call for help."

He studied her for a moment, picking his teeth with a soiled fingernail. "Cell's dead." He looked at the children. "Gas'll cost ya four bucks a litre. Cash."

Emma had forgotten about money. Her wallet had gone down with the *Lazy Bones*. "I lost my wallet," she said, reluctant to tell him more. "I could give you an IOU...."

"Yeah, right. Forget it, lady. Cash or no gas." He turned back to the house.

Unexpectedly, Skylar appeared behind her. "Here." From the pocket of her father's jacket she pulled a brown leather wallet and held it out. Hiding her surprise, Emma took it from her. Inside was an assortment of bills, and she pulled out a ten and twenty.

"I'll give you thirty bucks." She set the spare gas can on the dock. "And you fill it."

He swung around and scowled at the money yet made no move to take it or the gas can.

Emma's eyes narrowed. "Listen, jerk," she said, shoving the cash into her pocket. "The law says it's your responsibility to help boats in distress. Now you either move your butt and fill this gas can or I sic the cops on you and the owners of this floating fishbowl."

His eyes flickered when she mentioned the police, and she shivered beneath the venomous glare he fixed on her. Grudgingly, he picked up the can and headed for the shed. Emma jumped onto the float, causing the dog to bark with renewed frenzy, and followed the man into a metal shed filled with gas barrels. He opened a valve on the nearest one and, after unscrewing the cap from her gas can, inserted the nozzle.

"Where'd you say you was from?"

"I didn't." Emma handed him the money.

He stuffed the bills into his pocket before he turned off the valve. While he locked the shed, she lugged the gas can back to the boat where Caden and Skylar were trying to coax the border collie closer. Growling low in its throat, the dog crouched as if to spring.

The man walked over and knelt beside him as Emma hoisted the gas can into the zodiac.

"He don't like kids," he snarled at Caden.

Wide-eyed, the boy backed away from the platform and edged closer to Julie, who was seated on the far side of the zodiac. Skylar had already returned to her position near the bow.

"He's a stupid dog anyway," she said.

The man watched, unsmiling, as Emma started the motor and released the mooring ropes. When the zodiac was safely away from the float, she cast a quick glance backwards. He was still standing by the edge of the platform, only now he was holding the cellphone to his ear.

The channel soon opened into the grey-blue waters of the Queen Charlotte Strait. In contrast to the night of the storm, the water was now so calm that it reminded Emma of thick syrup. On the western horizon a white and black tug pulling a massive barge was heading north. To the east a prawn boat was slowly making its way towards Bonwick Island, and in the far distance she could see the purple slopes of Vancouver Island.

"Look!" Caden shouted, pointing off the port pontoon to a

large rock upon which dozens of fat sea lions were lounging. Emma slowed the engine and they heard a chorus of hoarse growls and barks as the lions waved their heads and lifted their flippers, as if shooing the intruders away.

Caden wrinkled his nose as the odour of old fish and sea lion feces drifted over them. "Stink-eee!"

Julie's face paled as she maintained her white-knuckle grip on the pontoon rope.

The sooner she gets off this water, the better. Emma opened the throttle to full speed and steered away from the rocks.

"No! Go closer!" Skylar cried. At the same time an especially large bull slid into the water just off the zodiac's stern.

"He's coming after us!" Julie shrieked.

The sea lion dove beneath the surface, then reappeared farther away from the boat.

"Aw, he wouldn'ta hurt us," Skylar said.

"Yeah, he could," Julie insisted. She didn't calm down until they were well into the strait and the lions were mere dots on the water behind them.

Hoping that no whales made an appearance, as they often did in these waters, Emma guided the zodiac across the strait, and gradually Julie began to relax. When Caden grew restless and leaned over the port pontoon to trail his hand in the water, she hauled him back onto the floorboards. Then, to keep him there, she started a game of rock-paper-scissors. Skylar kept her back toward them.

Their preoccupation gave Emma a chance to investigate their father's wallet. A simple leather billfold, it was worn smooth at the crease and contained little more than money, a driver's licence with a Campbell River address, and a social insurance card, both issued to Dennis Warner. In one pocket was a crinkled photo-booth picture of the children. A second pocket held a pay stub from the Silver Bay Logging Camp and three receipts, one from a restaurant in Port Hardy, and two for gasoline that were marked in pencil, "Charge to S.B." Silver Bay? She was surprised to find no credit cards. For several minutes she contemplated the licence photo that turned her image of the bearded stranger who'd grasped the rope she'd thrown during the storm into a human being with a rugged face and Skylar's eyes.

Slipping the wallet back into her pocket, Emma studied the child at the bow. Skylar's tangled blonde hair blew freely behind her as she leaned into the wind, clutching the safety ropes with small hands half-covered by the sleeves of the denim jacket. Emma wondered how anyone so tiny could be so tough.

⚓

Just off the tip of Malcolm Island, the sea grew choppy with such a strong tidal current that staying on course required all of Emma's attention and every bit of power that the Yamaha could produce. Intent on controlling the zodiac, she was startled when a blue speedboat zoomed past on her port side, heading towards Alert Bay.

"Hey! That's the boat from the fish farm," Skylar shouted.

Caden was more interested in a massive white cruise ship that seemed to fill the channel between Cormorant and Malcolm Islands. "I'm gonna ride on that boat," he said, earning a scornful look from Skylar.

⚓

Like many coastal towns that were originally accessible only by sea, Shinglewood was clustered just above the high tideline. Only recently had it begun to move westward following Flume Road, which wound from the public wharf up a long hill and disappeared from view as it angled through timberland to the main island highway. As they drew close, Emma could see the curve of the waterfront, backed by a business strip that included a bait shop, accounting office, barbershop, Sam Gabriel's law office, and Kate's coffee bar.

Carefully manoeuvring the zodiac around the boats tied to the public wharf, Emma found an empty berth and nudged the boat alongside the dock. The children were silent as she secured the ropes. With hands that had inexplicably begun to shake, she helped them onto the wharf and led the way to the gravelled lot where her "wreckmobile" was parked. A mid-eighties model, the blue Chevrolet crew-cab pickup was in good running order thanks to Twill, who conducted periodic tune-ups on the engine and supervised Emma's work on minor jobs. Today she felt as if the rusting fenders and cracked windshield were the battle scars of an old and dear friend — one that embodied all the familiar trappings of her life as it had been, before Sam sent her halfway up the coast and Arnold Forgessen had stumbled across her path. A lump formed in her throat as she knelt on the gravel in front of the truck.

"Is it broked?" Caden asked as she peered under the front bumper.

Emma swallowed back the lump. "No, Caden. I'm just looking for... this!" Her fingers grasped the magnetic box where she stored the extra keys, and she stood up again, but now her hands were shaking so much she couldn't insert the key into the lock.

"What the hell?" she muttered under her breath as the box and keys slipped from her fingers. Caden picked them up and handed them to her, and by holding the key with both hands she finally unlocked and opened the door.

A faint musty odour permeated the crew cab, which appeared even more dilapidated because the radio had been ripped out, and the upholstery resembled the shredded remains of a wild cat attack. These were some of the features that had knocked the price of the vehicle down to a level that Emma could afford. The blanket that usually covered the seats was in her dryer back at Windrush.

Skylar eyed the tattered seats with considerable suspicion.

"Are we going to Aunty Glenda's?"

Emma shook her head. "Campbell River is a two-hour drive from here, Skylar." She gripped the door handle. "Just get in... please."

Skylar stayed beside the rear wheel well, kicking at the pebbles beneath her feet.

"Come on," Julie said wearily as she helped Caden climb onto the back seat, then settled beside him. "We gotta do what she says."

Still, the younger girl refused to move, and Emma's temper flared. "Get in the goddamned truck!" she yelled. To her great relief, Skylar climbed aboard.

⁂

Staff Sergeant George Shuter was husky, and his thick, black hair was tinged with grey. Born and raised on a reserve in the interior of the province, Sergeant George, as he was known to everyone in town, had been assigned to the Shinglewood detachment five years earlier. He had quickly become an integral part of the village by organizing community sports events and antique car rallies, participating in fundraising drives, and frequenting the coffee shops and bars — not to drink, but to keep in touch with what was happening in his jurisdiction. Emma had often joined him for coffee at the Rusty Anchor, sharing a groan over Kate's bizarre pastry experiments and resisting his constant pleas to purchase her grandfather's 1953 Studebaker that was rusting away in the middle of a salmonberry thicket at Windrush.

He was talking with the clerk in the RCMP office when Emma approached the small reception window. Breaking off in midsentence, he stared at her in surprise.

"Emma? What's happened to you?"

With filthy, bedraggled hair and clothes and shadowed by three woebegone kids, Emma realized she must look a strange picture. But when she tried to explain, she couldn't find the words. "I… I… we were on the boat…." The warm room began spinning around her and she grabbed the counter for support. "… Captain Forgessen… he was bleeding and… and I'm trying to look after these kids and they were almost drowned and their dad's gone and…." Her voice broke and she closed her eyes.

"Hold on, Emma!" Sergeant George disappeared from the window and entered the waiting room from a side door. By then Emma was sobbing.

"It's okay," he said, putting his arm around her. "You're safe now."

Huddled close together, the children stared wide-eyed as he guided her to a wooden bench. He looked at them with concern. "Are you visiting Emma?"

Julie shook her head, and Emma gulped back a sob. "We were in an accident…." She broke off, overcome by a fresh wave of tears.

The sergeant thrust a box of tissues at her and called out to the clerk, "Get an ambulance, Carrie, and send Constable Schmidt out here." He scrutinized the children again. "Are you okay?"

They nodded, but their expressions as they crowded beneath the reception window told a different story. When a female officer came into the cramped waiting area and knelt beside them, Caden backed into Julie.

"Are we going to jail?" he whispered, his eyes wide.

"No way, honey," Constable Schmidt said. "We're here to help you." Julie and Caden relaxed slightly. The officer rose to her feet and guided them to a bench opposite Emma's. Skylar followed reluctantly, her face twisted in a scowl.

Sitting on a corner of the bench where she could face the three of them, the officer made eye contact with Julie. "Can you tell me your names?"

As Julie mumbled her introduction, Sergeant George returned his attention to Emma, who was wiping her eyes with a tissue.

"This is ridiculous," she said, but several more minutes passed before she could trust her voice enough to give him the basic details of what had happened. As she finished, two male paramedics entered the already-crowded waiting room. One, whom Emma had never met, stopped beside the children. The other, a young man named Paul Ruttledge, whom Emma knew from the fish hatchery, squeezed in front of Emma.

"I don't need...." She glanced at the sergeant, then held out her arm and allowed Paul to wrap a blood pressure cuff around it. While he shone lights in her eyes and checked her temperature, she correctly identified what day it was and named the current prime minister. After gently cleaning and bandaging a small cut above her forehead, Paul announced that aside from exhaustion, she was suffering no ill effects from her ordeal.

"I said I was okay," Emma repeated.

The children received a similar verdict, and as soon as the paramedics left, the clerk brought in a tray of muffins and hot chocolate, which even Caden ate without a fuss. Emma begged for a coffee, and by the time she had finished it, along with two muffins, she was feeling well enough to follow Sergeant George into his office to give him a more detailed account of the accident. In the waiting room, Constable Schmidt continued to interrogate the children in such an easygoing way that they didn't realize they were being questioned.

Emma was comforted by the sound of Caden's chuckle, and felt that she was finally gaining control over her emotions. Still, she needed both hands to hold her second cup of coffee.

The sergeant regarded her with worried eyes. "Feeling better?"

She pulled herself straighter in her chair and smiled faintly. "I'm sorry," she said. "I don't know where that came from."

"What's more important is what happened." He settled himself in front of his computer and switched on a recorder. "Tell me about this accident."

"It's a long story." She dodged back and forth from the beginning, when Sam sent her on the quest for Mary Dahl's signature, to the sinking of the *Lazy Bones* and the drowning of the children's father. He listened quietly until she mentioned how uneasy she had felt about the fish farmer.

"Where did you say this farm was located?" he asked.

"I'm sure the cabin we stayed in was on Topaz Island," she said. "The fish farm is right across from it."

The sergeant nodded and absently tapped his fingers on his desk. "I understand this is hard, Emma, but can you tell it to me once more from the beginning?"

She nodded, and in the second telling her voice was stronger, and she remembered a few more details. Sergeant George typed furiously as she spoke and when she finished, he led her through another round of questioning, his manner growing more brusque and official with each query.

"So, you were on this boat — the *Lazy Bones*? Okay. And what did you say happened to Captain Forgessen?"

"I don't know what happened to him, George. I came back into the cabin and he was lying on the floor. There was blood all over the place. I assume that he fell and hit his head against something. Probably the step to the co-pilot's chair."

"He was dead?"

"He wasn't breathing and I couldn't feel a pulse. Seemed pretty dead to me."

"And that's when the boat sank?"

"No! As I've already said, we hit a rock."

"And this Dennis Warner," he continued, fingering the wallet Emma had surrendered to him, "you say you never met him before?"

"Never."

Tapping the edge of the keyboard, he studied the notes on his computer monitor.

"The kids' aunt... Glenda ... where did you say she lives?"

"I don't know. Somewhere in Campbell River." Emma's head was beginning to pound. "Listen, George, I've told you everything that happened. Isn't that enough?"

He frowned. "Not when we have two irregular deaths to investigate. At this point, Emma, there is no such thing as enough." He returned to his notes. "Now, Sam sent you to Bear Creek Landing for what reason?"

"For the tenth time, I had to get a release signed by this woman — Mary Dahl. Ask Sam. He'll tell you."

Sergeant George met her gaze, then nodded and pressed a button that started a distant printer humming. "I'll just get you to sign this," he said, collecting a printout of her statement and bringing it to the desk.

Emma scrawled a shaky signature on the papers. "Does this mean I can go home?"

"I have to make a few calls first," he said. He walked back to the waiting room with her and motioned for Constable Schmidt to come back into the office. As the door closed behind them, Emma looked at the bench where Julie sat with Caden curled up beside her, thumb in mouth and Bear-Bear held close to his chest. Skylar, having pushed aside their cups and muffin wrappers, was perched on the coffee table. She looked as forlorn as her siblings.

Emma sat on the opposite bench and tried to think of something comforting to say. *They hate me and I don't blame them,* she thought. *But I can't help them. I'm a wreck myself.*

She got to her feet and went to the window. From here she could see Flume Road and along it the entrance to Bailey Road, which led back to Windrush.

I need to go home! Emma rested her forehead against the cool window glass. She was visualizing herself soaking in her old clawfoot bathtub when Sergeant George opened the door.

"Emma? Could I see you inside for another moment?" Once

they were back in the main office, he said in a conciliatory tone, "We have a slight problem."

"'We'?"

"Yes, well...." He cleared his throat. "I haven't been able to locate the children's aunt. Which means I'll have to transport them to Campbell River."

"Right...." she answered cautiously, aware that anything she said might be construed as an agreement to help him.

"The thing is, those kids are very frightened."

"Wouldn't you be?"

"Exactly! And since they do feel safe with you, it makes perfect sense for them to stay at your place tonight."

"Oh sure, George. A minute ago you were interrogating me as a murder suspect. Now you want to entrust children to my care?"

"That was just procedure. Besides, I checked your name through our system." He grinned. "You're clean."

"Gee, that's a surprise." Emma motioned towards Constable Schmidt. "What about Ann?"

He shook his head. "Her shift is almost over, and you know she has two toddlers at home."

Emma frowned.

"Sorry, but there's no way...." Suddenly she thought of Wendy Grieves. She was an ebullient social worker and Sam's greatest headache whenever he defended parents deemed unfit by the Ministry of Children and Families to retain guardianship of their children. Although Wendy had little patience for the failings of parents and Ministry bureaucrats, she fought like a tigress any time she thought the children in her care were getting a raw deal.

If anyone can help these guys, it's Wendy.

She presented the idea to the sergeant, but he shook his head. "I already checked. She's out of town until tomorrow at least, and there's no one else available in her office. It's either you or Family Services in Campbell River."

Through the reception window, Emma saw Skylar hunched forward on the coffee table, the back of her denim jacket pulled taut by her crossed arms. She was as close to tears as Emma had seen her.

"It's not a good idea for them to stay with me," Emma said. "I'm a wreck. And besides, they're already too attached to the idea that I'll look after them."

"Well, I don't think another night or two will make that much difference," said Sergeant George.

"It will tomorrow morning. I've been gone three days and I have a lot of catching up to do at work."

He smiled. "Already called Sam. He said to tell you to take the rest of the week off."

In the outer room Julie lifted her head. Her eyes were filled with so much hopelessness, Emma's stomach tightened into a knot. She knew that kind of despair and had experienced first-hand the helpless outrage that occurs when other people are making critical decisions about your life.

Her resolve weakened, and she turned back to the officer. "Tell you what, George. You rip up that fix-it ticket for my broken windshield and I'll keep the kids."

The sergeant's eyes widened. "You'd bargain with their welfare?"

Emma wouldn't but she was gambling that Sergeant George didn't know that. "I can't afford to fix the windshield right now," she said. "And since I hardly ever drive anywhere but here, it's not hurting anything."

He massaged his chin thoughtfully. "I won't rip it up, but I'll adjust the ticket to give you three months instead of three weeks."

"Works for me," Emma said. "So long as we're clear that I'm only keeping those kids until Wendy's back."

EIGHT

"I told you she wouldn't give us away!" Caden shouted as he unexpectedly launched himself into Emma's arms. Giving the sergeant a see-what-I-mean glare, Emma hugged the boy back. "It's only for tonight, Caden," she said. She set him down. "Tomorrow you'll go to a family that can take proper care of you."

"Yep, she's dumping us," Skylar said. But her expression as she followed her siblings out to the parking lot was one of relief.

Julie said, "Maybe Daddy will come by then."

Thankfully, Skylar and Caden were scuffling and didn't hear her.

"Everyone into the truck," Emma said. "We need to get something to eat that isn't full of sugar."

Just inside the entrance to the Rusty Anchor was a large sand-filled box that resembled a miniature beach. Backed by a mural of an old troller half-submerged in the sand, the box contained a large, rusty anchor, as well as an assortment of floats and shells, dried starfish, and odd-shaped pieces of driftwood. The rest of the room was decorated with fishnets, bits of marine equipment, and rustic galley tables with matching benches.

Emma chose a seat near the window with a clear view of the harbour. Kate Gabriel swooped down on their table before the children were even settled.

"What on earth?"

"Later," Emma said and, after hastily introducing the children, gave an order for bacon, eggs over easy, and toast. Then she noticed Caden's worried expression and added. "Make one of those eggs scrambled," she said, "And please make sure nothing touches."

⚓

Kate kept her curiosity at bay until she brought the meal to their table. "I still don't get it. Sam said you were coming down with some guy on a freight boat. How did you end up with these three?"

"She saved us," Caden said, eyeing the bacon as if he was trying to determine whether the individual streaks of fat, meat, and rind should be kept separate.

Skylar, who had already stuffed a large piece of toast into her mouth, said, "We saved her first!"

"It's a long story," Emma said, "and I'm way too tired to tell it now."

Kate studied her carefully then looked again at the children. "Whatever." She hurried off to make them more hot chocolate.

When she came back, Emma asked, "Is Sam in the office?"

Kate shook her head. "He's at home. Had a few too many at the conference yesterday." She nodded towards the empty glass case near the counter, where Emma's pottery was usually displayed. "By the way, I sold your bowls to a couple from California."

"Guess I'll have to make some more." Emma remembered her promise on the *Lazy Bones*. "Or not."

Kate tilted her head to one side. "Or not? Oh, please tell me that you've finally seen the light! Had an epiphany! Are ready to try something original!"

"Don't get your hopes up, Kate. I've simply decided not to make any more bowls. And I'm glad you sold those. I can put the money towards my roof."

"Well, you work for a cheap lawyer like my husband and that's what happens."

"Just remember, you said that, not me." Emma hesitated. "You think you could watch these guys for me while I pop into the office?"

"So now I'm a babysitter as well as a sales agent?" Kate waved her hand around the empty room. "Lucky for you we aren't exactly hopping here." As Emma stood, Kate added, "Make sure you come back before quitting time."

Right away Julie looked worried and Skylar hostile.

"She's just joking," Emma said, "and I promise I won't be more than a few minutes." She started for the door, then stopped and turned to Kate. "I forgot. I need to borrow your key."

Emma waved at Joe Spangle, the barber in the next building, as she unlocked the law office door and stepped into the large reception area. It was a simple room, with a few seaside pictures breaking the monotony of the pale blue walls and furnished with a desk, filing cabinets, and two leather easy chairs.

"Sam?" she called, in case he had returned to work without Kate's knowledge. Receiving no answer, she quickly checked the closet-sized equipment room that also served as a library, the slightly larger conference room, and finally Sam's office, which faced the harbour and the wharf leading to the bait shop. Everything was much as she'd left it. She paused. Was it really only four days ago? She inspected three new files that Sam had placed on her desk and found nothing that required her immediate attention.

Before leaving, she went into the washroom and gasped at her reflection in the mirror. *No wonder Kate was curious.* Her face was scratched, and her hair was matted and stiff. She cleaned herself up as best she could and tried to run a brush through her hair, making it look worse than ever. Giving up on further improvements, she switched off the lights, locked the office, and returned to the café for the children.

⁓

Bailey Road was a two-kilometre stretch that ran past several modern houses and a forested area before ending at an intersection with River Road, a gravelled track that forked west past Twill's house to the salmon hatchery where he worked and east toward Windrush. As she turned east, Emma glanced back at Twill's house, but saw no sign of him.

When she pulled up beside her house, Emma felt as if a great weight had been lifted from her shoulders. She was home. Kate might regard Windrush as a mausoleum, but to Emma it was a palace.

Clutching Bear-Bear tightly, Caden eyed the alder and maple trees shrouding the building. "Is this your house?"

"Yes, my boy, this is my home." Emma stepped out of the truck, grabbed the bag of groceries she had bought at the market, and led the way up three wide steps to the main entrance.

Skylar peered at the word Emma's great-grandfather had carved on the lintel when he built the house almost a hundred years earlier.

"Windrush," she read aloud.

Emma retrieved a key from under the mat. The door creaked as she opened it, reminding her once again to oil the hinges. Noticing how Caden's eyes widened at the sound, she said, "No one has died here, Caden, and there are no ghosts."

Caden, however, was staring into the wide hallway at Purkins, who was resting in a pool of sunshine. "Hey! A kitty!"

The cat arched his back as he eyed the three children charging toward him, then leapt through the kitchen doorway. Emma heard him skitter across the floor into the boot room. A thump of the cat flap signalled his escape.

"Purkins isn't used to children," Emma said. It would be a

long time before her pet forgave her for staying away, and she doubted that he'd ever forgive her for bringing the kids into his domain.

She deposited the groceries on the u-shaped counter in the kitchen, then opened a window above the breakfast table.

"This is nice," Julie said, turning in a circle as she surveyed the room. Blue-checked curtains graced the windows and a pink-flowered oilcloth covered the table. Pale green wainscoting on the lower third of the walls, topped with olive-leaf wallpaper, gave the room a garden ambience that was heightened by its sky-blue ceiling. It was tented in the corners with spiderwebs that Emma always intended to clear away but never quite got around to vacuuming.

"Spiders have rights, too," she once told Twill. "And what kind of world would it be without dust bunnies?"

While Emma put the milk and sandwich meat in the fridge, Skylar and Caden, explored the boot room. After an unsuccessful attempt at crawling through Purkin's flap, they peered through the window onto the narrow side yard overgrown with willow saplings and one large ornamental spruce.

"Aw, he's gone," Caden said, shifting his attention to the washer and dryer and taking turns with Skylar at amplifying their voices by yelling into the machines. Emma was grateful that the third door, which led to her studio, was closed.

Julie wandered across the hall to the dining room, where she ran her hand over the grand oak table. Emma's grandmother had served many family dinners at that table, back when the room had been filled with aunts and uncles and cousins. But it was the chandelier above the table that caught Julie's attention — a shaft of sunlight had transformed the elongated crystal raindrops into a cascade of colour. "It's beautiful!" she said. "Like millions of rainbows." She turned to Emma, watching her from the doorway. "Can we eat in here?"

"If you want," Emma said.

After storing the rest of the groceries, she showed them the other parts of the house, starting with the downstairs bathroom, which Caden insisted on trying out.

"Don't go anywheres 'til I'm done!"

"Oh, no," Skylar groaned, but still she wandered away to the living room door at the end of the hallway. There she waited until the toilet flushed and Caden and his bear emerged.

The living room was cluttered with newspapers and pottery magazines, and the rock fireplace held the blackened remains of at least two fires.

"Where's your TV?" Caden asked, and when Emma said she didn't have one, he gave her a pitying look. "You must be real poor."

"Aunty Glenda doesn't have a TV neither," said Julie. "She says they're bad news."

"Well, at least we agree on one thing," Emma muttered. She had given her television away following a solid week of watching reruns of New York's twin towers dissolving. "If the world is determined to go crazy," she had told Twill, "I don't need to mess up my day by watching it do so."

On the southern wall of the living room, set between two curtainless windows, was a pair of French doors that drew Skylar like a magnet.

"Hey! A river!" She unlocked one of the doors and headed out onto the covered deck, where a long staircase descended to a wooden landing. On one side of the stairway was a boat shed even older than the house, with rust-red shingles covering the outer walls. The other side was terraced from the conservatory windows down to a wooden bench on the grassy bank, where the lazy waters of the Stuart flowed past. With the recent rains and snow melt, the river had swollen to the size of a three-lane highway, and clumps of willows that were usually on dry land had been turned into small islands, their green branches grazed by early afternoon sunshine.

Whenever she was away from the Stuart, Emma seemed to lose an essential part of her being, experiencing a kind of emptiness that lingered until she returned to its banks. Today, as she stood on the deck and inhaled the marshy air, she could feel the river's strength regenerating her.

Skylar and Caden started down the stairs, but Emma called them back. "Not unless I have the time to be with you," she said. "And right now we need to bring in your gear."

"Is this where we're sleeping?" Julie asked a few minutes later as Emma, laden with two of the garbage bags, led them up the curved staircase at the far end of the lower hallway. Three generations of Phillips children had left numerous nicks and the occasional initial in the varnished banister and stairs. After a roof leak during one of the previous winter's storms, Emma had removed the carpeting from the upper hallway, revealing the original polished hardwood flooring. She dropped the bags in the corridor and went into her room, which took up the south quarter of this floor. Here the ceiling was stained with ever-widening brown circles, and the bucket she'd placed beneath the largest stain was half-filled with water.

Julie went to the bookcases that lined one wall of the room, but Caden and Skylar ran to a set of French doors, identical to those downstairs and also flanked by large windows.

"No!" Emma cried as Skylar reached for the door handle. "That balcony isn't safe."

"I was just gonna look," Skylar said, and stomped to a window seat in the corner.

The rest of the room contained an easy chair, a large old-fashioned dresser, and a double bed with nightstands on either side, both piled high with crime novels.

"This is where I'm sleeping!" Caden said, bouncing on the mattress.

Emma opened a window that duplicated the view in the den. "Not a chance, Caden. This is my room, and I'll thank you to stop destroying my bed."

Without knowing how she would divide the two remaining rooms, she ushered the children along the hallway, past a full bathroom and a second small bedroom on the left, to a pink-flowered bedroom on the right almost as big as her own.

"This was my room when I was younger," she said to Julie. "You and Skylar can sleep in here."

Skylar didn't seem happy with the arrangement, nor did Caden when Emma consigned him to the middle bedroom, but he did smile when he saw the *Bad Boys* poster tacked to the wall beside one of Wayne Gretzky and another of Dominik Hasek, both in full hockey gear.

"My grandmother fixed this room up for my boy cousins," she told him.

His smile disappeared. "Are they coming back?"

She gave his shoulder a reassuring squeeze. "No, they're all grown up and live a long way away. I hardly ever see them now."

"Good," Caden said, moving away from her. "'Cause I don't sleep with nobody but Julie. Not even Skylar."

Emma carried the bags to the girls' room and was just depositing them on the floor when she heard the front door open. A moment later a deep voice hollered up the stairs, "Emmie? You here?"

Followed at a safe distance by the children, she hurried downstairs to the lower hallway.

"Twill!"

"You were supposed to be back yesterday, young lady," he said with mock sternness. As she drew closer, he frowned.

"What the hell's happened to you?"

The fishy aroma emanating from Twill's plaid flannel jacket, the familiar cinnamon beard trimmed close to his chin, and the concern edging his voice pushed her close to tears once again.

"It's a long story," she said. Afraid that a hug would completely wreck her composure, she stepped back from him and turned to Julie, who had halted with Caden and Skylar at the foot of the stairs and was warily eyeing the stranger.

"Kids, this is my friend Twill Lafferty, and this," she nodded toward the children, "is Julie, Skylar, and Caden."

"Tu-u-will!" Caden said. "That's a funny name!"

Twill feigned indignation. "I'll have you know it's a fine old Newfoundland name," he said. "Twillingate Island is the place where my dear mutter was raised up."

"It's funny," Caden insisted.

"Methinks your handle's got its own brand of peculiarity," Twill said.

As the boy studied him uncertainly, Skylar pointed to a small disk on the back of Twill's head. "You got something stuck on your head."

Twill reached up and touched the disk. "Well, I'll be sniggered! Now how do you suppose that got there?"

"Let me see!" Caden said, positioning himself between Skylar and Twill so that he, too, could see the brown plastic disk, about the size of a loonie, connected with a wire to a small device in Twill's ear.

"It's for his hearing," Emma said. "Twill is deaf, but he has a machine that lets him hear."

Caden's eyes widened. "Like a super ear?"

Twill nodded. "That means I can hear *everything*. So you better not be keeping any secrets."

The three youngsters stared at him, clearly not willing to accept this, but obviously unable to dismiss the possibility that he might be telling the truth. Twill, in turn, studied them back. "And from which branch of the Phillips family tree do you lot spring from?" he asked.

"We're not branches!" Caden retorted.

Emma said, "I'm babysitting them for Sergeant George. Wendy Grieves is picking them up tomorrow." Before he could ask for an explanation, she added, "I was about to make coffee. Would you like some?"

Twill shook his head. "No, I've got to get back to the hatchery. There's a school group coming in about half an hour."

Skylar, who had been watching him steadily, asked, "Are you Emma's boyfriend?"

The two adults turned toward her.

"We're.... " Emma was unable to describe in words that an eight-year-old would understand the somewhat unusual relationship that she and Twill enjoyed.

"Well, now, my dear," Twill said, "methinks it's plain as the nose on your mug that I'm a man all right, and Emmie here's my friend. How you figure to put the two of them things together is pretty much up to you." Giving the child no chance to respond, he clapped his battered grey Tilley hat onto his head and escaped through the open doorway.

Emma followed him outside. "Twill, who's running the fish farm about twenty minutes north of Sea Lion Rock?"

"There's a lot of farms up that way. Why?"

She shrugged. "I can't go into it now. This one's across from Topaz Island."

He scratched at his beard. "Probably Northern Sea Farms. They have several in that area."

"Have you met any of their hired help?"

"Some of them. There was one guy who used to come by the hatchery. Apparently he left a couple of months back without giving a reason. Northern was scrambling to find someone to replace him but I think they finally got a guy from the Lower Mainland."

She had sparked his curiosity as well as his concern, but she knew Twill wouldn't press her for details.

"I'll come by tomorrow," she said. "Thanks for taking care of Purkins."

"No problem." He gripped her shoulder in a comforting gesture that came dangerously close to releasing the floodgates barely keeping her tears in check. Then, with a slight nod, he started down the steps.

Emma took a deep breath and let it out slowly, then returned to the hallway where Skylar and Caden were racing each other up and down the stairs, while Julie watched and kept score.

"How about you three play outside for a while?" Emma suggested.

With a loud whoop, Skylar headed out the door, chased by Caden and followed at a slower pace by Julie. Before closing the door behind them, Emma yelled, "And stay away from the river!"

Having ensured that the children were playing in the backyard nowhere near the water, Emma gathered together a clean set of clothes and a small glass of brandy and headed for the bathroom, where she filled the tub with steaming water. She gave a sigh as she sank into its warmth, stretching her legs out. Leaning back, with her head supported by the cool porcelain rim, she closed her eyes. But neither the warm water nor the brandy gave her the emotional release she was looking for. Instead she found herself listening for the children, imagining them sliding into the river and being carried away by deep undercurrents.

When her wrist began to ache from gripping her glass, she gave up and shampooed the salt and grime from her hair.

"And *this* is another reason why I don't have kids," she told Purkins, who had ventured back into the house and was now condescending to nibble at the treats she'd left in his dish beside the tub. As Emma climbed out of the bath, the cat looked up and meowed.

Julie had honoured her promise to keep her siblings away from the water by helping them build a three-sided fort at the base of a wide cedar tree. The boards they had used were the remains of a dismantled chicken shed that Emma had placed in a scrap pile, and she wavered between relief that the children were safe and annoyance at the thought of putting everything back after they were gone.

With Bear-Bear resting safely on the roof of the fort, Caden was patrolling a graveyard similar to the one he'd built on To-paz Island. On his shoulder was a stick he was using as a rifle. Julie was decorating the graves with ferns, bleeding hearts, and salmonberry blossoms. On the far side of the tree, Skylar was attempting to throw a rope over a sturdy-looking branch, but with each toss, the end of the rope snaked over the branch, then promptly slid back to the ground.

"Son-of-a-bitchin' thing won't stay there!" she said, unaware of Emma's presence.

Caden paused from his patrol. "I'm telling what you said."

"Who gives a shit?" With the rope in hand, Skylar climbed a stump next to the tree, grabbed a lower branch, and with some difficulty pulled herself up to the limb that she wanted the rope over.

Assured that the child wasn't going to fall, Emma retreated, leaving them to their play.

From the hallway she saw Purkins curled up on a window-sill in the living room, where he was soaking up the warm rays of afternoon sun.

"You get a longer reprieve," she told him on her way to collect the phone from the kitchen. Carrying it to the kitchen table, she sat facing the window, where she could catch the occasional glimpse of the children, and dialled her boss's home number.

"Gabriel residence." He sounded sleepy.

"Thanks a lot, Sam."

His innocent "For what?" didn't fool her.

"You know damned well what — for telling George I could take the rest of the week off." She visualized Sam shrugging.

"What could I do?" he asked. "I owe him for running a background check on the Dahls, and this was not such a bad way of returning the favour. We aren't so busy that a few days will matter."

"I'll remember that next time you want me to do a rush job."

"Which reminds me," he said, "where is that release? Please don't tell me it went down with the boat!"

"No, Sam. I grabbed my case just before I went into the water. Almost drowned from the weight of it, but by damn I saved it for you." He went silent, and she wondered if she had gone too far. Sam *was* her employer, she reminded herself. "It's in that waterproof pouch. If they find the boat, they can retrieve it."

"We won't get paid until they do," Sam said. "Anyway, what's this I hear about that boat carrying drugs?"

"What are you talking about?"

"You don't know? George suspects that Captain What's-His-Name was hauling pot for some growers up north."

Emma frowned. "It's the first I've heard about it."

"Well, I told him there was no way you would ever be connected with something like that."

"Thanks," Emma said dryly, but as she hung up the receiver, she wondered if Sergeant George shared her boss' opinion. Or did he think it a little too coincidental that Emma had hitched a ride with a drug smuggler who ended up with his head split open? She glared out the window.

If I'd checked the bloody hold of that boat before we left Bear Creek, none of this would have happened.

Suddenly she remembered the man who had been talking to Forgie on the dock at Bear Creek Landing. She hadn't mentioned that to Sergeant George. But when she rang the police station to correct her mistake, she was told the sergeant had gone home for the day. She left a message for him to call her in the morning, replaced the phone, and for several minutes stood lost in a fog of exhaustion and uncertainty.

Her reverie was broken by a shout from Caden ordering Skylar to "stop it!" Emma shook herself and glanced at the clock. She needed to make dinner and get the children bathed and in bed while she was still capable of functioning.

Caden's bath was the most difficult. He needed help washing his hair but refused to allow any of them into the room with him. Emma was dangerously close to exploding when Skylar suggested that he wear his bathing suit. Under those terms, Caden allowed Julie to come in for just long enough to scrub his back and wash his hair. Once he was dry and in pyjamas, Emma took over tucking him into bed, letting the girls go have their own baths. With his damp hair, the raggedy bear clutched in his arms, and half-smothered by the quilt that was far too big for him, Caden seemed so vulnerable that she couldn't resist hugging him.

Shrinking from her touch, he said, "I want Julie." Like a little mother, freshly scrubbed and in mismatched pyjamas, Julie came in carrying a worn storybook from one of their bags.

"I'll read to you, but I'm sleeping in the princess room with Skylar," she said before she began to read 'The Three Bears.'"

Emma slipped out of the room. Reassured that Skylar was out of the bath and in bed, she went to her own room and crawled under the covers. The last thing she felt before drifting off was a light thump as Purkins jumped onto the bed and curled himself into a ball near the crook of her knees.

Dark, foam-specked waves engulfed the man frantically wrestling the swirling waters. His hands reached for Emma, grasping her feet, preventing her escape. As she kicked desperately to break free of his hold, her feet slammed against Caden and Julie and Skylar. The children gripped her legs with one hand, while stretching the other toward the man, who was slowly disappearing beneath the sea.

"No!" Emma moaned as she woke with a start. Overcome by a sense of profound remorse, she turned on her side and stared into the black night, afraid of returning to the dream, yet too exhausted to keep her eyes open.

Eventually, sleep reclaimed her and she saw a thick mist billowing from the aisle of the *Lazy Bones'* cabin. From the depths of the mist Arnold Forgessen rose to his feet, blood pouring down his face as he lurched towards Emma, jabbing a stained finger at her heart.

She screamed, waking herself again. This time she sat up. A pulse throbbed at her temples, and a noise drew her eyes to the figure standing beside her bed.

"Julie!"

"Skylar took all the covers, and there's no room in Caden's bed." Julie shivered.

The darkness had given way to the soft light of early morning, and Emma peered blearily at the digital clock on the bedside stand. Just after four — far too early for rising. She wriggled to the cold side of the bed and patted the pillow beside her. "Then you'd better climb in with me," she said. Purkins raised his head, clearly annoyed by the disruption as Julie climbed under the covers.

She didn't, as Emma hoped, go back to sleep, but leaned over to Purkins and stroked his head. Instead of leaping away as Emma had expected, the cat moved closer to the girl.

"We had a kitty once," she said, "only Aunty Glenda said we couldn't keep him 'cause she's allergic." She looked around the room just visible in the predawn light. "This is nice."

"It used to be even nicer," Emma said. During their later years, her grandparents had been unable to do the maintenance work on the house, and although she'd tried to help them, most of her time had been consumed by crewing on her husband's troller and taking legal assistant courses during the off-season. In the six years since they'd died — events that were barely a year apart and coincided with the breakup of her marriage — Emma had tried to restore Windrush to its former glory. She started by rebuilding the river dock, then tackled the overgrown gardens. Last summer she put new wallpaper in the kitchen and bathrooms, and painted the outside walls. She'd even managed minor repairs on the roof, but the shingles were too old and the slope too high and steep for her to do an extensive job. Other parts of the house that were giving way to dry rot she didn't even want to think about.

"I wish Daddy would hurry up and find us," Julie said.

Emma remembered how she had played a similar pretend-he's-alive game following her own father's death. So long as she could believe he was coming back, she could also believe that the bad things happening around her were only temporary, that she and her mother would eventually leave the Okanagan and move back to their old house in Shinglewood.

"It'll work out, Julie. It just takes time."

She wasn't sure if the girl even heard her, for a moment later, Julie was snoring softly.

NINE

Just after ten o'clock the next morning, Emma drove through the gates of the Shinglewood Fish Hatchery and parked in front of a square concrete tank with a glass window that revealed about two hundred juvenile coho swimming in circles.

"See, there's the viewing tank I was telling you about," she said.

"Who cares about stupid fish?" Skylar said.

"Yeah, who cares?" Caden agreed. "We want to go with you."

"Well, you can't." Emma stepped out of the truck. "And you can suit yourselves: whether you want to sulk, or discover what a fish hatchery is all about."

Although she was feeling more in control of herself than the night before, Emma's patience was exhausted. Squinting against the mid-morning sun, she surveyed the grounds, but didn't see Twill standing among the huge circular fish tanks or the smaller pens that housed the trout that the Salmonid Enhancement Society raised and sold to offset the costs of their enhancement work.

She was heading toward the small cedar incubation shed when Twill's dog came tumbling down the steep metal staircase leading from the oxygenation tower. Barking and wagging his tail, he skittered to a stop in front of her.

"Hey, Rugrat!" She knelt to give him a pat, but the dog jumped away from her, his attention on the three children running toward them. "It's all right," she reassured him. "They're friends."

Following Emma's example, Caden knelt and held out his hand. "Come on, boy!"

The dog danced out of his reach.

"Here, I'll get him!" Skylar cried, circling behind, intent on trapping the dog between herself and her brother.

"Give him time, you two." Emma straightened. "He's got to trust that you're not going to hurt him, and then he'll be all over you."

Knowing that Rugrat was more than capable of handling three youngsters, she left them together and started up the steps of the tower, a two-storey concrete structure with a smaller third level rising from its centre. As she climbed, she could hear the soft humming of the pumps that were transporting water from the hatchery well to the top of the centre tower. Gravity-fed through a series of rectangular chambers filled with plastic cylinders, the water emptied into a narrow channel covered by a grated work platform that circled the upper structure, and down a wide pipe to a cistern in the ground, where it was piped to the fish tanks as needed.

Emma was stopped from proceeding onto the platform because a section of the grating had been lifted away from the channel. Here Twill was kneeling on a small ledge, his arm submerged past his elbow in the fast-moving water.

"Isn't that dangerous?" Emma asked.

Twill scowled and withdrew his arm. "Lost a bolt through the grating," he grumbled. "Thought I could grab it before it skittered into the pipe, but no such luck."

"Well, if you're not careful, you'll be following it," she warned. A year earlier, a summer student had walked onto the platform after dark, not realizing that the grating had been left open. She fell through, and it was only luck — and the strong arm of her companion — that saved her from being sucked into the drainage pipe.

Twill snorted. He replaced the grating, got to his feet, and glanced at the grounds below, where Skylar was toe-walking along the concrete edge of a fish tank less than half a metre above the water level. Julie was leaning over the edge, staring at the fish, while Caden was trying to lift Rugrat up to join Skylar.

"Jaisus Lord Tunderin'!" Twill shouted at them. "Get your arse off them pens!"

Skylar leaped to the ground, Julie jumped away from the fish tank, and Caden dropped the dog, who immediately ran to the tower. At the bottom of the steps he whirled around and barked at the children, as if to imply that it was all their fault.

"I have to go into town," Emma said. "I was hoping you would watch the kids for me." Twill paused at the entrance to the platform and turned to her. "I thought you said Wendy was collecting them today."

"She's going to — later. Right now Sergeant George wants me to come in and talk to some drug enforcement guy from Vancouver."

Twill's brow furrowed. "What's this all about, Emma?"

Briefly, she told him about the accident and how the police suspected that Forgie was transporting marijuana. "Now George seems to think I'm involved in a drug ring."

"He probably has some bureaucrat up his arse." Twill headed down the steps. "I wouldn't pay it much mind."

"Yeah, well, you're not the one under suspicion," Emma said. "Anyway, will you watch them for me?"

At the bottom of the steps, Caden was trying to coax Rugrat back.

"Come on, boy! I won't hurt you."

"His name's Rugrat," Twill said as he stepped around Caden and over to the girls, who were fidgeting on the pavement between the pens.

"Skylar didn't know she couldn't walk there," Julie said.

Twill ruffled her hair. "No harm's done, lass. I didn't want her skittering into the pond, is all."

Skylar glared at him. "You could have just said that."

He looked at her speculatively, then nodded. "Suppose I could have."

"So?" Emma glanced at her truck. "Can I leave them here?"

Twill frowned. "I do have a job to do, Emmie."

"Right, and part of it is guiding visitors through the hatchery. Since these guys have never seen one...." He showed no signs of softening until Emma offered to cook him dinner on the weekend.

"Fried chicken?" he asked. "With gravy?"

She nodded.

"One hour," he said. He turned to the children. "All right, you hooligans, come with me and I'll give you a firsthand look at the makings of a salmon."

Before Twill could change his mind, Emma escaped to her truck and drove away.

The Rusty Anchor was empty when Emma stopped by on her way to the police station. Kate complained as she wiped the counter, "They come, they drink, they leave, but their mess is still here."

"Well, give me a cappuccino and I promise I won't leave any mess," Emma said.

Kate turned to the coffee machines and began tamping grounds into the filter. She placed it in the espresso machine, shoved a metal pitcher underneath, and hit the switch. "So where are your kids?"

"They're not my kids, Kate," Emma said. "Wendy's picking them up this afternoon. And right now Twill's giving them a hatchery tour." She grinned mischievously. "I promised him a chicken dinner that I was already going to make him for taking care of Purkins."

Kate shook her head as she inserted the steam nozzle into a small pitcher of milk. "The man is a saint — all the things he does for you!"

"Hey! I help him too. Remember the fishing derby? And all the volunteers I find for clipping fins?" Once a year, the adipose fins were clipped on salmon smolts to identify them as hatchery stock before they went out to sea. With Emma's help, Twill had turned this difficult job into a community event. Kate, like most of the villagers, was perfectly aware of Emma's relationship with Twill, but by some unspoken agreement no one ever branded them as a couple.

With an exaggerated roll of her eyes, Kate said, "So now you're a big-shot television star, you think you don't have to be grateful, eh?"

"What do you mean?"

"Your picture was all over the TV news last night, along with a story about a boat sinking and some poor man with his head bashed in." Kate looked affronted. "All the juicy things you forgot to tell me yesterday."

"I couldn't tell you in front of the children," Emma said. "Did they really give my name?"

Her friend nodded. "If you had a television, you would have seen it for yourself." She smiled. "They had a great shot of the wharf, and in one clip you could see my sign." She poured the hot coffee into a disposable cup, added some steamed milk, topped it with thick foam and a generous sprinkle of chocolate, then handed it to Emma. "Enjoy."

The publicity might be good for Kate's business, but as Emma left the café, she was thankful she hadn't encountered the news teams, and even more thankful she did not have a television. *Let's just hope the police found the* Lazy Bones *and no drugs.*

<hr/>

Her hope dissolved when she sat across from Sergeant George.

"We haven't been able to find the boat," he said. "There's a team working on the wind and currents from that night. Factoring in Forgessen's prior routes and your information, they think they can figure out where she might have sunk."

Emma stared at him. "Prior routes?"

He cleared his throat. "Yes, well… an undercover crew has been following Forgessen for a while now, but somehow the wily old coot has always managed to give them the slip."

"In that broken-down tub?" Emma shook her head. "I can't see him outmanoeuvring a blind whale with a hearing problem."

"Yes, well, this time they thought they had him because they'd placed a tracking device on his GPS, but for some reason it wasn't working."

Emma chuckled. "Forgie must have dumped it. He told me it was in the shop."

The sergeant rolled his chair backward and got to his feet. "Anyway, a member of the surveillance team from the Landing is talking to some divers right now. He'll be out in a few minutes." He avoided eye contact. "Unfortunately, he wants you in the interrogation room."

Emma slowly got to her feet. "In the what?"

"It's only protocol." He led the way to a small, windowless room that was furnished with nothing more than a table and two metal chairs.

She stopped at the doorway. "No way I'm going in there, George. If he wants to talk to me, he can damned well do it out here."

"Oh, come on, Emma, don't make this difficult. Look, I'll

even stay with you." He went in and pulled out one of the chairs for her.

"The whole time?"

"If I can," he said, and breathed a sigh of relief when she finally accepted the seat. He closed the door and sat down next to her. *This is silly,* Emma chided herself. *I've done nothing wrong!* Still, her hands felt cold and clammy, and she jumped when the door reopened a minute later and a stern-faced officer entered the room. He held the door ajar.

"Thank you very much, sergeant. I can take it from here."

"All the same," Sergeant George said, his jaw set, "I think I'll sit in on this one."

Emma watched as the two men waged a silent face-off that ended with a soft tap on the doorjamb. Sergeant George looked up to find his clerk waiting with a message slip.

"Sorry, sir. I thought you would want this now."

The sergeant grabbed the note and frowned. With an apologetic glance at Emma, he got to his feet and excused himself from the room.

As the door closed, the officer slapped a pad of yellow, legal-sized paper on the table, went to an instrument set into the wall, and clicked a switch. Scraping the metal chair noisily against the tiled floor, he sat opposite her and pulled the writing pad toward him.

"I'm Constable Read," he said as he scribbled something on the top of the page, "and this interview is being recorded."

"Let me guess," Emma said, already irritated by the man's high-handed manner, "you're the bad cop, right?"

Constable Read glanced at her and frowned. "This is a criminal investigation, Miss Phillips." Returning his attention to the writing pad, he rattled off her right to have an attorney present and warned that anything she said could be used against her in a court of law.

Resisting the urge to give him a stiff-armed salute, Emma said, "I've already told Sergeant George everything I can remember. And that was also recorded."

The constable's eyes narrowed as he anchored his palms on the table and leaned toward her. "Is there a reason you don't want to help us, Miss Phillips?"

"Other than the fact that I do have a life, no reason at all, Constable." She was pleased to see a red flush creep over his face. "You did say you were just a constable, right? Not a detective or anything?"

The flush became a deep crimson. "You've got a pretty smart mouth for someone facing drug charges." She winced, and he relaxed back into his chair. "Your friend Forgessen was transporting marijuana from Bear Creek Landing."

"He isn't... wasn't my friend," Emma said, "and if I'd even suspected that he had drugs on board, I'd never have set foot on that boat. Besides, if you've been watching him so closely, you know damned well how I met him that morning." The constable busied himself writing, avoiding her glare, and suddenly an image of Forgie stepping onto the road in front of her rented car flashed through Emma's mind. "Oh my God! You lost him in the woods, didn't you? His truck never broke down at all!"

Dropping his pen, Read pressed his hands so hard onto the table his knuckles whitened. He thrust his face uncomfortably close to hers. "It is in your best interest, Miss Phillips, to cooperate with us."

Oh, hold me back! Emma choked down a laugh as she visualized the officer slogging through the mud as he searched through the woods for Forgie. *He's totally bluffing.*

Read straightened and grabbed his pen, jabbing the nib into his pad as he machine-gunned questions at her. "What did Forgessen say to you? Did he mention any names?"

Emma frowned and tried to recall her conversation with Forgie on the way to the Black Fly Ranch. "He rattled on about a lot of things, but I didn't believe any of them." She tapped her chin. "I remember one crazy story about a man being chopped up on some bluff by the Mafia." She shrugged. "I wasn't paying him much attention, not till he said he knew where Mary Dahl lived."

The constable waited.

"And there was a guy... the one I called Sergeant George about this morning. I saw him talking to Forgie when I got back to the boat."

"You didn't mention this in your earlier account."

Emma shrugged. "I didn't remember until last night."

"And what did this guy look like?"

"I was more concerned about the state of Forgie's boat, so I wasn't really looking at the man. As near as I can remember, he was a little taller than me... and I think he had light brown hair, cut short." She hid a smile. "Kind of like those six-dollar haircuts you cops get."

Read's jaw tightened. "Was he fat? Thin?"

She shook her head. "What the hell are you asking me for anyway? You should know exactly what he looks like." She touched her cheek with her index finger. "Oh, wait. That's right. You were watching the trees, not the man."

Constable Read frowned, ripped off the top sheet of paper, and pushed the pad and pen toward her. "You will provide a written account of everything that happened from the time you met Mr. Forgessen until the boat sank."

Emma made no move to pick up the pen. "I've already signed a statement for Sergeant George."

His lips thinned. "Are you refusing to write down what happened, Miss Phillips?"

She got to her feet. "Without my lawyer present, I'm not

writing a damned thing. And as far as I'm concerned, unless you're charging me with something, this interview is over."

Constable Read had also risen to his feet and blocked the door. She scowled, hating the fear she felt as he towered over her. Nodding toward the wall, she said, "I believe that recorder is still on."

He looked from her to wall, then back again. "You're making a serious mistake," he said, but he stepped aside.

Emma swept past him and slammed out of the room. She glared at Sergeant George as she stomped past his office.

"I'm turning that Studebaker into an outdoor fire pit!"

Twill's truck was still parked at the hatchery, but the gate was locked and there was no one about. Hoping he'd taken the children to his house, Emma drove back along River Road. Nestled beside the Stuart River, the wooden hexagon that Twill called home had been erected at the height of the hippy era by a transplanted New Yorker who envisioned it as the nucleus of a massive commune. Although both the New Yorker and his devotees had long since departed, their odd-shaped sanctuary remained and was now locally dubbed "The Castle" because of the six-sided turret that formed the upper storey of the house. Emma had always thought it looked more like the Mad Hatter's hat. The whole building was badly in need of a paint job, and its cedar-shake walls were weathered grey and streaked with green algae. The deck that encircled the entire building drooped in several places, and the floor wobbled and creaked beneath her feet as she walked across it to the screen door. But it wasn't the condition of the house that troubled her.

There should be more noise, she thought as she knocked on the door. *Why am I not hearing the kids?*

"Anybody home?" she called.

When there was no answer, she opened the door and entered the cluttered living room. "Twill?"

A light glowed in the far right corner of the room where Twill was hunched over his fly-tying desk, intent on winding a feather around the shaft of a small hook. He didn't respond, and as she made her way across the room, detouring around an easy chair on which rested two crab traps and avoiding a side table piled high with books and newspapers, she saw why. The magnetic disk that connected his speech processor to the electrodes implanted beneath his scalp was dangling from his ear, so he was unaware of her presence until she touched his shoulder.

"Did you talk to the sergeant?" he asked too loudly.

Emma nodded and pointed to his disk. He grinned as he put it in place.

"Where are the kids, Twill?"

"They're not here?" He peered into the shadows of the room and scratched his head. "They was here a while ago. The dog was making a helluva racket, so I pulled this thing off. They're probably hiding somewheres."

"Why aren't they at the hatchery? With you?"

"They got hungry. So I brought 'em here and they made some sandwiches." He got to his feet and surveyed the room once more. "Dog's not around either." He walked with her out to the deck, put his index fingers to his lips, and gave a piercing whistle. As the sound died away, Emma cupped her hands around her mouth and yelled. "Julieeeee! Skylaaaar!" There was no response. She yelled again.

"Maybe they went back to your place," he said. "I showed 'em where the trail was."

"Jesus, Twill! They could get lost!"

"Now, Emmie, when you was their age you lived in them woods." He patted her shoulder. "They'll be fine. They've got Rugrat, and they couldn't have been gone long. I only tied one fly."

"Well, thanks for being so conscientious. Now I'll go and see if I can find what's left of them."

The mossy trail between the Castle and Windrush was well marked and separated from the river by a thick growth of willow trees and salmon berry bushes. Emma could have walked it blindfolded, but today she was watchful as she searched for any sign of the children. Every few minutes she stopped to yell.

"Julie-e-e-e-e!"

The moss had been disturbed near a giant red cedar, and a little further on she found leaves from salal and salmonberry bushes scattered over the ground. Around a sharp bend a freshly broken willow branch had been dropped on the trail, and she remembered seeing Skylar whip the bushes on Topaz Island with a similar stick.

"Skyla-a-a-r!" she yelled, climbing to the top of a small rise where the remnants of an old wooden water barrel lingered from the early logging days. Nearby was a mound of fresh bear scat. "Ca-a-a-den!"

Her concern increased when she saw small footprints near a slippery, fragile section of riverbank, and she was only a little reassured to find the moss torn up again further along the trail.

Damn! I should have taken them with me. She jogged around an old cedar stump. *Skylar's way too unpredictable for Twill to handle.*

At the river landing the boathouse was locked, and there was no evidence that the children were anywhere close, but as she started up the steps to the house, she heard Rugrat barking. She glanced up at the top floor balcony and gasped.

"Oh my God!"

Skylar was perched precariously on the narrow cedar guard-rail. She seemed unaware of the fragility of the structure, or of the distance between it and the glass roof of the conservatory below. As Caden and Julie watched open-mouthed from the French doors in Emma's bedroom, and Rugrat pranced back and forth between them, the girl stretched both arms outward and took one wobbly step and then another. Midway through the third step, the dog barked and Skylar tottered, her foot searching for the rail. Emma sucked in her breath and held it until the child regained her footing.

"Skylar," she called as calmly as she could manage, "I'd like you to get off there."

The girl looked down. Her expression showed no fear, and Emma realized with shock that Skylar was fully aware of the danger she was in.

"*Now*, Skylar. Get down." Emma repeated, resisting an impulse to race up two flights of stairs and pull her to safety.

After a few heart-stopping moments, the girl took one final step and jumped safely down onto the deck. By the time Emma had let herself inside and raced upstairs, the children were in the girls' room. Julie was playing with a collection of miniature dolls on the bed. Skylar and Caden were on the floor playing tug-of-war, using Rugrat as the rope.

"What the hell do you think you were doing?" Emma grabbed Skylar's shoulders and gave her a shake.

Skylar twisted away from her and grabbed the squirt gun from the bed. "Don't touch me!" She brandished the gun at Emma as if it was real. Rugrat barked furiously and jumped back and forth between them.

Julie watched from the bed. "I told you she'd be mad."

"I coulda' done it if I wanted," Caden said.

"And I could take you all straight back to the police station!" Emma saw the fear that sprang into their eyes. "But I won't." She looked at Skylar. "How did you get into the house?"

"We climbed through the window downstairs," Julie said. "We didn't go by the river," she added, "... except on the trail."

"You should have stayed at Twill's place," Emma said. The faint ringing of the doorbell drifted upstairs. Ordering them to stay out of her room and off the upper deck, she hurried down to the front door.

"Thought maybe you'd run away!" Wendy Grieves said when Emma waved her into the hallway. A yellow visor cap was perched on top of the woman's prematurely grey curls and her face was creased with a jovial smile. Her bright cotton sundress and sandals matched her cap and made her look, Emma thought, like a huge ball of sunshine. The bulging briefcase that she clutched in one hand was the only indication that this wasn't a fun visit.

"Tempting, but no," Emma said as she led the way to the kitchen. Before she could invite Wendy to sit, Caden and Skylar stormed into the room, both talking at once and accompanied by Rugrat barking his own opinion.

"We're going out to our fort," Caden announced as they headed for the door.

Julie followed behind them. "I'll make sure they stay...." Her face paled when she saw Wendy, and her voice trailed away.

"Well, now, aren't you a happy bunch!" Wendy said. As the social worker's words reverberated through the kitchen, Skylar and Caden moved closer to Julie. Rugrat growled low in his throat.

"That's enough, you," Emma said to the dog. Then she turned to the children. "Kids, this is Wendy Grieves. She's going to look after you."

"I'm certainly going to find someone who will!" Wendy studied Julie's wary expression. "You've all been in care before, haven't you, dear?"

The girl's eyes grew bright, and her lower lip trembled as she nodded.

Skylar balled her fists. "They were mean to Caden."

Scarcely above a whisper, Julie added, "That's why Aunty Glenda took us."

"Well, I'm hoping your aunty will take you again," Wendy said. "Only we're having a hard time finding her." She turned to Emma. "Seems she left on a retreat without telling anyone where it was. In the meantime we'll have to find places for them to stay."

"Can't we stay here?" Julie asked. "Until our daddy comes?"

"Your dad?" Wendy glanced at Emma, who shook her head. "Well… I'm not sure, sweetie," the social worker said. "But you don't need to worry. We'll work something out. Now, why don't you children run along while I talk to Miss Phillips?"

Needing no further encouragement, Caden raced outside, followed closely by Skylar and Rugrat. Julie stood uncertainly. "If we go someplace else, Daddy won't know where to find us."

Wendy patted her shoulder and guided her to the laundry room, which led to the back door. "Don't worry, dear. We'll take care of everything."

Returning to the kitchen, the social worker settled at the table, opened her briefcase, and pulled out a thick manila file folder.

"Haven't been here since your grandma passed away," she remarked as she removed the visor cap. She patted her curls back into shape and tucked the cap into her briefcase. "Sergeant George said their father was dead."

"He is." Emma sat across from her. "We all saw him fall into the water, and he never came back up. But Julie thinks he swam to an island."

Wendy nodded. "Denial. Seen it happen before. We'll have to get her some help for that."

"You said you'd find *places* for them," Emma said. "Does that mean they won't be together?" She flinched as Wendy's laugh erupted. Neither of them heard the click of the side door opening.

"Now, Emma, you've been associated with this business

long enough to know that foster parents don't grow on trees. Especially ones who can take three children without notice."

"But you are going to keep them together, right?"

"I have to make an assessment of their situation." Wendy shifted her weight on the chair. "Check with the foster parents on my roster. If I can't find a local placement for them, I'll have to contact Campbell River."

"And in the meantime?"

"Why, they'll stay here, of course."

"With me? I don't think so!" Emma leaned forward, hands on the table. "I've got things to do, Wendy."

"Like what?"

"I work for a living, remember? And I'm behind in my potting and fixing up my roof and getting my driver's licence back and cancelling my credit cards." When Wendy remained silent, Emma added, "Besides, they're getting too attached to me."

Wendy pursed her lips. "Why do I get the feeling that it's not their attachment you're worried about?"

"It doesn't matter. Anyway, if you're so concerned, why don't *you* keep them?" As soon as the words were out, Emma's cheeks reddened with shame. She knew the social worker's history because Sam had represented Wendy's husband, Colin, in a pension dispute with Veteran's Affairs in Ottawa. Colin served in the first Gulf War and was hospitalized with severe post-traumatic stress disorder, and although he was eventually released, he couldn't stand to be around people. Just going to their mailbox was an ordeal for him. As a result, Wendy gave up her job as a supervisor with the Ministry of Children and Families in Campbell River and they moved to a cottage in the woods on the outskirts of Shinglewood. Here Colin gardened or read or listened to classical music. He rarely left the property and avoided children because they triggered images of the mutilations he'd witnessed.

Wendy never complained about the family she couldn't have or the administrative career she'd abandoned that might have enabled her to effect real changes in the Ministry. Instead, she contented herself with her job as a small-town social worker, actively participated in community events, and always found something to laugh about, unless it had to do with the unfair treatment of the children in her care.

Her eyes were sad. "You know I'd take them in an instant if I could."

"I'm sorry," Emma said. "But I'm tired as hell, Wendy, and I need time to sort things out. The kids have to go."

A noise from the laundry room caught her attention. Julie and Skylar were standing near the open door, and their expressions showed they'd heard what she said. Emma looked away.

"I thought you wanted me to find them a place together," Wendy said.

"I did. I do. Just not with me." Emma felt mean, but she couldn't back down. If she showed any weakness at all, Wendy would pounce.

The social worker clicked her tongue. Heaving herself to her feet, she turned toward the laundry room, where Caden too was now watching. "Well, kids, I guess you're going to have to come with me after all. You go along and get your things and meet me at the door."

"Rugrat went home," Julie said as she and Caden and Skylar filed past the two adults, keeping their distance from Wendy. As they clomped up the stairs, Emma heard Skylar say, "I'm not goin'!"

Wendy gave no indication she heard. "It would be better if you could keep the children until I find a permanent placement for them, Emma," she said as she headed for the hallway. "These temporary solutions are hard on kids."

"Getting attached to me and having to leave will be even

harder on them," Emma said, but she was no longer certain whether she was trying to convince Wendy or herself. "Anyway, I'd better go help them. Their bags are heavy."

She felt her resolve waver when she saw Caden standing outside the girls' room, Bear-Bear clutched in his arms.

"Skylar's not comin'!"

Julie was in the middle of the room, putting the last of her dolls in a garbage bag. She pointed to the closet. "She's in there."

"I'll get her," Emma said. "You two go on." Neither child moved. "If you don't go down, Wendy will come up."

Caden glued himself to Julie's side.

"It'll be better if I talk to Skylar alone," Emma said.

With a final peek at the closet, Julie took her brother's hand and trudged from the room. "It's only 'til Daddy finds us, Caden."

Emma opened the door to the closet. She didn't relish a battle of either strength or wills with Skylar.

The little girl was huddled in the darkest corner of the cedar-lined enclosure with her back to the door.

"I'm not going," she said.

Not sure what to do next, Emma sat on the floor, legs crossed and elbows resting on her knees. "So you're going to stay here in the closet?"

"What do you care?"

"Well, it is my closet." Emma studied the small shoulders hunched beneath Dennis Warner's oversized jacket. "Just because I can't keep you doesn't mean I don't care."

Skylar turned and glared at her. "It's your fault Daddy fell in the water."

"So you keep telling me." Emma held back her own opinion of their dad's incompetence. "But I did get you to a safe place."

"Not anymore."

"Well, Wendy... Mrs. Grieves... did say your aunty might take you."

"Aunty Glenda's weird, and she has a slobbery boyfriend." Skylar's voice broke and her body grew rigid. Emma tried to block the images the child's words brought to her own mind. The creaking of the door opening into her bedroom. The smell of her stepfather's breath on her face. She shuddered and forced her attention back to the girl.

"Maybe we can talk to your aunt about that." She knew how useless the suggestion was even as she made it. Her own mother would never have believed anything bad about Emma's step-father, and she would never have confronted him. She was too afraid he would leave her.

Skylar swiped at her eyes with the sleeve of her jacket. As the silence stretched between them, Emma reached up and pulled the string that dangled from the closet ceiling. An overhead light came on.

"Look," she said, pointing to a seascape carved into the cor-ner walls. Amid the wooden waves were tropical islands, sail-ing ships, and swashbuckling pirates. "My grandfather carved this when he was a little boy. His mom died, and since his dad was a fisherman, he was alone a lot with just a housekeeper to look after him. If he was scared or upset, he'd hide in here and make up stories. Then he'd carve a part of the story into the wall, and by the time he was done, he wasn't scared anymore." She leaned forward and traced the outline of the mermaid bowsprit. "This was always my favourite part. I used to pre-tend she was real and I'd tell her things I couldn't tell anyone else."

Skylar glared at the carving. "If I was a mermaid, I'd swim away and no one would ever catch me." She let out a deep breath. "Daddy's dead. He's not coming to get us."

"Maybe for a little while Julie needs to believe he's alive," Emma said. "Maybe thinking he's gone hurts too much."

"It doesn't hurt me." Skylar tightened the jacket around her.

"He doesn't want us anyways. Aunty Glenda don't neither. Nobody does."

There was no self-pity in Skylar's words. They were a flat statement of an ugly truth. And suddenly Emma was consumed with the need to protect her, no matter the cost.

"Tell you what, Skylar. You can stay with me until Mrs. Grieves finds a place where the three of you can be together." As soon as the words were out, Emma panicked. *What the hell am I saying?* Striving for damage control, she added, "But you have go without a fuss when that happens, even if it's with your aunt."

The girl rested her forehead against the mermaid. "Okay," she said, her voice resigned.

Berating herself for giving in to what was nothing more than a short-lived attack of altruism, Emma crawled from the closet and held out her hand. Skylar ignored it and came out on her own.

An hour later, as she watched Wendy's car disappear down the road, Emma fingered the bandage on her forehead and wondered if her fall from the *Lazy Bones* had wiped out a few brain cells. It was the only way she could explain her insane offer. She wasn't comforted when she returned to the house and found Purkins streaking across the yard with Caden in hot pursuit.

TEN

Emma was frying bacon on Friday morning when the side door opened and Twill walked in, followed by Rugrat. The dog immediately bounded over to Caden, who was standing on a stepstool handing dishes down to Julie and Skylar. Caden almost dropped the plate he was holding as he jumped from the stool to wrap his arms around the dog. A moment later they were both rolling on the laundry room floor.

Stepping into the kitchen, Twill sniffed the air appreciatively. "Smells mighty good."

"You're welcome to stay," Emma said, lifting the bacon onto a plate and cleaning the grease from the pan so she could scramble eggs in it. "I was going to fry them, but apparently eggs with yolks in the middle represent two things that touch."

He shook his head. "I'm not even going to ask. And I'll pass on breakfast." He inclined his head toward the children, who had followed Rugrat outside. "Wasn't Wendy supposed to pick them up yesterday?"

"Don't even go there," Emma said. Working on the counter beside the electric range, she broke a half-dozen eggs into a bowl and grabbed a whisk. "So if you're not going to eat, why are you here?"

"I have to take a rain check on that dinner you were going to make me."

Emma stopped whisking and tilted her head to one side. "What's up?"

"Northern Sea Farms wants me to watch their Topaz Island farm until Sunday."

Her eyes widened. "That's the one...."

"Where you got gas. I know. The guy from Northern said the caretaker took off without giving notice." He watched as she went back to whisking, then dumped the egg mixture into the pan.

"Doesn't surprise me." She deposited the bowl in the sink. "That guy was a capital-C creep."

"More than that," Twill said. "Apparently he was cooning fish from the pens and hawking them on the side. He must'a got word that Northern was doing some checking, and after you came by, he figured it was time to pack her in. Anyway, they're offering a full month's pay for two days of easy work."

"What about the hatchery?"

"Leonard Smythe's going to handle things for me." He reached across to the bacon plate and nabbed a rasher. "Anyway, I wanted to warn you that there's a she-bear with a cub hanging around."

Emma jabbed at the eggs with a turner. "Yeah, I saw fresh scat on the trail yesterday."

"Well, this one's got herself a real attitude," he said, munching the bacon. "Almost wrecked the door on the feed shed trying to get in last night." He wiped his hands on his pants. "Anyway, I've gotta get back and pack up my fishing gear."

"So when *do* you want dinner?" Emma asked, spooning the scrambled eggs onto four plates.

"Sunday would be nice," he said. "You can make it at my place and afterward we'll have a listen to that Oscar Peterson record."

Emma noted the look that passed between the girls as they came back inside and took their places at the table.

132

"Better have it here," she said, "in case Wendy hasn't found a home for the kids by then."

She followed Twill outside, where Caden was still wrestling with Rugrat. As soon as he saw his master, the dog ran to his side.

"Can't he stay?" the boy asked.

"You'll have to ask him," Twill said, but when he opened the truck door, the dog jumped into the cab and took up his usual place on the passenger seat. No amount of coaxing on Caden's part would move him.

The boy's face was glum as he watched the truck disappear down the drive.

"Come on," Emma said, putting her arm around him. "Breakfast is ready, and I've got a surprise for you." Inside she presented him with a ceramic plate that was divided into three separate sections, each containing a single breakfast item. "I made it for serving appetizers, but I thought you'd like it."

Caden looked at the plate and then at her. "You made it?" Then he flashed her a smile that seemed to stretch from ear to ear. "Su... weet!" He turned to his sister, who was already attacking her meal. "Hey, Skylar! Look what I got!"

That afternoon, while the children worked on their fort, Emma went to the conservatory. Although it smelled a little musty, the room was awash with afternoon light from the floor-to-ceiling windows that made up three of its walls, and as she gazed out at the silently flowing river, she had an overwhelming sense of peace and contentment. Even her muse was in place, for Purkins had crept in through a window she always left open and was now curled up on an easy chair.

"So what should we create today?" she asked the cat as she crossed the room to her supply cupboards. She extracted a bag of clay and carried it to an old-fashioned wooden kitchen table that stood in the middle of the room. Her grandfather had constructed the table and it always reminded Emma of him: sturdy and practical. He could build anything he put his mind to, including the conservatory, which he had designed on an envelope one night after her grandmother had complained that Shinglewood's growing season was too short. He retired that fall, and by the following spring had turned the design on the envelope into a reality.

When her grandmother elected to take up potting — having read an article about how art exercised the mind and kept dementia at bay — the greenery was evicted and Grandfather Phillips found another envelope to draw on. Emma had just returned from a summer of crewing on the *Twillingate* and was able to help him do the building. Through an ad in the local paper he located an electric kiln, which came with a potting wheel and several boxes of clay and glazing materials that the disillusioned owner never wanted to see again. He installed the kiln beneath a lean-to shelter outside the greenhouse door, next to the rock chimney that served the main-floor fireplace.

The third mess of clay her grandmother splattered around the room prompted Emma to enrol in classes with a local potter. There she discovered what her grandmother didn't know — that the splash pan had to be raised and fastened in place prior to spinning the wheel. She also discovered she had a gift for working with clay herself. She loved the feel of it in her hands and the magic of turning a mental image into a bowl or a dish that people would actually pay money to own. When her grandmother gave up the hobby in frustration, Emma took over the studio. A few months later she registered for evening classes with a more innovative potter who was teaching hand-building and there she learned that whimsical creations were much more fun than bowls and dishes. She could lose herself for hours in a world of shapes and textures and experimenting with various glazes. Opening the kiln after a firing was like unwrapping presents at Christmas. Then she married Tommy, and between looking after him and his boat, there was never time for her own projects. It wasn't until she returned to Windrush and was desperate for a way to make extra cash that she went back to potting — only this time she concentrated on making practical bowls and cups she knew she could sell.

Now, as she absently wedged the lump of brown clay, she remembered her promise on the *Lazy Bones*. Today, she decided, she would create something that would express the helplessness she experienced when the boat was sinking and in the horrifying nightmares now haunting her dreams. From a shelf in the supply cupboard she retrieved a binder with pictures of animals and shapes she liked and flipped through the pages. She stopped when she found a photo of an eagle and suddenly remembered the eagles she had seen from the deck of the *Lazy Bones*. As if it were happening again right in front of her, she could see one of the eagles swooping down and grabbing a fish. *That's how I felt when the boat went down. Like that fish. Helpless.* She propped the book on the table.

Maybe a plaque, she thought. *Something I could hang on a wall.*

As the image slowly took shape in her mind, she rolled the clay to a form a base. By now the scene she envisioned was clear: a large eagle swooping down on a terrified rabbit. She began to shape a head and became so engrossed in curving the beak, making it both strong and fearsome, that everything else slipped so far from her consciousness she didn't hear Julie until the girl was right behind her.

"Jeez!" Emma jerked her hand and dropped the eagle's head onto the base. "Don't sneak up on me like that!"

"Can I make something?" Julie asked.

Emma eyed the collapsed head. *You've got to stop being so jittery, Phillips! Or start locking the damned doors.* Then she looked at Julie's eager face and some of her annoyance ebbed.

"Where's Skylar and Caden?"

"They're looking for bugs for Skylar's zoo."

"And you don't like zoos?"

"I don't like bugs."

"Then I guess this is a good place for you," she said. "Pull up that other stool and sit over here." She peeled the bag back from the clay and, with a fish line looped between two bolts, cut a pound-sized slice from the slab. When the girl was seated on the stool, Emma showed her how to wedge and roll the clay. Finally she motioned to a cutlery tray filled with makeshift tools: metal quills, curved molding sticks, old toothbrushes, and a few spoons.

"You can use these to make patterns or hollows, or to mould something into the shape you want." She demonstrated how to cut the clay with a needle-thin rod fastened to a wooden handle.

Julie picked up the roller and awkwardly ran it over her clay. With each roll she became bolder, and the worry lines on her brow gradually faded. Emma could almost see the world retreating from the girl's consciousness.

Returning to her own creation, Emma tackled the eagle's head with greater confidence, adding a line here and creating a tuft there, gradually fashioning a powerful bird of prey. Finally she brushed the edges of the head with a moistened toothbrush and secured it to the base. Now, even from a distance, she could feel the eagle's menacing intent.

She glanced at Julie, whose face was tight with concentration as she put the finishing touches to a lumpy human shape with wings extending from either side. A flattened ball was crudely attached to the shoulders, and above it was a large clay ring.

"That's a very nice fairy," Emma said.

Julie frowned. "It's not a fairy. It's an angel, and she's showing Daddy where to find us."

"Of course it's an angel. They do look a lot like fairies, don't they?"

The next morning, as she wavered between sleep and waking, Emma found herself staring at the dust canyons on her dresser, illuminated by the bright sunlight streaming through her window. "Oh God," she said. Blurry-eyed, she surveyed the clothes and shoes scattered about the rest of the room. "What a mess." Reluctantly she rolled out of bed, grabbed some clothes from a basket of clean laundry, and stumbled into the upstairs bathroom for a brisk shower. She was just pulling on her T-shirt when she became aware of frantic whispering in the hallway. Scrambling into a pair of denims, she followed the whispering to Caden's room, where three very worried youngsters stood in front of the bed. Behind them, the mattress was skewed sideways, and the sheets and quilt were heaped on the floor between the bed and the door.

"What's going on?" Emma asked. She stepped closer to the bed and saw the large wet stain on the mattress that the children were trying to hide.

"Caden had an accident," Julie said, putting a protective arm around her brother. His eyes were round with apprehension.

Skylar positioned herself in front of him. "He can't help it," she declared hotly. "He's only six."

Emma looked back at the mattress. It had been in perfect condition; now it would have to be replaced.

"I'm sorry, Emma," Caden said, edging closer to Julie. His lower lip trembled and Emma felt her annoyance evaporating. *I never get company anyway, so what does it matter?*

"Hey, accidents happen," she said, rumpling his hair. "We'll dry the mattress out today and put some plastic on it for tonight."

The children's relief was instant.

"We're going to wash the sheets," Julie said.

And Caden grinned. "Yeah, I'm gonna put in the soap!"

"Sounds like a plan," Emma said, and led the way downstairs.

After breakfast, while the children were perfecting their forts, Emma hauled a ladder to the side of the house and climbed up onto the roof. By scraping the moss from between the shingles, she hoped to prevent the water from future rains backing up, and thus eliminate the leak above her bedroom. It was a tedious, messy task that took over an hour, and when it was done she still wasn't sure if it would solve her problem. Only the next rain would prove her right or wrong, but to be on the safe side she found a large sheet of clear plastic that she tacked onto the peak and draped over the side. She was grateful she was able to finish the job before Skylar discovered the ladder.

For the rest of the morning she worked in the garden, which the rain had endowed with a fresh crop of weeds. At first she enlisted the children's help with the weeding, but when Skylar and Caden dismantled half of her rockery in a frenzied quest for "damngod beetles" and came within a hair's breadth of trampling the only tulips that had actually managed to bloom, she banished them to their fort, allowing just Julie to stay. She liked the way the little girl was rearranging garden ornaments and creating scenes with rocks, shells, and odd-shaped pieces of driftwood from the scrap pile. There was a companionable silence between them, and Emma realized she was actually enjoying Julie's company.

They lunched on tomato soup and ham sandwiches, which Caden could pull apart and eat separately. When they were finished, Emma hauled a plastic tub from the hall closet.

"Some of my younger cousins left these," she said, lifting the lid to reveal an enormous collection of Lego pieces. "I thought you might like to play with them."

Caden and Skylar were soon absorbed in constructing battleships and tombstones, allowing Emma and Julie to slip away to the conservatory to resume work on their sculptures. Julie peeled back the plastic with which they had shrouded their work to keep it moist.

"When you're finished building your angel, she will dry faster if you hollow her out," Emma said, and showed the girl how to use a metal quill to drill upward from the bottom of her angel and scoop out the clay.

Returning to her own sculpture, Emma began fashioning the rabbit's head, a task that proved harder than she had imagined. An hour later, as she frowned down at her work and debated whether to leave it or start all over, she glanced at Julie, who was staring despondently at the angel in her hand.

"Is something wrong, Julie?"

"Skylar says Daddy doesn't want to find us. She heard him tell Aunty Glenda we're trouble he can't handle." She looked at Emma. "Are we really bad kids?

Emma shook her head. "Absolutely not. You and Skylar are beautiful and smart, and Caden's way too little to be anything but good."

"Then why hasn't Daddy come?" Julie's voice broke, and her eyes filled with tears.

Because he was dumber than a fence post! Emma stifled the thought. "Maybe he can't, Julie. Maybe he...."

"But I saw him!" Julie said desperately. "I saw him go into the forest!" As the little girl's face crumpled, Emma went to her side and awkwardly patted her hair. Unexpectedly, Julie wrapped her arms around her waist, buried her head in Emma's shoulder, and cried.

"It's okay, child." Emma soothed, wishing she could think of something uplifting to say, something that would give the child hope. "It's okay."

Gradually the sobs subsided and Julie pulled away. "Maybe he got lost," she said, wiping her eyes with the back of her hand. "Maybe Aunty Glenda can help him find us when she gets back."

It was a perfect opportunity to encourage Julie to face the fact her father would never find them, but Emma couldn't do it. Instead she dug a tissue from her pocket and handed it to the girl.

"Here, sweetie. Blow your nose and wipe those tears, and we'll go and make some ice cream cones. Would you like that?"

Julie nodded and offered a faint smile of thanks.

Emma replaced the plastic around the angel, but when she started to do the same with her own work, Julie peeked over her shoulder.

"That's a nice horse!" she said. "I bet that eagle's gonna land right on its head!"

Sunday was Mother's Day, an event that Emma had ignored ever since the package she had sent to her mother the year after leaving home had been returned unopened. Emma never knew whether it was her mother or her stepfather who had sent it back.

This year, however, the occasion was forced upon her when, shortly after eight o'clock, a soft tap on the bedroom door woke her from the first sound sleep she had enjoyed since leaving for Bear Creek Landing. She barely had time to mumble, "Who is it?" before Julie entered her room bearing a tray laden with coffee, two slices of toast smothered with jam, and a bowl of cornflakes drowning in milk.

"Happy Mother's Day, Emma."

As the tray wobbled in Julie's hands, Emma hastily bunched pillows behind her back and accepted the breakfast. Beside her, Purkins burrowed deep under the covers.

"But..." she began, intent on pointing out that she wasn't a mother in any sense of the word. She stopped when she remembered Julie's tears from yesterday. "My goodness!"

Feet scuffed the hallway floor and Caden, clutching Emma's only blooming tulips, shuffled into the room.

Emma managed a faint smile. "What have you got there?"

In princely fashion, he marched to the bed, his jam-smeared face beaming as he held out the flowers. "They're for you!"

Skylar followed him into the room but stopped just short of the bed. Her face tense and with one hand behind her back, she watched Emma manoeuvre the breakfast tray to a sturdier position on her lap and accept the bouquet from Caden's sticky fingers.

"They're beautiful, Caden. Thank you."

He smiled with satisfaction.

Skylar's scrutiny continued. Clamping one hand on her hip and keeping the other hidden behind her back, she said, "You're not our Mom."

"Absolutely not."

"But you're making them keep us together?"

"I'm... going to try."

The girl's blue eyes narrowed. Then her thin shoulders relaxed and she thrust a weather-polished piece of driftwood at Emma. "Here."

Setting the flowers on her tray, Emma took the gift. She turned the rectangular block this way and that, searching for a recognizable shape. "It's a... a...."

"Tugboat!" Caden said, coming to her rescue. "Skylar says it's just like you."

"I look like a tugboat?"

With a giggle, Skylar shook her head. "No. Tugboats take care of all the other boats." She pointed to the tray. "Aren't you gonna eat?"

"How could I not?" Emma asked. "Everything smells so wonderful!"

While the three children watched expectantly, she sampled the charred toast and took a sip of the coffee, which was so bitter she was sure they'd used half the contents of her canister to make it. Somehow, she managed to swallow without grimacing.

"Skylar made the coffee," Julie said.

"It's... very strong." Emma set the cup down.

Skylar nodded with satisfaction. "I told you it needed more," she informed Julie. She turned back to the bed. "Can we go outside now?"

"You certainly can."

The two youngest children ran from the room, but Julie lingered by the bed. Emma looked at her. "How did you know it was Mother's Day?"

"My teacher told us," Julie said. "We were growing plants for our moms." She fingered the tulips on Emma's tray. "I was growing one for Aunty Glenda, but then Skylar made her mad and she said we couldn't stay with her."

"Well, maybe she's not mad anymore," Emma said.

Julie shifted her weight from one foot to another. "That woman phoned."

"Woman?"

"The one that's gonna take us away."

"Wendy Grieves? But it's Sunday...."

Julie pursed her lips in a reflective manner. "She's gonna be here at... ten."

Emma glanced at the bedside clock. It was now almost nine. "I'd better get dressed," she said. Setting the tray aside, she slid out of bed and tried to ignore Julie's woebegone expression.

If Wendy has a home for them, they'll have to go, Emma told herself sternly. And lest she waver and make more foolish promises, she gently but firmly propelled the child out the door. "Thank you for the breakfast, Julie."

While she gathered her clothes, Emma felt a strange mixture of relief and sorrow. The prospect of regaining her freedom, of having her home to herself once more, was almost intoxicating.

But when she looked at the tray and the gifts Skylar and Caden had brought her, she felt sick to her stomach.

It has to be done, she told herself, and kept repeating the words while she showered and dressed.

All three children disappeared as soon as the social worker drove into the yard.

"I didn't think you worked on Sunday," Emma said as Wendy settled into a chair at the kitchen table.

"I don't normally, but I got a call from the Campbell River office. Glenda Duncan has contacted them." She paused. "It seems the Warner children may be with you a little longer than we anticipated." She eyed the cup of Skylar's coffee that Emma placed before her. "At least until their aunt makes up her mind about their guardianship."

Emma surveyed the mess the children had left on the table, and began piling one cereal bowl into another and splashing leftover milk onto the oilcloth. "What's to decide? They're her family."

Wendy shrugged. "It's got something to do with consulting her angels for advice. Apparently there's a waiting list." She rolled her eyes heavenward.

"A waiting list?"

"Who knew?" Wendy lifted her briefcase, which seemed to have expanded since her last visit. "I always thought that when you needed your guardian angel, you just called out, and a light would flash, and poof — there she'd be!" She glanced at the jam-smeared tabletop, then set the case on her lap and began searching through the contents.

"Well, I can't keep them," Emma said, dumping the bowls into the sink. "I have a job to go to tomorrow morning."

Wendy oozed sympathy. "Of course you do, Emma. In fact...." She paused to inspect the form that she had pulled from a file folder. "I'm going to see about getting you some financial assistance from the department."

Emma ran hot water over the dishcloth and wrung it out. "So what part of *I'm working tomorrow* aren't you getting, Wendy?" She returned to the table and mopped up the jam, milk, and burned toast crumbs.

"Of course you have to work," Wendy agreed, squeezing the form back into the file and continuing her search. "And we've got that all figured out. My supervisor and I have concluded that it would be in the children's best interest to enrol them in school."

"That's crazy! They're still in shock, for God's sake. It's only been five days since their father drowned in front of them!"

Wendy frowned at the contents of another folder. "We are aware of all that, my dear. That's why grief counselling is being arranged for them."

"A little late." Emma tossed the dishcloth into the sink and settled into a chair.

"Going to school will give them a sense of normalcy, Emma. They've already missed over a week of classes." She arched her eyebrow. "You wouldn't want them to be held back a grade, would you?"

"I hardly think that another few days will make much difference," Emma said.

Wendy cleared her throat. "Yes, well, it may be a little more than that...."

"Why?"

"Glenda's gone on another retreat."

Emma stared at her. "How the hell does she expect an angel to find her if she's never home?"

"The way she tells it, the angels are off looking after other souls. For something this big, she has to go to a place where there's the right kind of energy and send them a message through this spiritual guide, who may or may not be busy himself. Or herself." She shook her head, clearly mystified.

"And there's no one else? No other family?"

"Only Glenda," Wendy said. "I've been searching, believe me, and I did find places for one or even two of them, but none for all three."

Emma peered out the window, checking for some sign of the children. She thought she saw a cedar bow moving near the fort area, which meant Skylar was probably conquering another tree.

"I don't know, Wendy. These kids have issues that I don't have a clue how to deal with. Julie thinks her dad's still alive and Skylar's climbing everything she sees." She glanced at the door to the laundry room. "And the other night Caden wet the bed."

Wendy looked at her sharply. "So what did you do?"

"About the bed-wetting? What could I do? It wasn't his fault and he was really upset." She described how Caden helped the girls put the sheets in the washer.

"Sounds like you handled it beautifully," Wendy said, nodding her approval. "According to his file, Caden's last foster mother made him wear those diapers they've got for older kids, which wasn't a bad idea except that she presented them to him in front of the other children she was caring for."

Emma remembered the fear she'd seen on Caden's face when she found them in the bedroom. "Aren't you supposed to screen these people?"

"With more kids than homes to put them in," Wendy said, "you sometimes have to take what you can get. Our priority is for the children's safety."

Emma glanced out the window. The cedar bough was moving more vigourously now. "I should never have promised Skylar they could stay here."

"But you did." Wendy met Emma's gaze and held it. "Anyway, I'll get the necessary paperwork done and meet you at the school tomorrow morning." She removed some pamphlets from the file she was still holding and set them on the table. "This is some information on helping children who have undergone trauma. It might help you to understand what they're going through." With visible relief, she took a sip of coffee. Emma grinned as she watched her try to swallow the bitter liquid.

"Skylar made it," she said.

Wendy set the cup down and pushed it aside. "Which leads me to ask: where are the kids? I haven't seen them."

"I think they're hiding," Emma said. "They figured you were here to take them away."

Wendy got to her feet and collected her briefcase. "Never mind. I'll be seeing them tomorrow morning."

Caden and Julie were crouched inside the fort, but Skylar wasn't in the cedar tree as Emma expected.

"She's up there," Julie said, pointing to the ornamental spruce near the side of the house.

Emma went to the base of the tree and peered up through the branches to where a denim jacket was barely visible among the bluish-green needles.

"Skylar?"

"She was gonna climb into our room," Julie said.

Pushing back a memory of doing exactly that on a similar spruce, Emma raised her voice an octave. "The bedroom window's locked and Wendy's gone, so you can come down from there!"

Skylar didn't move.

"She's stuck," Caden said.

"Am not!"

"Then get down," Emma said. "*Now*."

"Don't want to." Skylar moved closer to the trunk of the tree, anchoring her runners more firmly onto the branch.

Julie shrugged and twirled an index finger near her ear.

When Emma's third order to come down had as little effect as the first two, she said, "Fine. I'm going to town for groceries. You can come or stay." When the child still made no response, Emma stepped away from the tree and motioned for Julie and Caden to follow her. "Maybe we'll stop for hamburgers and ice cream on the way home," she said loudly.

"Wait!" Skylar shouted. "I'm coming, too."

Emma paused. "I haven't got all day. If you don't come now, we're out of here."

A silence followed, and Emma's neck began to ache from staring up at the tree. "Skylar?"

"I'm stuck."

"I thought you weren't?"

"You've gotta get me out of here," she bellowed with the force of a field marshal.

Emma grinned. "That's where you're wrong, Skylar. I don't 'gotta' do anything."

"She can't get down herself," Julie said.

"So I guess she needs to ask for help just like anyone else who gets in trouble."

There was no sound from the tree, and finally Emma started for the truck. "Come on, you two."

"All right!" Skylar shouted. "Help me!"

"Help you what?"

"Help me get out of this damngod tree!"

Emma remained where she was.

Finally Skylar said, "Please."

"Well, then...." Emma returned to the tree, pushed some branches aside, and peered upward. "Let's see what we have here." A quick inspection showed that, as Skylar had started down, a lower limb had slid up the back of her jacket, the smaller branches now hooked over her collar, locking her in place.

"You'll have to take the jacket off," Emma told her.

Skylar hugged the tree trunk. "I can't let go!" She demonstrated how her fragile perch wobbled.

Emma swore under her breath and began climbing the tree, keeping her weight close to the trunk. By balancing on a limb below the child, she was able to pop the snap fasteners on the jacket and hold the child until she had wriggled her arms free. Once on the ground, Skylar grabbed her coat and headed for the truck, her expression furious.

"You're welcome," Emma called after her.

Without a word, Skylar climbed into the back seat and snapped her seatbelt into place. As Emma got into the driver's side, she saw a glint of moisture in the child's eyes.

That evening, while Julie was peeling potatoes and Emma was frying chicken, Twill came in through the laundry room. He was carrying a bag of fish, and if he was annoyed by the continued presence of the children, he gave no visible sign.

"Jigged me a halibut," he said, holding up the bag. "Thought you might be wanting to cook us up a slice."

Emma manipulated pieces of chicken from the frying pan into a roaster. "Put it in the fridge," she said. "I'm not sure if the kids even like fish."

He stowed the package and sat at one end of the table, sniffing the air. "I see you've got yourself a first-class lumper," he said, nodding toward Julie, who flashed him a shy, slightly confused smile.

"He means you're a good helper," Emma told her, then glanced apologetically at Twill. "I'm afraid I'm a little late. We went into town for groceries and ended up at the playground." She transferred the roaster into the oven, closed the door, and leaned back against the counter. "So I thought you were going there to manage fish, not catch them."

He grinned. "Well, now, there's no law I know about that says you can't do both. And I was watching them pens almost the whole time I was fishing."

"Did you hear anything more about the caretaker?"

"Just that they found the company's boat tied up at the dock in Shinglewood. Manager from Northern figures he's back on the mainland by now. There's a warrant out for him, but no one's holding their breath. Far as the cops are concerned, he's small potatoes."

Drawn, no doubt, by the aroma of chicken baking, Caden appeared in the doorway.

"Where's Rugrat?"

Twill shook his head. "I'm afraid, my son, that dog had other ideas. Guess he figured I was going back to the fish farm and he didn't want to come. Last I saw he was heading into the back forty after a squirrel."

Caden's enthusiasm vanished, but he lingered in the doorway, absently outlining a floor tile with the scuffed toe of his shoe.

Twill removed a long piece of string from his pocket and began threading it around his fingers, making an intricate web. When it was finished to his satisfaction, he flipped it over and it turned back into a single strand. By the time he'd dissolved his second web, Skylar was also watching from the doorway. Emma took over peeling the potatoes so Julie could watch, too.

Glancing up, Twill appeared to be astonished that he had acquired an audience. "Well, now," he said, winding the string around both hands and holding them out to Caden, "maybe you can give me the help I needs on this project. If you'll take this from me, I can make the next move...."

Caden refused to come forward.

Emma put down the potato she was peeling, held out her hands to Twill, and deftly removed the beginning of a cat's cradle from him. She made another twist to the pattern before transferring it intact back to him.

"There," he said as Emma returned to the sink. "Now wasn't that an easy thing?" He turned back to Caden and added, "I'll bet you can do the next step even better."

But it was Skylar who marched across the room to stand in front of him. Hands outstretched, she followed Twill's gentle instructions and took the cradle, but as she made the next twist the whole structure collapsed. She scowled at the mess.

"It's stupid," she said, thrusting the string back into his hands. Caden drew closer. "Let me do it!"

Twill nodded at him. "In a moment, my son," he said, wrapping the string around his fingers again. "First we've got to give your sister another chance." Once more he held the web out to Skylar, who crossed her arms and backed away from him. Turning to Caden, he transferred the string to the boy's hands. Caden furrowed his brow and clamped his lips as he concentrated on keeping the string taut. With stiff, awkward movements, he made the twist and transfer.

"I did it!" he shrieked when Twill held up the cradle.

"See, there's nuttin' to it, my son."

Skylar unfolded her arms and held out her hands. "I can do that." This time she successfully managed the next twist. She transferred the string to Twill and stepped back with a disdainful, "too easy."

"But I done it first," Caden reminded her.

Following Julie's turn, Twill produced a second string so that two of them could work together, and while Emma finished preparing the rest of supper, the four of them took turns creating new cradles.

After dinner Caden and Skylar took both strings and headed outside, but Emma soon called them back. "Baths and bed," she said.

Skylar eyed her suspiciously. "Why? It's not even dark out."

"Because tomorrow you're going to school."

"No way!" Skylar and Caden protested in unison.

Skylar added, "Daddy said we don't gotta go no more."

Emma began clearing plates from the table. "Well, Wendy Grieves says you do, and I don't think now is the right time to tick her off."

Julie took her own plate to the sink. "It'll be fun," she said. "We can read books and do projects."

Skylar made a face at her. "It sucks, Julie," she shouted, "and they're gonna call us names again!"

"I'll shoot 'em," Caden said.

Twill laughed. "Well, now there's a fine solution," he said, handing Julie his dishes. "And I'm sure you'll have a high time in prison with all them other scalawags that didn't go to school."

"Maybe these kids will be nicer," Julie said.

"You'll be okay," Emma told her. "Anyway, there's only a month before school's out for the summer."

"Yeah, right," Skylar said, marching out of the room. She stomped upstairs and a moment later the door to the girls' bedroom slammed so hard the house shook.

Twill slapped his knee. "Well, that's that, then," he said, pushing away from the table. "I think I'll take myself off to my own place. Good night, kiddies, and thanks, Emmie, for a delicious dinner. Your old grannie would be proud of you."

As he started for the door, Emma turned to Julie. "Will you see to it that they start their baths?"

Julie nodded. "Come on, Caden," she said. With a last, wary look at Twill, the boy scooted out of the room ahead of her.

Emma followed Twill outside. As they walked to his truck, she slipped her hand into his. He gave her fingers a gentle squeeze.

"You haven't forgotten we're having the release party next Sunday, have you?" he asked.

She slapped her forehead with her free hand. "Oh God!" she groaned, feeling overwhelmed and guilty at the same time. The full-day release party marked both the conclusion of the coho salmon's stay at the hatchery and the beginning of their journey into the open seas, an occasion that the volunteer directors of the hatchery considered worthy of a major celebration. It always ended with the release of the salmon smolts into the Stuart River, and as one of the directors, it was Emma's task to organize the event.

Twill looked at her sharply. "You did put the notice in the paper?"

She nodded, thankful that she had remembered to do so the day before she left for Bear Creek Landing. Hoping to cover the fact that since her return she hadn't given a thought to the preparations, she said, "I just have to ask George if his club will run the barbecue, and talk to Kate about the catering."

Twill frowned and withdrew his hand. "It's not like you, Emmie, to be putting off stuff as important as this."

They had reached the truck, and she stopped short and put her hands on her hips. "Yeah? Well, you try doing anything with three kids yammering at you night and day."

Twill was not sympathetic. "So get Wendy to take them. That's her job."

Emma shook her head. "If she takes them, she'll put them in separate homes."

"You're not thinking this thing through, Emmie." Twill climbed inside the truck cab and slammed the door. He added through the open window, "Every day those kids are with you they're getting more attached."

"You think I don't know that?" She kicked a stick out of her path. "I've been trying to get that across to Wendy, but she can't find them a place together."

He glared at her. "Then maybe they need to go to separate places for a spell."

"No!" It came out sharper than she intended. She softened her tone to add, "Twill, I promised Skylar that wouldn't happen. I *promised*."

"You had no right to do that, Emma." He leaned forward and inserted his key in the ignition. "You have to let them go." Without waiting for a response, he started the truck and backed out of the drive.

"You're wrong about that, Twill." Emma turned on her heel and walked back to the house. "I don't *have* to do anything."

ELEVEN

That night Caden wet the bed again. In the morning Emma found him attempting to lug his blankets down the stairs to the laundry room.

"How about I dump these in the washer, and you hop into the bath?" she suggested, gathering up the bundle and trying hard to ignore her watch.

Caden looked cautiously around and whispered, "Don't tell Skylar."

Remembering how fiercely Skylar had defended him the first time he'd wet the bed, Emma suspected it was really his own shame that made him want to hide the blankets. But she promised anyway, and while he trudged back up the stairs, she carried the bedding to the washer. After setting out milk and cereal for breakfast, she began throwing together peanut butter sandwiches for lunches as well as one meal of a plain slice of bread, a separately wrapped wedge of cheese, and an apple. When Julie came into the kitchen, Emma dashed up for her own shower.

Barely ten minutes later she returned with a towel wrapped around her damp hair to find Skylar and Julie embroiled in verbal combat. It was several minutes before she was able to sort out that Skylar had grabbed the milk jug from Julie, spilling milk onto her own jeans.

"It's your fault," Skylar shouted, brandishing the jug and wiping her pants at the same time.

Julie backed away. "Is not, Skylar. You...."

Emma grabbed the container. "Break it up, you two!"

"It's not fair," Skylar yelled as she stomped upstairs to change.

Emma heated a cup of yesterday's coffee in the microwave and choked down a few gulps.

"Oh God! We are so late," she cried, glancing at the clock. She grabbed the dish towel and swiped it over Caden's milk moustache. "You two get your jackets on."

In her bedroom she made a quick change into a blouse and slacks, glanced at the dress shoes lining the closet floor, then slipped her feet into a pair of sturdy sandals. As she raced back downstairs, she ran a comb through her hair.

"Skylar, we have to go!" she yelled over her shoulder, but it was minutes before the girl appeared.

"I don't want to go to that stupid school," she said.

"Right now, Skylar, I'm not a damned bit interested in your wants. I'm late for work so move your little butt or I'll move it for you!" As Skylar trudged outside, Emma slammed the door and locked it, then hurried to the truck and climbed into the cab. "Anyone not in their seat and belted up by the time I get this thing started is walking."

She shoved her key into the ignition and twisted. Nothing happened.

"What the hell?"

A second and third attempt produced the same result. Emma checked the dash and discovered the switch that had drained the battery. The children watched from the back seat.

"Who was playing with the lights?" she demanded, glaring at each child in turn.

Skylar backed against the door. "I was looking for string."

"Well, you've drained the bloody battery!" Emma grabbed her purse, jumped from the cab, and stomped around the yard until she was able to count to ten without cursing between the numbers. Then she returned to the children. "In the future," she said, enunciating each word, "do not get into this vehicle without my permission. Is that clear?"

Three heads nodded in silence, and she ordered the children out of the truck. Skylar complied with such enthusiasm that Emma wondered if leaving the lights on had been a deliberate act of sabotage. *Impossible*, she told herself. There was no way an eight-year-old kid, even one as bright as Skylar, could be that clever. But the girl's delight evaporated when Emma announced they were now going to walk to school and led the way along a nearby trail.

"What about bears?" Skylar called after her. "You told us there's bears!"

"My dear, you're making enough noise to scare away a whole forest of bears!" Emma said. "So move it."

When the weather was fair, she often walked to work along this rugged track, which twisted through salmonberry bushes and swampland before rising steeply up to a high cliff. The trail was often impassable during the winter rains, but this morning it was dry, though deeply rutted from runoff during last week's storm. At the top of the cliff Emma paused to give the children a brief rest, and for a moment they stood looking out at the water and the islands of the archipelago.

"This is one of my favourite spots," she told them. "Up here, everything I'm worried about kind of floats away."

Skylar pointed to a passageway far beyond the cliffs. "That's where we were," she said, identifying the route they had taken around Malcolm Island. Emma stared at her in surprise. *Maybe she was smart enough to sabotage the battery.*

"Hey, look!" Caden cried.

Emma swung around to find him pointing at a fresh pile of bear scat.

Julie wrinkled her nose. "Eeww! Dog poop!"

Skylar turned thoughtful as she studied the pile, but before she could say anything, Emma herded all three of them back onto the trail.

The route down the cliff was easier, the track eventually morphing into Ocean Avenue, a road that had been put in by a development company several years earlier. There had been talk of a huge housing project on the hillside, and one of the developers had even approached Emma to sell her viewpoint property. A few months after her refusal the investors had pulled out, leaving only the road to indicate the plan had ever existed.

Near the intersection of the trail and the road stood a deserted house and barn surrounded by the gnarled, moss-covered remains of a once-thriving apple orchard. The owners had left long before Emma arrived to live with her grandparents, and the empty buildings seemed to grow shabbier with each passing year.

As they walked past the driveway, Skylar looked sideways at her brother. "I bet it's a ghost house. And that's a ghost barn where people got murdered to death."

"Don't scare him," Julie said, as Caden edged closer to her side.

Emma shook her head. "You'll make a marvelous writer when you grow up, Skylar. If you survive that long."

The girl toed a pebble onto the blacktop. "Nope. I'm gonna be a mountain climber."

"Skylar can climb anything!" Caden said.

"So I'm discovering," Emma said. But it wasn't the conquest of physical heights that she was thinking of. As far as she was concerned, it was the emotional mountains Skylar was scaling that were far more daunting.

The elementary school was noisy with children and the foyer outside of the office seemed like a war zone. Emma parked herself and her three charges on a bench inside the main office, Caden situated between her and Julie, and Skylar grudgingly perched on the far end, ready to bolt at the slightest provocation. Clutching the plastic-bagged lunches Emma had made for them, they watched the secretary bustle from her desk to the counter as she answered phone calls and dealt with students and parents who came with late notes or requests for materials. Finally the bell rang, and a few minutes later a short, plump lady waddled into the office, issuing orders and admonitions as she progressed. She had arrived in Shinglewood last fall, and although Emma had seen her in the village before, they had never formally met.

"I'm Mrs. Pfluger," she said, then beamed at the children. "Who do we have here?"

"These are the Warner children," Emma said.

The principal turned to her expectantly.

"Wendy Grieves said they were to be enrolled here." When Mrs. Pfluger still showed no sign of comprehension, Emma said, "She was supposed to make all the arrangements."

"Well, I'm afraid she hasn't done so." Mrs. Pfluger smiled, but Emma got the distinct feeling she was the one being reprimanded. "Are you their mother?"

"God, no!" Emma said, earning a severe frown from the principal. "I'm looking after them on a temporary basis. Very temporary. I'm Emma Phillips."

Recognition illuminated Mrs. Pfluger's face. "Yes! You work for Sam Gabriel. I saw you on the news." Emma shrugged. "Well, they're here now," Mrs. Pfluger continued, "so if you have their records, we can go ahead and register them."

Skylar glared at the principal. "Daddy says we don't gotta go to school."

Mrs. Pfluger raised her right index finger. "We don't *have* to go to school," she corrected. She studied Skylar. "And which Warner are you?" There was a sternness to her voice that made the girl's bravado falter.

"She's Skylar," Julie answered, her voice scarcely a whisper. "This is Caden and I'm Julie."

The principal nodded. "Well, Skylar, Caden, and Julie, I'm sure you would like very much to do as your father says. However, the law is *very* clear that little children must go school." As if that settled the matter, she continued, "Now if you'll be patient for a little longer, your... Ms. Phillips and I are going to have a private chat."

She instructed the secretary to give each child a "comfort," then led the way to an inner office where she settled into an oversized chair that only emphasized her gnomish appearance. On a smaller chair facing her desk, Emma gave a brief account of the accident.

"That's pretty much what they said on the news," Mrs. Pfluger said. "But if they'd never met you before, why are they with you now?"

"Trust me," Emma said, "they're leaving as soon as Wendy can find a foster home that will take all three of them."

"She never gave you any transfer forms? Or authorization slips from the Ministry?"

"No, but according to Julie, she's in grade five, Skylar's in grade three, and Caden's in grade one."

Mrs. Pfluger pursed her lips. "This is highly irregular." She surveyed Emma as she might a naughty child. "I can't possibly register them without proper documentation."

"Well, you'll have to do something," Emma said, glancing at the clock on the wall. "I'm late for work."

A familiar burst of laughter exploded outside the principal's office, and a cheery voice boomed, "So you made it!"

Emma envisioned the children's terror as the social worker

loomed above them. "I've brought you some backpacks," Wendy said from the other room, "and I put some books and pens in them. We'll get the other things you need when we find out what they are."

A moment later Mrs. Pfluger's door flung open and Wendy stepped into the room. She looked down at Emma. "Well, I see you got here okay. I'm afraid I had a bit of an emergency this morning." From the dark circles that makeup had been unable to erase from beneath Wendy's eyes, Emma suspected that Colin Grieves had suffered an episode in the night. In their case against the government, Wendy had cited numerous occasions when she found her husband hiding beneath a table, sheltering from explosions that existed only in his head. It often took her hours to talk him back to reality.

Pushing aside her sympathy for the woman, Emma got to her feet. "Now that you're here," she said, edging between Wendy and the door, "I'm going to work." Before anyone could object, she left the office and closed the door behind her.

On the bench, Skylar had moved so close to her brother that their arms touched, and for once he didn't object to her presence. Each child was now burdened with a colourful backpack, a lunch, and a small cereal bar, which Emma suspected was Mrs. Pfluger's "comfort."

"I'll pick you up after school," Emma said, avoiding their eyes as she attempted to hurry past.

Skylar beat her to the door and blocked her path.

"Are you coming back?" she demanded.

Emma felt a twinge of guilt. The thought of walking away from the whole damned mess had occurred to her several times that morning. She met Skylar's gaze.

"We have a deal, remember?" She gave the child a gentle shove toward the bench. "I've got to go, Skylar."

They'll survive, she assured herself. Still, as she cut across the schoolyard to a landscaped park that bordered the marina parking lot and the strip mall, she couldn't dismiss the fear she'd seen on the children's faces. It was the kind of fear she believed no child should ever have to endure.

Sam came into the reception area just as Emma entered the office.

"So you finally remembered you have a job," he chided with a pointed glance at his watch.

Emma slammed her lunch bag into a drawer and struggled to keep her temper in check. "You're the one who sent me to the middle of nowhere, Sam," she said. "And it was you who told Sergeant George I could look after those kids." She thumped her purse beside the lunch bag. "Now they figure I'm the damned answer to all their troubles!" She rammed the drawer into place, then looked at the cup in Sam's hand. "You actually made coffee?"

"I got a thermos from Kate." He waved at a large file on her desk. "Which is fortunate because I've been on the phone since I arrived. Kazinski wants his release, the Dubois are asking why their closing didn't happen last week, and that pompous new McFamily director is riding my ass because Ted Holloway didn't show up for the hearing on Friday." He glared at Emma as if the whole mess was her fault.

"Did you try getting Ted at Crab Bay?" she asked, heading for the coffee room. "His girlfriend, Tamara, watches camp there for Timberline Logging. He and young Keith usually go up for the weekend." Always good-natured, Ted Holloway was one of Emma's favourite clients. The 24-year-old was working hard to make a home for his adolescent brother Keith, who had been orphaned a year earlier when their parents were killed in a car accident. The boy had Down syndrome, and it infuriated her that the Ministry of Children and Families was making it so difficult for Ted to become his legal guardian.

Sam followed her as far as the doorway and watched as she

dumped the remains of last week's coffee into the small sink and rinsed out the pot before filling it with fresh water.

"That can't be good for his custody case," he remarked. "The boy's supposed to be in school."

Emma shrugged. "If the director had taken the time to study his file, he would have seen that Keith's schoolwork and social skills have improved one hundred per cent since he left that group home they put him in and started living with Ted." She filled the coffee bin, clipped it into place, and switched on the machine. "Anyway, Wendy owes me big time right now, so I'll get her to smooth things over with the director and arrange for a new court date. As for Kazinski, I'll send an email advising that the release has been signed and will be forwarded to them by the end of the week."

"I thought it was at the bottom of Queen Charlotte Strait. "

"Trust me, they'll find the boat, which means they'll also find the briefcase. At any rate, the email will get Kazinski off our backs and give me time to work on the Dubois closing."

While the coffee slowly dripped into the pot, she turned her attention to the cups scattered over the counter. "Couldn't you have cleaned up after yourself?" she asked, running hot water into the sink. As Sam made a hasty departure for his own office, she called after him, "Don't forget you're tending bar at the salmon release on Sunday."

⚬⚬⚬

For the rest of the morning Emma played catch-up. She started by emailing Kazinski & Sons, then dialled the Children and Family Services office, where she left a message for Wendy. Her next call was to the Crab Bay logging camp.

"I've been here since Thursday," Ted told her. "There was a teacher's conference, so Keith didn't have school on Friday. Tamara was going to bring us out in the crew boat, only the camp manager needed it to check some timber up the coast.

Now we have to wait and see if there's room for us on the boat going back to Shinglewood tonight."

"You should have phoned, Ted. A court hearing is important." She thought for a moment, then asked, "Isn't there a road into that camp?"

"A rough one. You'd need a four-wheel drive."

"Well, stay close to the phone 'til you hear from me."

She refilled her coffee mug and turned her attention to the closing documents for the Dubois' new home, working steadily through the morning. It felt good to be back in a world she understood, where she felt competent and in charge, and being so busy kept her from thinking about the children huddled on the bench outside of Mrs. Pfluger's office.

At lunchtime Sam emerged from his office. "I'm having lunch with the Dubois," he said as he headed out the door. "I assume that I can tell them the papers will be ready for signing tomorrow morning?"

"All I can do is try," Emma said, but her response was lost in the slamming of the door. "Right," she muttered, pulling the peanut butter sandwich from her drawer. She was chewing when the phone rang. Gulping a mouthful of cold coffee and struggling to release the peanut butter grip cementing her tongue to the roof of her mouth, she grabbed the receiver.

"Gabriel's Law."

"I've spoken to the director," Wendy Grieves said, "and he's agreed — very reluctantly, I've got to tell you — to give Ted and Keith another chance if they show up for a meeting at four this afternoon."

Emma glanced at the clock. Although the journey from Crab Bay took less than half an hour by water, it would be after five before the crew boat left the camp.

"They'll be there," she promised. As soon as she disconnected, she dialled Sam's cellphone.

"Pick them up? Emma, we're not running a charity here. This *is* a pro bono case, remember?"

"But it's not Ted's fault that the crew boat didn't go back this morning."

Sam exhaled loudly. "All right. Go get them."

"I can't, Sam. I've got to collect my own kids from school at three."

"Your own kids?"

"You know what I mean. Anyway, my truck didn't start this morning, so there's no way I can go."

"Use mine," he said, "and get Kate to watch your kids until you get back."

Before Emma could respond, Sam hung up. She stared at the receiver for a second, then dialled the number for the Rusty Anchor.

"I'm just heading out for a dentist appointment," Kate said. "Call Twill. You said he owes you."

"He doesn't think so."

As she expected, Twill was more than annoyed by her request.

"What the hell do you think I'm doing here, Emma? Running a bloody nursery?"

She bit her tongue to keep from reminding him that's exactly what a hatchery was. "Just one hour, Twill. If I leave now, I can make it up to the camp at Crab Bay and be back by four. As soon as I drop the Holloways off, I'll collect the kids." She let a silence fall between them. Further pleading would only cement Twill's resistance.

"Well, since I'm almost quit for the day, I'll do it. But if you're going to start taking on other folks' kids, woman, you'd best be losing my number. Me and youngsters aren't meant to be on the same page."

"I'll keep that in mind," Emma promised, too relieved to argue.

The road into Crab Bay was worse than the pot-holed ones she had driven at Bear Creek Landing searching for Mary Dahl. Fortunately, Ted and Keith Holloway were both waiting outside of the camp office. Emma felt a sharp stab of emotion when she saw them, both dressed in ill-fitting suits, Ted tall and rake-thin, Keith much shorter, his plump face beaming at her.

"Hello, Emma Phillips," he said with a learned formality. "My brother and I are going with you now to see Sam Gabriel."

"Yes, you are." Emma smiled. She turned to Ted. "Isn't Tamara coming?"

He shook his head. "The first aid man was sick, so she's taking his shift." He helped Keith into the back seat of Sam's pickup, then climbed in himself. "But she sent a letter saying she's going to help me with Keith." He patted an envelope protruding from his suit pocket. As they started back along the logging road, he said, "Thank you for picking us up. It's a long way to come."

She smiled. "No problem. You and Keith can pay me back by hauling all the tables from the community hall and setting them up at the hatchery on Sunday."

Emma walked home along the cliff trail and stopped at the house long enough to change from her work clothes and feed Purkins. She filled his bowl with his favourite salmon dinner, but instead of racing toward it as he usually did, the cat sat in hallway, his head turned towards the girls' room, and meowed. Emma stared at him.

"Oh God, not you too?" She shook her head in disbelief. "Well, don't worry, my friend. They'll be back."

As she walked slowly along the path to the Castle, Emma wondered how serious Twill had been when he said she'd have to lose his number if she planned on keeping the children. Not that she was considering such an insane idea. Still, she resented his remark. Did their relationship really mean so little to him?

She was still pondering the question when she climbed the steps to his porch. There was no sound from inside the house, and she felt her irritation rising. *Don't tell me he's let them go off on their own again!* However, as she entered the living room, she saw Twill, Caden, and Julie grouped around Skylar, who was seated at the fly-tying desk, Rugrat nestled at her feet.

"Okay," Twill said, "make the final knot. That's right. Now clip her off." With her face screwed up in concentration, Skylar picked up a small pair of scissors and cut the thread she had used to tie a rather lumpy black fly. Releasing her masterpiece from the vise, she held it up to the others. "It's a real bug!" she said triumphantly. "Just like Daddy used when him and me went fishing."

Twill straightened and slapped his knee. "Well, that's that, then."

"Now it's my turn!" Caden said, attempting to push his sister off the seat.

"Sorry, my son," Twill said, pulling him away. "Your turn's going to have to wait for another day."

"I thought there wasn't going to be another day," Emma murmured.

He looked at her sharply. "And I thought you had enough smarts not to sass a man that's just saved your arse."

Caden raised his voice. "You said I could have a turn after Skylar!"

Julie was stuffing books and crayons into her pack. "You gotta pick up your things, Caden," she said, earning a scowl from her brother.

"It was still my turn," he said, but he moved reluctantly away from the vise and began gathering some papers from the coffee table.

"I have burgers at home," Emma told him. "And lots of fries that you can eat one by one."

Skylar swept the flies she had constructed into her hand. "*Your* home," she said.

Emma paused, then nodded. "Right. My home." As the children finished gathering their gear together, she told Twill about her arrangement with Ted Holloway. "Tomorrow I'll check with George to make sure he's bringing the barbecue, and we're all set."

"That's the good news," Twill said, accompanying her outside. "Bad news is there's a storm brewin' for Friday." He looked around the driveway in surprise. "Where's your truck?"

"Battery was dead this morning," Emma said with a conspiratorial wink at Skylar. "I have to put it on the charger tonight."

On her way to work the next morning, Emma stopped at the Rusty Anchor, and since there were few customers, she sat at the counter to drink her coffee while Kate filled the espresso hopper with coffee beans.

"Sam says you're getting real serious about those kids," she said. "Enrolling them in school and everything."

"Not my idea," Emma said as she eyed the pastry shelf, wondering if she dared add a slice of carrot cake to the breakfast she'd already eaten at home. "The bureaucrats seem to think it's the best thing for them. Of course, they didn't have to spend two hours last night listening to Skylar condemning every teacher in the building to eternal damnation." She shook her head. "I can't believe the mouth on that girl."

Kate frowned. "Sounds like she might have Tourette's syndrome. Didn't you say she was supposed to be on some kind of medication?"

"According to Julie, she is. Wendy hasn't mentioned anything about it." Deciding against the cake, Emma sipped her coffee then set her cup down. "Personally, I think all she needs is a little stability in her life. Skylar's as sharp as a new tack. She made a rope swing on that old cedar behind my place — you know, the one with the wide base? Climbed up and fastened the rope herself. I don't think I could have tied a better knot than she did."

"She sounds a lot like you." Kate closed the hopper lid, folded the paper bag that had held the coffee beans, and tossed it into a small recycling bin. "Looks after herself and doesn't take crap from anyone." She wiped her hands on a towel. "Those kids might be good for you, Emma. Stop you from hiding away at Windrush."

"I'm not hiding anywhere," Emma said, before Kate could launch into her favourite rant. "Not everyone has to have people around them all the time."

"I can already see them making a difference. You've never stopped in here on the way to work before."

Emma glanced at the clock. "Which is probably a good thing." She grabbed her coffee and headed for the door. "It's made me late for the second time this week — and it's only Tuesday."

Kate chuckled. "See what I mean? You're not nearly as up-tight as you used to be."

                           ⁂

Sam was at the filing cabinet in the front office searching through a stack of folders.

"The Dubois will be here in ten minutes," he grumbled, "and I can't find their file."

Emma set her cup down. "It's on your desk," she said as she dumped her purse and lunch into the drawer. "I put it there yesterday."

"I don't believe it," he said, following her into his office. She pointed to the folder nestled atop his inbox. "Hmph!" He shook his head. "I'm sure I checked there first."

"Right. Musta been those gremlins again." She started to

leave then turned back. "How did Ted Holloway's meeting with the director go?"

Sam settled into his chair and opened the file. "He's giving Ted another chance. Which reminds me…." He looked at her sternly. "If you're going to be late so often, you need to get your cellphone working."

"After drowning it in salt water, I don't think there's any hope of that," she replied. "But if it's really so important for you to be able to reach me, you could always buy me a new one." She hid a smile, knowing she had him in a corner. For Sam, spending money was almost as painful as backing down.

He scowled at the closing document on his desk. "Fine. Pick one up during your lunch break. But just something basic — no frills."

At the electronics store in the mall, Emma watched as the young male clerk set an array of cellphones on the counter.

"This one takes the best video clips," he said, holding up a flat-surfaced model. "And with this palmtop, we're offering a discount on a data recovery software package."

He thrust the box in front of Emma, and she picked it up. "What's it for?"

"If your palmtop is damaged, you can use this program to retrieve any data you have stored in it."

"I took a picture!" Emma exclaimed.

The clerk shook his head. "Excuse me?"

She waved the software box at him. "Would this allow you to get pictures from a cellphone that's been dunked in water?"

He frowned and said, "Cellphones should never be immersed in water."

"But if they were, could you get the pictures from them?"

"Yeah… there's probably a lab somewhere that could. Now, could I recommend…."

"Nope." She pointed to the simplest and least-expensive phone on the counter. "I'll take that one, if you can activate it in the next ten minutes."

As soon as the purchase was complete, Emma drove to the police station, where the receptionist showed her into the sergeant's office. He listened quietly while she described how she'd taken the picture of the wharf at Bear Creek Landing.

"That guy I saw talking to Forgie might have been in it," she said. "I figured the phone was toast, but this guy at the computer store thinks the picture can be retrieved."

Sergeant George leaned forward. "You never told me you still had the phone."

"It's in the pocket of that floater coat I was wearing. To tell you the truth, I'd forgotten I even had it." She looked at him searchingly. "So is the guy at the store right?"

He shrugged. "Depends on the damage. There's a techie in Victoria who's pretty good." He rested his elbows on the desk and tapped his fingers against each other. "Hard to say if it's worth the expense. Salt water's pretty corrosive, and you're not even sure the guy's in the picture."

Emma was disappointed. "So I should just toss it, then?"

He lowered his hands. "No. You can bring it in. I just wish you'd let us know earlier." He paused. "They found the boat this morning."

Her heart skipped a beat. "Where?"

"Near the Numas Islands. Tug going past at low tide saw the tip of the mast sticking out of the water."

"And Forgie?" The name came out as a croak and she shivered as she pictured the bloody face and lifeless eyes of the man she'd left crumpled on the floor of the *Lazy Bones*.

"Divers brought his body up about an hour ago." He looked at her soberly. "They're going to do an autopsy. Until that's complete, his death is being treated as a possible homicide. I'm supposed to make sure you don't leave town until that's confirmed."

"They think I murdered him?" Emma searched his face. "Jesus, George! Why the hell would I murder him? I only met the guy that morning!"

His expression hardened. "Forgessen's forehead was bashed in, Emma, as if he'd been assaulted. The fact that there was no other person on that boat makes you a pretty good suspect."

"But I told you what happened." Her stomach knotted. *Surely he wasn't serious?* "Why the hell would I want to kill him?"

He looked away, and she felt the knot tighten.

"What?" she demanded.

"The boat's cargo hold was full of marijuana."

She sat back abruptly. "Oh, crap."

His desk phone purred. He glanced at the call display and picked up the receiver. "Sergeant Shuter."

As he dealt with the call, Emma tried to absorb the mess she had stumbled into. She couldn't imagine anyone seriously thinking that she was involved in smuggling marijuana or any other drug, never mind killing someone. And yet she knew if Constable Read had his way, she would have already been tried, convicted and sentenced.

I should have just waited until that damn plane came back!

Sergeant George replaced the receiver. "Now, where were we?"

Emma cleared her throat. "Does this mean Read's going to be harassing me again?"

"Constable Read wasn't harassing you, Emma," he said sharply. "He was conducting an investigation. And I don't know if he'll want another interview." He raked a hand through his hair. "For some reason I'm being kept out of the loop."

She met his gaze and held it. "From now on, unless Sam's with me, I'm not talking to anyone, George."

"Fair enough," he said. He rolled his chair away from the desk and got to his feet. "I'll walk out with you."

As they left his office, Emma remembered the salmon release party. "You're getting your kinsmen to bring the barbecue and man it, right?"

He stopped, and a slight smile played on his lips. "I thought you were going to use your grandpa's old Studebaker for that."

"Well, if you bring your barbecue, I won't have to, will I?"

He laughed. "In that case, I'll have the crew there as promised." He led the way to the reception area and held the door for her. "If that phone doesn't look too bad, I'll send it off. There's a slim chance it might help."

"I hope so." Emma's shoulders drooped. "I just wish I hadn't let Sam talk me into that trip." She thought of the document that had started the whole mess. "Do you know if they've recovered my suitcase? That release Mary Dahl signed is inside."

"They never mentioned it," Sergeant George said, "but I'll see what I can find out."

⚜

Emma worried about the interview as she drove to the schoolyard.

How could I not have suspected Forgie was hauling dope? she asked herself for the umpteenth time. She thumped the steering wheel and cursed herself for being so focused on getting the document signed and going home that she ignored the warning signs that, in retrospect, seemed so bloody obvious. *He practically told me he was running drugs!*

Caden, clutching Bear-Bear to his chest, was waiting inside the school's entrance door. Julie stood beside him, holding a note from Mrs. Pfluger.

"You gotta go to the office and get Skylar," she told Emma.

"Yeah," Caden said cheerfully. "She got in a fight."

Julie frowned at her brother. "She was sticking up for you,

Caden." She turned back to Emma. "Some of the boys were teasing Caden for bringing Bear-Bear to school."

"They said I was a baby," Caden said indignantly, "an' Skylar said they was assholes."

Emma rolled her eyes. "You two wait here." She headed across the foyer to the office, where their sister was sitting on a bench. Her blonde hair was tangled, her right arm sported a deep purple bruise, and her forehead was plastered with a Band-Aid. On her face was an expression of unrepentant fury.

"What did you think you were doing, Skylar?"

"That lord t'underin' turd pushed Caden!" the little girl protested, just as Mrs. Pfluger appeared.

"We don't use that kind of language in this school, young lady." She turned to Emma. "I think it would be best if Skylar waited here while we have another private chat, Ms. Phillips."

Promising herself that she would talk to Twill about his language, Emma followed the principal into her office. The chair groaned as she sat down. "I wasn't told that Skylar was a special needs child," she chided as if Emma had deliberately kept this information from her.

Emma remained standing. "She seems like an okay kid to me," she said, adding to herself, *if you don't count a fiery temper and a foul mouth.*

"And since these children are going to be with you for such a short time," Mrs. Pfluger went on, "it is difficult to plan special programs for the girl. We'll receive no extra funding and we're short-staffed as it is." Her fingers drummed the desk then abruptly stopped. "She is taking her medication, isn't she?"

"What do you mean?"

"Skylar was diagnosed with attention-deficit hyperactivity disorder at her last school. It's a behaviour — "

"I know what ADHD is," Emma said, remembering the fight

Ted Holloway had with Family Services when Keith was incorrectly diagnosed with the disorder.

Mrs. Pfluger frowned. "Yes, well, according to her records, she was prescribed medication for the condition. She should be taking it every day."

Emma thought of Skylar sitting for hours at the bow of the boat and of her tightrope walk on the balcony. Certainly the girl had excess energy and nerve, but Emma remembered being the same way when she was a kid. In those days they just called her a tomboy. "Skylar's doing fine, Mrs. Pfluger. She's been with me for over a week now, and except for being exceptionally smart and resourceful, I haven't seen her acting abnormally."

"I am sure you may think so, Ms. Phillips, but professionals in the field have determined that Skylar has ADHD. Normally it would be my job to ensure she is put in a program that will address her special needs. However, since the child won't be staying long, there doesn't seem to be much point in designing a program for her. But she certainly cannot be allowed to continue her attacks on the other children. Medication is the only answer until she gets more settled."

Emma leaned forward. "If anyone should be put on medication, it's the child who pushed Caden in the first place. Don't you have some kind of policy about bullying around here?"

Mrs. Pfluger was unmoved. "Throughout her life Skylar is going to encounter aggressive behaviour. She needs to learn to deal with it appropriately."

"What Skylar needs is a stable environment and someone to love her and take care of her," Emma said. "The last thing she needs is to be doped up. Not after seeing what that did to her Mom."

With gnomish affront, Mrs. Pfluger squared her shoulders and pursed her lips. "I certainly would not compare the child's prescribed medication with the street drugs her mother used.

Andrea Warner was an addict. And while I agree that Skylar needs a home and love, that is certainly not part of my responsibility."

With an effort, Emma faked an expression of camaraderie. "Look, the kid has just lost both of her parents. She saw her father die right in front of her. She's bound to act up because of that."

"I'm not insensitive to her situation, Ms. Phillips," the principal said, spreading her hands palm-up in the air. "There is simply nothing I can do to change it."

Fighting back a volcano of fiery expletives that would rival Twill's repertoire, Emma leaned toward the other woman. "What if I can get Skylar to behave? Would you lay off on the medication?"

Mrs. Pfluger looked at her sadly. "My dear, I'm afraid you really don't understand the power of ADHD. It is not something you or Skylar can control."

"Still," Emma pleaded, "if she doesn't get into any more fights — if she behaves — will you leave her be? I mean, you said yourself, she's only going to be here for a short time."

The principal's fingers resumed drumming. Finally she said, "Ms. Phillips, I have the welfare of almost two hundred other students to consider. If I feel Skylar's behaviour threatens their safety... or even their feeling of safety... I'll be duty-bound to urge Mrs. Grieves to consult a physician and have the child placed back on medication."

It was the best she would offer, and Emma was forced to accept the decision. All the same, as she returned to the bench where Skylar was waiting, she was determined to prove the principal wrong.

That evening Julie took Caden into the living room to read him a story, leaving Skylar completing a page of sums at the kitchen table. Emma watched the girl's pencil skip from one column to the next.

"You're fast," she said. She sat in a chair across from the girl and added, "I used to sit here doing my homework with my grandmother. If I got all of the answers right, she would give me a cookie and some milk and read me some of the animal poems she made up."

Skylar shrugged. "We don't got a grandma. Just Aunty Glenda." She printed a number beneath the column she had just added.

Emma did a quick calculation in her head to confirm the answer and nodded her approval. "It was nice that you stuck up for your brother at school."

"That kid was gonna throw Bear-Bear in the toilet!" Skylar shoved the completed assignment into her backpack.

"He was probably just teasing," Emma said, "like you were doing when you told Caden there were ghosts in that farmhouse."

Skylar tossed her head contemptuously. "Well, I didn't hurt Bear-Bear."

"No, but it doesn't matter, Skylar. Fighting is against the school rules, and if you keep doing it, they're going to make you take those pills again."

"No way, Emma! Daddy said...."

"It doesn't matter what he said. He's not here anymore. If you fight, Mrs. Pfluger will make you take the pills."

"Well, that sucks!" Skylar flung her pack onto the floor and glared at Emma. "I told you I didn't want to go to that stupid school!"

As she stomped out of the room and up the stairs, Emma yelled after her, "Just stop fighting, Skylar!"

A moment later the bedroom door slammed shut.

"Well, there goes my psychology degree," Emma told Purkins, who had just padded in from the boot room.

TWELVE

On Wednesday, Emma and Wendy met for lunch at the Rusty Anchor. Over a somewhat wilted salad, Emma recounted her quarrel with Skylar.

"She needs help, Wendy, and by that I don't mean taking pills."

Wendy speared a crouton with her fork. "The councillor monitoring the kids says they're making great progress."

"Right. Caden wets his bed and builds tombstones, Julie talks to angels, and Skylar's become the new Terminator. A real healthy bunch."

Wendy waved her fork in Emma's direction. "You need to read those pamphlets I left you. What you're talking about are typical reactions to the kind of trauma the children have experienced."

"Like watching both parents die in less than a year?"

"More than that, I'm afraid." She rested her fork on her plate. "I spoke to the family supervisor in Campbell River. She said Andrea — the kids' mother — had been mixed up with a bad crowd as a teenager. She straightened out after she met Dennis, and was clean when she had Julie a year after their wedding. He was working for a local forest company and they were saving for their own home."

"So what happened?"

"House prices went up, and they had two more kids. He thought he could make more money by working at a logging camp, only it was the kind that didn't take families, so Andrea stayed in town." Wendy shook her head despairingly. "She wasn't the type that could handle being on her own with three small children. Long story short, she got back with her old crowd and was doing all kinds of drugs. He came out of camp and found the kids alone while she was at the bar with another man. When she returned home, they had a huge fight that left her with a swollen lip and a black eye. He threatened to go to the Ministry and she countered with an assault charge. The court, in its infinite un-wisdom, put a restraining order on him. Still, he tried to get Family Services to investigate her, but everything seemed fine on their initial visit to the house — it was clean, the children were happy — so they figured he was just trying to get back at her. They'd just lost half their staff and before they got around to making a second visit, Andrea had overdosed."

Emma twirled her fork in her salad, her appetite now vanished. "Julie thinks her mother was sick."

"Probably because she found her mother lying in her own vomit with a needle stuck in her arm." Wendy shook her head. "Amazing that the child isn't a basket case."

"Which brings us right back to the fact that they have issues I'm not capable of dealing with," Emma said. "Especially Skylar."

"I'm not so sure, Emma. From what I can determine, Skylar is behaving better now than she ever has." She reached across the table and patted Emma's hand. "You're doing a good thing here, lady. No matter what else happens to them, you've provided those kids with the feeling that someone in this godforsaken world cares about them."

"I wish I could believe that." Emma pushed her plate aside.

Through the window she watched a large troller pull away from the marina. Wendy followed her gaze.

"I heard they found the *Lazy Bones*."

Emma nodded. "They're doing the autopsy on Forgie today." With a sardonic lift of her eyebrows, she added, "So you might want to reconsider my qualifications as a temporary guardian for those kids."

"What do you mean?"

"I've heard, unofficially of course, they're treating his death as a homicide, and I'm the number-one suspect."

The social worker's belly laugh resonated throughout the café, earning them a curious glance from Kate as she walked past with an order of grilled burgers and crisp-fried potatoes. Wendy eyed the hamburgers longingly, then sighed and turned back to her salad. "Those boys need to upgrade their training in behavioural profiling."

"Speaking of behaviour," Emma said, "are your fiddlers still on for the salmon release?" Several years earlier, in an effort to steer local youth away from drugs, Wendy had worked with a violin instructor to organize a fiddle club. It became so successful that the youngsters were now playing for audiences across the province and had become a traditional part of the salmon release festivities.

"They'll be there."

Kate appeared with a coffee pot. "Have you talked her into keeping those kids?" she asked Wendy.

"Your husband's already ticked off because I'm coming in late every day," Emma said sharply. "A few more weeks of this and I'll be out of a job."

Kate splashed coffee into Emma's cup. "Sam will just have to install a computer at your house so you can work from home." She turned back to Wendy. "Emma would make a great mother, don't you think?"

Emma scowled. "Back off, Kate. I like my life just the way it is. Or was," she added darkly.

Wisely, Wendy chose that moment to stuff a forkful lettuce into her mouth. By the time she swallowed it, Kate had moved on to another customer, and Emma was able to shift the subject back to the salmon release party.

Later that afternoon, Emma was sorting through folders and filing them in the cabinet by her desk when Sergeant George stopped by to deliver her briefcase.

"Your suitcase was a write-off," he said, "but this wasn't too bad."

The leather case was stained with salt, and so was the plastic pouch that Emma retrieved from inside it. Holding her breath, she opened the Ziploc seal and removed the document Mary Dahl had signed. It was perfectly preserved.

"Sam will kiss you for this."

The sergeant made a face. "I hope not. But you might want to. The initial autopsy report came in this morning."

Emma looked at him warily. "And?"

"Seems your friend Forgessen died of a heart attack before he landed on that step."

Her eyes widened with surprise and relief. "So I'm not a suspect?"

The sergeant grinned. "Never were in my books. And because of that picture you took, Constable Read's got a new lead in the drug case."

"They were actually able to download it?" Emma placed the release on her desk. "And the guy was in it?"

He nodded. "The image was fuzzy, but there was enough detail for them to identify him. They've always suspected he was the buyer, only they haven't been able to make a firm connection. Now, thanks to you, they might even have enough evidence to arrest him. Or at least to get a search warrant for his warehouse in Port Hardy."

"And I'll bet Read takes all the credit," Emma said, feeling too relieved to be annoyed. The sergeant gave a wry smile. "Anyway, I thought I'd bring this over and give you the good news myself."

As the door closed behind him, she picked up the release and smiled. Life was beginning to look good again. The bonus she'd now get from Sam would bring her savings account very close to what she needed for her new roof, and by fall it might actually become a reality. And she wasn't going to jail.

Screw you, Constable Read!

⚜

Emma's day just kept getting better. She cleared up several files, got to the school on time and found the children in high spirits. Julie had even made friends with a girl who had a collection of pocket dolls.

"They're just like the ones Aunty Glenda bought for Skylar and me," she said, climbing into the back seat beside her sister. "We're gonna bring our extra ones to school and trade."

"You can have mine," Skylar offered. "They're stupid."

"Skylar won a goal in soccer," Caden said from the front as he fastened his seat belt.

"Way to go, Skylar!" Through the rear-view mirror, Emma saw Skylar duck her head.

"It hurt my foot," she grumbled, but she sounded pleased.

"Maybe we can get you some proper soccer shoes," Emma said, then gave herself a mental kick. *Stop encouraging these kids to think this is a permanent arrangement!*

"My teacher's gonna give me her kid's shoes," Skylar said indifferently. "She's too big for them."

"Well, that's... good," Emma said, but as she backed out of the schoolyard, she felt strangely deflated.

At Windrush the children headed for the kitchen, dumping their packs on chairs and announcing that they were hungry. Emma was ready with a full box of chocolate cookies.

"I made a picture for you!" Caden said after inhaling two cookies and a glass of milk. Digging through his backpack, he withdrew a paper that had been folded several times and handed it to her. The page was filled with crosses. Beside them a large stick figure and three smaller ones stood close together. Emma couldn't decide whether this was a good sign or something more sinister.

"That's you an' me an' Julie an' Skylar," he said, pointing to each figure in turn.

"And who are the graves for?"

Caden shrugged. "Dead people." He reached hungrily for the package of cookies. "Can I have another one?"

Emma nodded. "One more." It was clear that she wasn't going to get anything more from Caden about his picture. She placed it on the fridge door, holding it there with one of the fish-shaped fridge magnets she'd made. "Then you guys can go play so I can do some potting." Between making meals, washing dishes and clothes, and handling the dozen or so daily disasters that seemed to crop up with the children, Emma hadn't been back in her studio since Saturday. Although she really wanted to work by herself, she asked Julie, "You coming?"

Julie shook her head. "I've gotta get my pocket dolls ready for tomorrow. You go ahead."

Feeling as if she'd just been patted on the head and sent on her way, Emma went into the conservatory. She scowled at the empty wicker chair.

Even Purkins has deserted me! But as she carefully removed the plastic from her sculpture, the cat bounded into the room and gave a loud, cranky meow. Dressed in a frilly doll's gown with an even frillier bonnet, he paused in the centre of the room as if he didn't know which way to turn.

Emma raised an eyebrow.

"You do realize you look totally ridiculous."

Glaring, Purkins meowed once more, leapt onto the chair, and curled into a dissatisfied ball with his back to Emma.

"That's exactly how I feel," she said, and, bending over her plaque, began shaving clay from the eagle's prey in an attempt to transform the horse into a rabbit.

Twill appeared the next afternoon as Emma was taking two rhubarb pies out of the oven.

"Smelled them things all the way over at the hatchery," he said, hanging his jacket over the back of a chair and settling at the kitchen table. He had left Rugrat outside with Caden, who was dodging the soccer ball Skylar was kicking from one side of the driveway to the other.

"It's for dessert," Emma said. "But you're welcome to stay for supper. Macaroni and cheese with smokies."

"Don't mind if I do." He crossed one leg over the other and leaned forward, resting an elbow on his knee. "So how are you coming with them plans for Sunday?"

Emma removed her oven mitts and laid them on the counter. "Ted and Keith Holloway are looking after the tables, Sam's tending bar, George has the barbecue and his guys lined up, and Wendy's booked her fiddlers." She pulled a pot from a lower cupboard and began filling it with water. "I even got Kate to donate coffee and pastries. She figures if we put out a donation pot rather than setting a price on them, we'll make a lot more."

He rubbed his chin thoughtfully. "Sounds like it should all work out. I'm thinking we might need a big tent in case those rains come like they're predicting."

She stood for a moment, lost in thought, and then said, "The

Scouts used one at their jamboree last year." She set the pot on the stove and adjusted the heat. "I'll call George tonight and get the name of whoever was in charge of it."

Twill got up and peered out the window to the drive where Rugrat was attacking Skylar's ball. "Where's the oldest one?"

"Julie? She went to Corinna Blake's place. You know, that new couple running the pet store?" He nodded. "Corinna's mom is going to drive her home...." She turned to the clock above the sink. "... Any time now."

He moved behind her and massaged her shoulders. Relaxing, she leaned her head against him.

"Don't suppose there's any chance Wendy'll find them a place by Saturday?" he asked hopefully. "So we could maybe get together after the party?"

Emma heard Caden laughing in the yard. He was happy. They all were.

She nuzzled his neck. "No reason we can't do that anyway," she said.

He pulled away and returned to his chair. "Me an' kids don't mix, Emmie. You're not listenin'."

~~~

Emma was serving dinner when Julie arrived, so excited about her adventure that she dominated the conversation, telling them all about Corinna's "absolutely perfect bedroom" and her "awesome" playhouse that included a swing set and climbing gym.

"Who cares about her stupid playhouse?" Skylar exclaimed as Julie launched into a second round of description. "I like it way better here 'cause there's trees to climb and you can build your own forts."

"Yeah!" Caden piped up between mouthfuls of the chocolate ice cream he'd chosen over the rhubarb pie. "An' we got Purkins."

"There's lots of homes even better than Emmie's," Twill said slyly. "Like your aunt's house, I'm betting."

Skylar snorted. "Aunty Glenda's got nothing but dead people at her house."

Emma began gathering their plates. "You can help me with dishes," she told Twill, forestalling any further discussions on where the children should live. "And the rest of you can do your homework."

"I don't have any," Skylar said.

Twill ignored the tea towel Emma was holding out to him. Instead, he reached into the pocket of his jacket and turned to Skylar. "Maybe you can be occupyin' yourself with this." He held out a small fly-tying vise and a plastic bag that held an assortment of hooks, thread, and other materials for building flies.

Skylar gaped at the gift. "For me?" When Twill nodded, she took the vise and turned it reverently in her hands as if she'd never seen such a magnificent tool.

Twill set down the plastic bag and moved some dishes from the end of the table. "I think it'll fit good here," he said. She brought the vise over and he showed her how to fasten it to the edge. Without another word she settled onto a chair, dumped out the contents of the bag, and began poking through them.

Twill grinned and turned to the dishes, piling them into the dishwasher in such a disarray that Emma finally shooed him away.

"You can help Julie with her fractions," she directed, having noted the troubled expression on the older girl's face as she stared at her math book.

Twill leaned over her shoulder and studied the assignment.

"Well, now," he said straightening, "that don't seem too hard, dividing a half by a quarter." He looked around the kitchen and spied the half pie left over from dessert. Carrying it to the table, he said, "See this pie? Now there's just half left, and if I was to divide that into four pieces...."

Emma shook her head. "I don't think that's right, Twill. The problem is to divide one half by one quarter. What you're doing is dividing by four."

Julie pointed at the problem in her textbook. "I think my teacher said I had to turn something upside down."

Skylar left the fly she was tying and went to her sister's side.

"It's easy," she said and, picking up the knife, cut the half evenly into two pieces. "See? Now it's one quarter and one quarter, and that makes two."

Twill's focus switched from the pie to the textbook. "Now how the dickens did you figure that out?" he asked, eyeing Skylar with new respect.

Skylar pointed to a picture on the opposite page of a half circle divided into two pieces. "It says so right there." While Twill scratched his head and stared at the diagram, Skylar went back to her vise and the fly in progress.

"Well, I'll be jinkered if I can figure how you get a whole number out of two fractions," Twill muttered. Pulling out a chair, he sat beside Julie and took the book. "Lemme have another go at this."

Emma smiled and returned to her dishes. She was sure that the last time Twill had been bested by an eight-year-old like Skylar was years ago when he had lost a bet to her over the correct spelling of "driver's licence"— he'd insisted it ended with "se." Only after he checked his wallet did he hand over the $20 that she'd won. He never noticed during the entire argument that she had been staring at the fishing licence tacked to the cabin of his boat.

On Friday morning, when Caden ran into the kitchen for breakfast, he exclaimed, "I didn't wet the bed!" And he whirled about to show that his pyjama bottoms were dry.

"Right on, Caden!" Emma held up her hand for a high-five. As his small hand met hers, she felt a connection that went far deeper than their two hands touching. It was like a warm current running through her, and for the rest of the morning she smiled every time she remembered the sensation.

Later that afternoon, as Emma was closing another real estate transaction and planning a frozen pizza dinner that would give her an extra hour or two in the studio, Wendy entered the office. There was an aura of despondency about her as she sagged into a chair beside Emma's desk.

"Let me guess," Emma said flatly, "the aunt won't take them."

Wendy shook her head. "Worse than that. They've located the children's father... or what was left of him."

Emma winced. "Are they sure it's their father?"

"According to his dental records it is. Apparently his body had drifted under a boom of logs that was being towed to the mill at Beaver Cove. They found him when they were pulling the logs out of the water." She leaned forward, resting an elbow on the desk. "The councillors and I feel that it would be easier for the children if you told them about his death."

"No way, Wendy." Emma shook her head emphatically. "I'm not watching Julie's heart break in front of me. Not a chance."

Wendy sighed heavily. "I was afraid you'd feel that way. We just thought it would be more bearable coming from someone they trust." Pushing her hands down on the desk, she heaved herself from the chair. "So I guess it's up to the councillors and myself."

With mixed emotions, Emma watched the social worker walk to the door. She remembered the day her own father died. Clay Phillips had been the baby of the family, and her grandmother was devastated by his death. Yet she had put comforting Emma above her own anguish, choosing a quiet spot by the river to tell her about the accident and holding her tight as she cried. She had buffered Emma's pain with the reassurance that she was safe and loved. Unfortunately, there was no loving grandmother around for the Warner children.

"I'll do it," she said.

Wendy swung around, relief lightening her features. "Thank you."

All the way home from school, while the children chattered about their day and their plans for the weekend, Emma rehearsed what she was going to say to them. Pulling up in the driveway, she turned off the engine, and before Skylar could bolt from the truck, she held up a brown paper bag of chocolate-coated bear claws Kate had given her. "I thought maybe we could have a treat by the river."

Julie and Caden greeted the news with enthusiasm. Skylar, her hand already on the door handle, swung around and stared at her. "Why?"

"It's a nice day," Emma began, but when she saw the disbelief in Skylar's eyes, she added, "and I have something to tell you."

A scowl distorted Skylar's face. "You're dumping us, aren't you?"

"No. It's not about that." Emma opened her own door and stepped from the truck. "Let's just get some milk and glasses and go down to the river bench."

Julie brought her pocket dolls, and Caden dragged Bear-Bear along, insisting his teddy get an equal share of the treats. Scorning both toys and treats, Skylar ran down the stairs and when she reached the grass began searching between tufts of grass for flat rocks to skip across the river. Just a few yards from the bench she discovered a large pile of fresh scat, which she quickly pointed out to her siblings.

"Hey! Bear poop!" She eyed Caden and pretended to shiver.

"Maybe the bear will come and eat us!"

"What makes you think it's bear scat?" Emma asked to distract Skylar from teasing Caden.

"I saw some at school," Skylar said, nudging the pile with the toe of her runner. "Danny Shuter was throwing it at the girls at recess."

"Yeah," Caden said, "an' Skylar throwed it back at him."

Emma raised an eyebrow. "I hope you washed your hands." Skylar detoured around the scat and continued her search for pebbles. "Yeah. They smelled like shit." She picked up a quarter-sized stone. "Daddy says flat rocks are best, but I can make any rock skip."

"Actually," Emma said slowly, sitting on the bench and patting a spot on either side of her, "it's your Dad that I need to talk to you about." The three children stood before her, their faces tense and their eyes focused on her face. She leaned forward, hands clasped on her lap, and as gently as she could, told them that their father's body had been recovered near a logging camp. When she finished, Caden turned to Julie, his expression confused.

"You said he was in a forest!" His eyes filled with tears.

Skylar glared at her sister. "You're a liar!" she shouted. Then, throwing her rock at the water, she swung around and raced up the stairs to the house.

"Skylar, wait!" Emma pleaded, but the girl was already out of earshot.

Julie sat on the bench. She didn't cry, as Emma had expected. Instead, there was a vacancy in her eyes that was far more distressing than tears. It was as if all hope had evaporated from the little girl's soul. Emma put one arm around her and reached for Caden with the other.

"There's nothing wrong with hoping for something," she said. Julie remained rigid, refusing comfort. "I'm going to find

Skylar," she said, pulling away from Emma and dumping her dolls on the bench. When her brother tried to follow her, she turned on him with uncommon fierceness. "Stay away from me, Caden! I'm not your damned mother!"

The little boy stood uncertainly, halfway between the stairs and Emma. His lower lip trembled as Julie trudged up the steps and didn't look back.

Emma pulled him onto her lap. "You've still got me, little one," she said, tucking Bear-Bear into his arms. Caden resisted for a moment before grief and confusion got the better of him and he wilted against her. Rocking him gently, Emma let him cry and even after his tears stopped and he began to suck his thumb, she continued to rock until he was sound asleep. Leaning back, she stared at the slow-moving river. Near the far bank she could see a beaver pushing a small tree limb as it swam silently toward the shore, and for a moment she envied the simplicity of the creature's life, much like her own had been prior to meeting the Warner children. And yet, as she rested her chin on Caden's head and smelled the sweet, sweaty scent of his hair, she felt an earthy kinship with the beaver.

Before going to bed that night, Emma checked on the girls. Julie was asleep — or pretending to be — with the crook of her arm over her face. Skylar was sitting cross-legged on the bed, pulling apart the flies she had tied, tossing bits of feather and dubbing onto the floor. With a shock, Emma saw her father's jacket discarded in a heap in the corner.

"I told Julie he was dead," Skylar said.

"Yeah, you did."

"He should'a swimmed." She glared at Emma. "You swim-med."

"You said he didn't know how to swim. And maybe he hit his head."

Skylar cupped the hooks in her hand and threw them at the jacket in the corner. "He was a damngod stupid asshole!" she cried, her voice breaking.

Emma sat on the edge of the bed. "It was an accident, Skylar."

The girl's lower lip quivered and she screwed her face into a tight knot. "He would'a dumped us anyways," she choked.

"Maybe." Emma searched for what to say next. "But he did come to get you."

Skylar slid under the blankets and covered her head with the sheet.

Emma rested a hand on her shoulder, then got to her feet. She went around to Julie's side of the bed and snugged the coverlet around her. "Goodnight, sweetie," she whispered, but Julie gave no indication that she had heard.

A few hours later Emma found the sisters curled together, with Skylar cradling her father's jacket in her arms.

THIRTEEN

Emma woke before dawn on Saturday to the sound of rain pounding on the roof. She peered groggily out the window. A wind had come up and the sheet of plastic that she had secured to the roof was now billowing past the window. Then a softer, dripping sound inside the room caught her attention, and she turned to find a large puddle of water in the middle of the floor. *Damn!* Pushing Purkins off her stomach, she jumped out of bed, padded barefooted downstairs, and returned with a mop and the drip bucket just as Caden appeared, dragging his bedding.

"Leave it," she said. "I'll put it in the washer and you hop into the tub."

Breakfast was a continuation of what was rapidly becoming a day from hell.

"There's no more cereal," Skylar said, thumping her empty bowl onto the table.

"Yes, there is." Emma went to the cupboard. "I bought a new package the other day." But there was no cereal on the shelf where she had stored it. "Julie! Where did you hide the bloody cereal?"

Avoiding Emma's gaze, Julie plodded past her to the stairs. It was several minutes before she returned with the box of Cheerios.

"Packrat!" Skylar taunted. She tried to snatch the box from Julie's hands, but Emma grabbed it first. Ripping off the top, she poured some into each of the three bowls. But this didn't stop the sisters' bickering, which escalated from criticizing the way Skylar toasted the bread to a discussion of Julie's snooty friends at school. After retreating to the bathroom and screaming into a towel, Emma assigned them all separate chores, hoping this would keep them from killing each other.

"We're not your slaves," Skylar declared, and instead of dusting the living room furniture, she turned the feather duster on Caden and began copying everything he said until he stormed up to his room in tears. She then went back to tormenting Julie.

Afraid that if she didn't get the hell out of there, she would be the one doing the killing, Emma donned her rain gear and went outside to salvage her roof.

The rain and lingering moss on the shingles made the steep surface so slippery that she decided to install a safety line before venturing onto the roof. It took three attempts for her to hurl a length of rope over the roof peak to reach the lower deck railing, where she secured it with a reef knot. Then tying the opposite end around her waist, she crawled onto the shingles and made her way to the area above the upper den.

The downpour limited her ability to see where she was going, and even creeping about on her knees, she had to rely on the safety line more than once to maintain her balance. She tried first to rescue the plastic sheet, but as she was hauling it back to the peak, the wind ripped it from her fingers. In dismay she watched it tumble away like an ungainly kite, until it flopped over her rock garden. For a moment Emma contemplated climbing down to retrieve it but decided instead to focus on the roof. One by one she inspected the cedar shingles above the area of her room. Near the peak she found one that had rotted through, and was lifting a piece of it up when she sensed a movement behind her. She turned to see Skylar crawling up the slope of the roof.

"No!" Emma shouted at her. "You can't be up here, Skylar!"

The girl kept coming, the impact of her boot toes sending bits of dark green moss tumbling to the ground. Furiously, Emma jabbed the fractured shingle back into place, then turned to tend to the child, inadvertently pressing down on the damaged area. With a sickening crunch the shingle collapsed inward, knocking her off balance and forcing her arm and shoulder into the opening. Her arm scraped painfully against splintered cedar as she pulled herself free. A jagged hole gaped into the attic.

"Jesus!" Rubbing her arm, she glared at the mess she had made. Now the hole was far too big for patching. Even worse, the leak could not be contained by buckets alone.

By now the cause of the disaster had crawled up beside her.

"Damn it, Skylar! Why the hell don't you listen?" she shouted over the wind. "I told you to get off this goddamned roof!"

Skylar gaped at the hole and at Emma's angry face, and began backing down the slope.

"Grab onto the rope," Emma yelled, anchoring herself and holding the line taut. But Skylar ignored the rope and continued inching down until she lost her footing and slid backwards. With a frightened yelp, she reached for the line and missed.

"No!" Emma scrambled toward her just as Skylar's foot hit the ladder frame, stopping her fall. Without a word, she wriggled onto the rung and disappeared from view.

Emma climbed back up the roof and stared gloomily into the crawl space above her bedroom.

No way I'm fixing that hole today. I'll have to borrow a tarp from the hatchery.

She didn't know how she was going to manage a large tarp in this wind when she hadn't even been able to hold onto the plastic one, but she had to try. She arranged the broken shingles over the hole as best she could and hoped that the wind would leave them in place until she could collect the tarp.

It won't keep out the rain, but it might slow it down, she reasoned as she crept backward to the ladder. Once she was on the upper rung, she released herself from the safety line.

Her feet had barely touched the ground when a car crunched onto the gravel drive.

"Not now!" she groaned. Wendy Grieves, sporting a bright yellow rain poncho with matching hood, emerged from her car.

"Don't you ever take a day off?" Emma asked, doffing her hat and jacket before leading the way into the kitchen.

Wendy's usual jolliness was absent as she draped her own hat and cape over a chair. She sat heavily in the only other chair that didn't have milk spilled on it, and leaned an arm on the table, carefully avoiding a knife smeared with peanut butter and jam.

"So how did the children take the news about their father?"

As they usually did when the social worker appeared, the children had vanished, but Emma could hear footsteps and an assortment of thumps and bumps overhead.

"About as well as you might expect," she said, still irritated that she had to be the one to tell them. "Skylar got mad, Julie was heartbroken, and Caden cried. This morning has been hell."

"It was good of you to do it." Wendy looked longingly at the coffee pot.

Ignoring the silent request, Emma leaned against the counter, her arms crossed. "I've got to get back to the roof."

"Right," said Wendy. "Well, the office called to say Glenda Duncan got in touch with them. She's flying back from Toronto this morning and she wanted to inform us right away that she wouldn't be taking the children. Apparently her angels have decided that doing so will impede her spiritual development."

Emma's bad mood darkened. "So what happens now?"

Wendy squared her shoulders. "I have a home lined up in Campbell River for Caden and Julie, and there's another family in Victoria with experience in dealing with children who have ADHD that is willing to take Skylar."

Emma unfolded her arms. "But I promised...."

"I know you did, dear." Wendy nodded vigorously. "And you've tried your best."

"But...." Emma paused to close the hallway door. It had been several minutes since she had heard any noise from upstairs, and she suspected the children were listening to every word being said. "Skylar needs to be with Caden and Julie," she said quietly.

Wendy nodded again. "I agree, Emma. But the fact remains there just aren't that many homes available for three normal children, never mind one with behavioural problems."

Emma went to the table and began stacking bowls and plates together, giving herself time to think. A part of her screamed, *It's not your problem. You have your own life to live.* A stronger part of her remembered her vow on the *Lazy Bones* to make her life count for something.

"What if I kept Skylar?" As soon as the words were out she regretted them, and a voice inside her head groaned, *Oh crap, here we go again!*

Wendy's eyes widened. "You?" She tilted her head questioningly. "I thought you didn't want kids."

Exactly.

"I don't mean forever. Just until they get a place together." She raised an eyebrow. "They *will* eventually be placed together, right?"

"That's the desired outcome, but it's hard to say if that's what will happen." Wendy studied Emma thoughtfully. "Why Skylar?"

Emma carried the stack of dishes to the counter. Why *was* she so concerned about the least likeable of the Warner children? Skylar was bad-tempered, ungrateful, and totally unpredictable. She didn't sugarcoat her words, and when someone threw shit at her, she hurled it back in their face. *Skylar's a lot like you,* Kate had said, but to Emma the child was more like her grandfather

199

and Twill, individuals who were imprisoned by the very conventions that made other people feel safe.

She grabbed a towel and swiped it over the seat of a chair, then twirled the chair around and sat on it, her arms resting on top of the back support.

"Skylar needs someone who understands her, Wendy. Someone who won't stuff her full of drugs."

"Emma, administering prescribed medications to control hyperactivity does not constitute stuffing someone full of drugs," Wendy said stiffly.

Emma snorted. "Right. The emphasis being on control."

"And that," Wendy snapped, punctuating the words with her index finger, "that is exactly why you can't look after her. Not right now, anyway."

Emma winged her hands palms-up. "Hello? I've been looking after her for the past two weeks!"

"Yes, but the director's been getting irate phone calls from Mrs. Pfluger about your refusal to accept Skylar's... behavioural problems. She's advocating the children be removed from your care as soon as possible."

"What the hell's with that woman?" Emma demanded, jumping up from the chair and slamming it against the table.

Wendy glanced at the closed door and lowered her voice. "The school doesn't get funding for those kids because they weren't enrolled in the fall. Which wouldn't be so bad if they didn't need special care, but the cost of assigning a special needs teacher to Skylar this late in the term will come right out of Pfluger's budget."

Emma shook her head in disbelief. "So it's all about money? Skylar's sacrificed so the school can balance its budget?"

"Bureaucracy is an evil thing," Wendy agreed. She got to her feet too. "You can still put in a request. I'll drop the forms off on Monday when I pick up the kids."

"That soon?"

Wendy nodded. "The director wanted them out today, but their placements won't be ready until Monday and I assured him that I was closely supervising their care." She wrapped the yellow poncho around her shoulders. "You've done the best you can, Emma. It's not your fault."

Emma followed her to the door. "Maybe I should have tried harder to get along with Pfluger," she said glumly. She stood on the porch and watched the social worker plod through the puddles to her car.

How the hell am I going to tell them?

She ran her fingers through her hair, still damp from the rain and heaved a sigh. Then she turned back to the kitchen and opened the door to the hallway. "You can come out now."

Only Caden appeared, sporting a chocolate moustache left over from the cocoa Emma had made him for breakfast. Worry lines creased his forehead. "Julie said we can't stay here no more." His eyes begged her to refute the statement.

Emma knelt beside him. "Julie's right, Caden. Wendy has found a really nice family for you." His eyes widened with fear and she put a comforting hand on his shoulder. "It won't be like the last one, Caden."

He looked at her closely. "Does you know them guys?"

"The family?"

He nodded.

"No," Emma admitted. "But Mrs. Grieves wouldn't let you go to some place that wasn't nice." Caden looked at the floor. His shoulders slumped as he turned away from her and trudged down the hallway, then slowly made his way up the stairs.

Did you really expect him to believe another promise?

Emma clenched her fists and tried to focus on her roof and the flood of water that must be pouring into her bedroom. She needed to go back outside. Instead, she followed Caden to the girls' room.

Julie appeared even more downcast than her brother. Her hair in tangles, she sat on the bed and quietly stroked Purkins, who had curled up in her lap.

"Where's Skylar?" Emma asked.

She pointed to the closet where Caden was guarding the door, an angry scowl marring his face. "Skylar won't let me in!"

"She probably wants some time alone," Emma said, then contradicted herself by suggesting they all go to the hatchery to pick up a tarp for the roof.

"I want to stay here," Julie said.

Caden crossed his arms. "Me too!"

There was no response from the closet.

"Rugrat will be there, Caden," Emma said, but even the promise of a romp with Twill's dog didn't sway him. He climbed onto the bed where Bear-Bear was resting on a pillow, and huddled beside his sister and the cat. "I'm staying with Julie."

Emma looked up at the ceiling. There was no evidence of any leaks in this bedroom, but she could hear the rain pounding on the roof. She needed that tarp.

"I can babysit," Julie said. "I done it for Aunty Glenda lots of times."

"I don't know...." Emma fell silent as she weighed the risks of leaving them alone against the misery she would cause by forcing them to accompany her. Abandoning the roof was not an option. Finally she nodded. "All right. Just don't go near the stove, and absolutely don't go outside. I'll be back as quick as I can."

As Emma expected, the drip from the bedroom ceiling had become a steady stream, and the bucket she'd placed under it was overflowing. She emptied and replaced it, mopped up the worst of the water, and threw an armful of towels under two new drips. Then she headed for the hatchery.

She found Twill working in a swirling pool of muddy water

with Leonard Smythe, the hatchery's wiry assistant manager. Though known for his easygoing manner, Leonard's face was tense as he and Twill tried to clear out the intake channel that carried water from the river to the oxygenation tower.

"There was a landslide upstream," Twill shouted as he lifted a shovelful of mud and tossed it up onto the bank. "Sent a load of silt down, plugging up the pipes. If we don't get it cleared out, them fish are all gonna die."

"I need a tarp," Emma shouted back. "I've got a big hole in my roof."

Twill nodded toward the hatchery buildings and immersed his shovel again. "In the storage shed. You'll have to get it yourself."

Leonard dumped more mud onto the pile. "We're gonna need volunteers," he panted. "We'll never clear this ourselves."

Twill surveyed the muddy channel and looked pleadingly at Emma. "There's a list by the phone in the office, Emmie. Call as many as you can."

Emma shook her head. "I've got to get back," she yelled. "The kids...." Her voice trailed away. Twill had gone back to shovelling.

"Oh, this day just keeps getting better and better," she fumed as she turned on her heel and plodded through the rain to the office. "Forget about the kids. Forget about the roof. Just save the damned fish!" Without removing her gear, she began dialling numbers. By the time she had run through the list and was heading for the storage shed, the first of the volunteers was arriving.

Back at Windrush, Emma lugged the tarp to the side of the house, where the ladder was still leaning against the edge of the roof, then went inside to check on the children. She had barely closed the side door when Caden came running into the kitchen.

"Skylar's runned away!" he shouted. "And Julie's crying an' crying an' crying."

Swearing under her breath, Emma kicked off her boots and headed for the girls' room, where she found Julie sobbing into her pillow. The closet door was open, and in front of it a wingless clay angel sagged in a pool of purple liquid, discolouring the hardwood floor.

"What's going on?" Emma demanded. "Where's Skylar?"

"Skylar said angels are booshit," Caden offered helpfully. "So Julie throwed her juice all over Skylar's coat an' Skylar runned downstairs and got Julie's angel and...." He shrugged dramatically and held his hands out to the mess on the floor.

"Julie threw her juice?" Emma stared at the girl crying on the bed and tried to figure out what the hell she should do next: clean up the mess, comfort Julie, fix the roof, or search for Skylar? She rubbed a hand, still wet from the rain, across her eyes and forehead, then turned to Caden, who was toeing the edges of the juice pool.

"You," she said firmly. "Get a towel and mop up that juice. And Julie, I need you to stop crying and tell me where you've looked for your sister."

"Every place," Caden answered.

Julie sniffed and nodded.

"Well, check the house again," Emma said. "Every room, closet, and cupboard. I'm going to search outside."

Without waiting for a response, she headed back outside, where it seemed to be raining harder than it had all morning. She searched the obvious places first: the fort the children had built, the reachable branches of the nearby trees, the woodshed. There was no sign of Skylar. With growing alarm she went around to the river side of the house to check the garden, the boat shed, and the bench where she'd told the children about their father's death. For one long moment she studied the river itself, swollen and muddied from the landslide. Pushing aside a fear too horrifying to contemplate, she returned to the house.

Julie rushed into the boot room as soon as the door opened.

"Did you...?"

Emma shook her head.

Worry lines creased Julie's forehead. "She's not anywhere here neither," she said.

"Yeah," Caden said. "She's not in the closet. Not nowhere!" He flung out his arms to demonstrate, and Bear-Bear slammed against the wall. Caden looked down at the stuffed animal and his eyes widened. "Maybe a bear...."

Emma pulled off her coat. "Don't even go there, Caden. Skylar's just hiding somewhere, but I think we're going to need some help finding her."

She called Wendy Grieves' cellphone first, and the social worker promised to be at the house in ten minutes. As soon as she disconnected, Emma dialled the police station.

"I'm alone here," Constable Schmidt said. "Everyone else is attending a three-car pile-up on the highway."

"So a little girl out in the worst storm of the bloody season doesn't count?"

"Now, Emma," the constable said in a carefully controlled tone, "children hide all the time. Nine times out of ten they're within a few feet of their home. That little girl's probably somewhere perfectly safe."

Through the boot room door, Emma saw Skylar's pack lying on the floor where she'd dropped it on her return from school the day before.

"Not if she's out on one of the trails," she said. Keeping her voice low so Julie and Caden wouldn't hear, she told the constable about the bear scat they'd seen.

There was silence on the line. "I'll contact Sergeant George. And I'll call the ferry manager and get him to watch the shoreline for her."

"Thank you. And while you're doing that, I'll check the trail to the hatchery."

"I'm sure she's fine," said Constable Schmidt again.

Emma let out a deep breath. "I hope you're right."

She hung up the phone and made a hasty check of her bedroom, and by the time she had emptied and replaced the bucket, there was a knock at the door. Handing Julie and Caden more towels to spread on the floor, Emma ran downstairs and let Wendy in.

"How can I help?" she asked.

"Just stay with Caden and Julie," Emma said. Pulling on her raingear once more, she gave a hasty synopsis of her conversation with Constable Schmidt then hurried back outside.

The trail through the woods was sodden, and in many places she had to wade through puddles that came close to the top of her gumboots. Wherever there was a patch of mud, she carefully knelt to search for footprints. She found none. *That doesn't mean she didn't come this way,* she thought, fighting back panic. She called out Skylar's name again and again, but there was no answer, and no sign she'd been on the trail at all.

Emma's panic escalated when she reached the Castle and a quick inspection of the house and outbuildings yielded the same result.

Where is she?

The volunteers had cleared most of the silt from the channel when Emma arrived at the hatchery. Twill and Leonard were taking apart the pipes leading to the oxygenation tower and cleaning them.

"You get the tarp on?" Twill asked, removing a section of pipe and handing it to Leonard to flush out.

Emma shook her head. "Skylar's missing," she said. "I've searched everywhere I can think of, and she's nowhere at my place or yours. I was hoping she might have come here."

"She's probably hiding somewheres," he said, echoing Constable Schmidt. He walked over to the volunteers clustered around the channel.

"Any of you folks see a kid on the road when you drove in?"

An older man looked at him sharply. "Like who?"

Twill held his hand waist-high. "Little tyke about this tall. Blonde hair."

The man shook his head. "No, but that don't mean she wasn't there. Hard to see anything in this rain."

"What about the tower?" Emma asked Twill.

He frowned. "What the hell would she be doin' up there?" He leaned his head back and, shielding his eyes with his hand, surveyed the walkway around the top of the tower. "Nah. Anyways, I think we would'a seen her." He rested his hand on Emma's shoulder and she suddenly felt like crying.

"Hey, now," he said gruffly, giving her a gentle shake. "She can't have gone far, Emmie. You go ahead and check up there just the same." He pushed her toward the tower and swung around to face the men. "Joe, maybe you could give Leonard a hand with those pipes. The rest of you, help me look for the kid." As one of the men walked toward the lunchroom, Twill yelled, "And boot that good-for-nothing dog of mine outside. He'll probably head right for her if she's anywheres around here."

Emma took a deep breath, forcing back her panic, then grasped the metal railing and slowly climbed the slippery steps to the top of the tower. Although there was no water running through the system, she was worried about the wide pipe that ran down to the cistern. However, when she reached the platform she saw that the grating was securely fastened. For a moment she stood at the railing, peering through the rain at the hatchery grounds. As far as she could see, there was no sign of a little girl in a blue denim jacket.

Sergeant George was waiting for her at the foot of the steps. He squinted at her from beneath his hooded poncho. "Where have you looked so far?"

"I walked the trail here," Emma said, wiping rain from her face. "And I looked all around Twill's place and Windrush. I don't know where the hell else she might have gone."

Together they walked to the office and listened as Twill received a similar verdict from the volunteers.

"No one has seen her at the ferry terminal," the sergeant said, "and the highway crew attending the accident are sure she didn't pass that way." He turned to Twill and Leonard. "Get your volunteers to do another check back along the trail and the riverbank. There's a chance Emma might have missed something. Meanwhile, I'll head back into town. Could be she went to the school or some place like the Rusty Anchor — a place that's familiar to her."

"If she went to the school, she probably took the cliff trail," Emma said as she and Twill followed him to his car. "Drop me off at my place and I'll walk the trail from there and meet you at the school."

Twill nodded regretfully at the tower. "I've got to get this thing unclogged or them smolts won't be long for this world," he said, "but take the dog wit' you. If your girl's about, he'll be finding her." As he headed towards the men working on the pipes, he called over his shoulder, "And keep an eye out for that she-bear!"

With his coat now soaked through, Rugrat had shrunk to half his size, and he was not at all eager to climb into the police cruiser until Emma lifted him onto her lap.

⁂

Julie's tearful face dispelled any hope that Emma had of Skylar's spontaneous return home.

"Child's been crying ever since you left," Wendy said as

Emma slammed the coat room door against the wind. "Seems to think it's her fault Skylar ran off."

"It is!" Julie sobbed, wrapping her arms around Emma's waist, oblivious to the water streaming from her raincoat. "I shouldn't have made her so mad!"

Emma placed both hands on the girl's shoulders and pushed her gently away. "Skylar isn't mad at you, Julie," she said firmly. "When we find her, we'll sit and talk this all out."

Caden was watching them, his eyes wide and his lips trembling as if he, too, was about to cry. "Is Skylar gonna die like Daddy?"

Emma shook her head. "No, Caden. Rugrat and I are going to find her. I promise."

She told Wendy of her plan to walk the cliff trail. "I'm meeting Sergeant George at the school. One of us is bound to find her," she said, as much for her own sake as for Wendy and the children.

Back outside, she started up the trail with the dog running ahead of her, nose to the ground. A muddy river coursed down the hill from the cliffs, trenching the path, and while Rugrat found the situation delightful, Emma was forced to push her way through the brush to maintain her footing. She couldn't imagine Skylar making her way up the incline, but halfway along she was sure she saw the partial outline of a child's footprint in the mud.

Straightening, she cupped her hands and yelled, "Skylaaaar!"

All she heard in response was the rain pounding against the sodden ground.

Rugrat sniffed the area carefully before he dashed on ahead, disappearing around a corner near the crest of the hill. Emma followed at a slower pace, pausing every few moments to call out. But there was no sign of Skylar.

Emma thought of what she'd said to Caden. *Why do I keep making promises I can't keep?* she chided herself. *I promise to make life count for something. I promise Skylar I'll keep them together. Keep them safe. And what have I've done? Lost a little girl in the pouring, frigging rain!*

She'd almost reached the spot where Rugrat had disappeared when the steady pounding of the rain was shattered by an explosion of terrified shrieks, vicious barks, and snarls.

"Skylar?" she shouted hoarsely.

She scrambled the rest of the way up the cliff and tore through the brush to a small clearing. Skylar was clinging to the lower branch of a cedar tree. Beneath her, Rugrat was charging the heels of a massive brown bear that snarled and whirled, swiping at the dog, who was managing to stay just out of reach. At the same time, Emma glimpsed a movement on her right, and a small, furry cub swept past her and disappeared into the brush bordering the trail.

She froze, unable to decide what to do. All she could think of was the warning that had been drummed into her from time she was a little girl — never get between a mother bear and her cub. Only none of the warnings had come with instructions on how to deal with the situation if it actually happened. She stared at the mother bear, who seemed to swell to mammoth proportions, and she had a horrifying glimpse of teeth as the bear roared and slashed at Rugrat, her sharp claws grazing the top of the little dog's head. He yelped and leapt out of reach.

Skylar screamed again and now Emma sprang into action, grabbing the remains of an old alder limb that was lying by the trail.

"Aarrrgh!" she yelled, swinging the limb over her head as she advanced toward the tree where Rugrat continued his frenzied lunging at the bear and jumping back, barely evading its slashing claws. Yelling even louder, Emma thumped the limb against the ground and it instantly disintegrated, leaving her with nothing more than a rotten stub. Tossing it aside, she edged sideways, keeping her eyes on the fray, snatched up a sturdier limb near the tree, and shook it at the bear. This, combined with Skylar's screams and Rugrat's unrelenting attack, was suddenly too much for the bear. With a final roar and swipe of her paws, she turned and lumbered into the bushes to find her cub. The dog tore after them, barking furiously.

"Rugrat! Come!"

Ignoring Emma's command, the dog disappeared beneath a clump of salal, his bark growing fainter as he went deeper into the woods.

"Rugrat!" she screamed, to no avail.

A sob drew her attention from the dog, and she turned to Skylar, who was still clinging to the tree, her fingers wrapped around the limb above her.

"We've got to get out of here, Skylar!" Emma shouted, reaching her arms up to the girl.

"No!" Skylar tightening her grip on the limb. "The bear's gonna come back!"

"That's why we have to leave!" Emma grabbed hold of girl's legs to pull her from the tree. "Please, Skylar! I won't let the bear hurt you!"

Even as she said it, Emma knew Skylar had no reason to trust her, but at that moment the child let go of the branch and slid into her arms. Maintaining a stranglehold around Emma's neck as she stumbled away from the clearing, Skylar cried, "Where's Rugrat?"

"He'll be okay," Emma gasped, heading back toward town. She was certain the scruffy little dog was doomed, but was too intent on maintaining her footing and hanging onto Skylar to dwell on the thought. Slight as the child was, wearing the water-logged denim jacket and rigid with fear, she was rapidly wearing Emma down. Her heart was hammering hard, and she was wheezing and thinking she would have to stop and rest when she saw a flash of orange on the trail ahead. A moment later, Twill appeared.

"What the hell happened?" he asked.

"The bear... and her cub...." Emma said, resting against a stump and fighting for breath. "Rugrat's gone after them."

"He's gonna die!" Skylar sobbed. "You gotta save him!"

Rain dripped from Twill's black sou'wester hat onto his raincoat as he awkwardly patted Skylar's shoulder.

"Hey now, don't fash yourself," he soothed. "We'll get him back." He turned to Emma. "What way were they headed?" She nodded toward the brush behind him, then winced as he gave an ear-splitting two-fingered whistle. When he got no response, he whistled two more times and then gave up.

"We'd best be moving on," he said, lifting Skylar from Emma's arms. "No telling when our friend might come back." He kicked a small mound of mud out of his way. "Dog was nothing but a nuisance, anyways." With Skylar rigid in his arms, he stomped down the hill to his truck, which he had parked as close as he could to the trail. As soon as Emma climbed into the cab, he transferred the girl to her lap, then spun around to whistle one last time. Emma focused on Skylar, who was shivering violently. Her pants and jacket were soaked through.

"We've got to get you out of these wet things," Emma said, reaching for the snap fasteners on the jacket.

"No!" Skylar screamed, crossing her arms tight across her chest. "It's my jacket! It's mine!"

Emma jerked her hand away.

"Okay, okay," she said soothingly.

Instead, she grabbed the blanket that Twill kept in the truck for Rugrat to sit on, and wrapped it around the child's wet clothing. By the time Twill slid behind the steering wheel, Skylar's shivering was already starting to calm.

"What's going to happen to Rugrat?" the girl asked as he started the truck.

"He knows the way home." Twill began manoeuvring the vehicle back and forth until they were facing the road. As they bumped along the track, he growled, "What in the billy blue blazes were you doing out here anyways, girl?"

Skylar stiffened. "She promised we'd stay together."

Ignoring the self-righteous look Twill shot her, Emma said, "I tried, Skylar."

"It's 'cause I'm bad, isn't it?" the girl asked. "I heard that lady. She said Mrs. Pfluger hates me."

The truck jolted as one of the wheels slipped into a pothole and bounced out.

"That woman's an interfering, dunderheaded bitch, if you ask me," Twill growled, forgetting that he had once advocated the same course of action as the principal.

Emma winced at the thought of Skylar's expanding vocabulary of obscenities, but she said, "You're not bad, Skylar. And Mrs. Pfluger doesn't hate you. She just thinks you'll be better off with someone who... with someone else."

Skylar's face twisted as she fought a flood of fresh tears. "You promised!" She leaned away from Emma, resisting comfort. "You promised." Emma kept her arms around the girl, holding the blanket in place.

"Sometimes, Skylar, people want something so bad they make a promise without really understanding that some things are just beyond their control. I truly wanted for you and Julie and Caden to stay together."

Skylar searched Emma's face, then wilted against her. "I don't want to be all by myself," she said, almost inaudibly.

Emma tightened her grip on the girl. "Don't worry, sweetie," she said. "I'm not giving up. I'll make sure you stay together if it's the last thing I do."

Beside her, Twill cleared his throat, but wisely remained silent.

⚜

Sergeant George was standing beside his police cruiser in the school parking lot, and Twill stopped to let him know Skylar was safe. After radioing the news to the station, the sergeant waved his hand at the rain. It was pouring harder than ever.

"You still having the release party tomorrow?"

"Rain don't hurt the fish," Twill said, "and tomorrow's the best moon and tide for releasing salmon. Besides, weather report says this storm's supposed to end later today."

The officer nodded. "Well, if it doesn't, I'll see if I can get the big tent from the Scouts." He tipped his hat to Emma and Skylar. "I'm glad it all worked out," he said, then turned and got into his cruiser.

⚜

Wendy had built a fire, and Emma was grateful for the warmth that enveloped her as she and Skylar and Twill trooped into the laundry room. Sergeant George had already called to say they'd found her.

"You gave us quite a fright, young lady," Wendy boomed, on her way to hug the girl until Julie and Caden crowded in front and wrapped their arms around their sister.

"I'm sorry I wrecked your coat," Julie apologized, tears spilling down her cheeks.

"Did you really see a bear?" Caden asked.

Skylar nodded, her eyes brightening. "Two," she said, raising her arms to mimic the mother bear. "They were climbing up the tree to eat me, an' Rugrat...." Suddenly her face crumpled. "Rugrat got killed," she cried.

Caden stepped back and shook his head. "Nu-uh," he said as a small, furry bundle bounded into the room. "He's right here! He came back!"

214

Skylar dropped to her knees and flung her arms around Rugrat's neck, giggling as he licked her face.

Wendy grinned. "Came back ten minutes ago," she said. "Looked like a drowned rat, so we dried him off with your last towel." She grimaced apologetically at Emma. "I'm afraid it's never going to be white again."

Emma knelt beside Skylar and patted Rugrat's head. "I don't care if it's black as night," she exclaimed. "I'm just glad to see this brave little beggar."

Twill, who had been watching the exchange, slapped his knee. "Well, that's that then," he said. "Now I'd best get back and see if there's anything left of the hatchery."

Emma got to her feet and touched his hand. "Thank you."

He grunted and whistled for the dog. Rugrat gazed up at him and wagged his tail, but didn't move away from Skylar. Twill eyed him with mild amusement. "Guess he's had enough rain for one day," he said. He turned to Emma. "I'll come back later and give you a hand with that tarp," he added, then stepped outside and closed the door.

Wendy collected her coat from the kitchen. "I'll head out, too," she said. "Colin will be wondering where I'm at, and I'm supposed to meet the fiddlers at the school in half an hour for a final practice."

Emma returned from seeing Wendy out to find Julie apologizing once more for ruining Skylar's jacket.

"Actually," Emma said, "I don't think you ruined it, Julie. I promise...." she glanced at Skylar. "... I *bet* we can wash that stain right out."

Skylar eyed her suspiciously. "Really?"

"I have a trick," Emma said. "If you give me your coat, I'll see if I can perform some magic."

"Yeah, right," Skylar scoffed.

"Just try it, Skylar," Julie said. "Please?"

"Yeah, I wanna see the magic," Caden chipped in.

Skylar looked at the large purple blotch staining the front of her coat. "Do you gotta wash the whole jacket?" Emma nodded, and the girl's expression grew even more troubled.

Kneeling beside her, Emma said, "If I can get it to work, it'll be done in a few hours. Either way, as soon as the coat's out of the dryer, you can wear it again."

"But it won't smell like Daddy no more," Skylar whispered, so low that only Emma heard. "No, it won't," she agreed, "but that juice will get mouldy in a few days and start to stink. Then it won't smell like your Daddy either, will it?"

After almost a full minute of contemplation, Skylar solemnly shook her head and slowly undid the snaps on her jacket.

Praying that her grandmother's recipe for stain removal actually worked, Emma plugged in the electric kettle, and when it was boiling, held the jacket over the sink and poured hot water over the purple blob. The children watched in amazement as the grape juice liquefied and disappeared down the drain.

"Now," Emma said with considerable relief, "while it's in the washer, Skylar, you can go up and have a hot shower."

"There's no more towels," Julie reminded her.

Emma frowned, then remembered the sheets from Caden's bed. They were still in the dryer, along with two large towels. Relieved, she grabbed one of the towels and held it out.

Skylar glanced at the doorway, where Caden was watching. "What if Caden takes my jacket? He said he would."

"'Cause you were gonna take Bear-Bear!" Caden said.

Emma rolled her eyes. "If Caden sets foot in the laundry room, I'll wring his neck!"

A hint of a smile touched Skylar's lips.

"Okay," she said, accepting the towel. Still, she insisted on supervising the laundry project herself, standing on a stool as she watched the water pour over the jacket. Finally, with a regretful sigh, she closed the lid. As she passed Caden on her way upstairs she said sternly, "Don't touch it or she's gonna wring your neck!"

Emma was upstairs installing a larger bucket under the worst of the leak and placing the old bucket under one of the new ones when pandemonium broke out below. She rushed downstairs and found Julie trying to pull Skylar away from the side door.

"What on earth...? " Emma said as Twill pushed the door open, sending Skylar stumbling backward, barely missing a collision with her sister. In an instant, Caden, who had been trapped out on the porch, squeezed between Twill and the door and stormed over to the dryer, followed by a drenched Norfolk Terrier.

"I'm gonna get it!" Caden vowed, opening the dryer door.

Rugrat barked fiercely as Skylar pushed her brother aside.

"No!" she shrieked. "Emma said you can't!"

Julie shouted, "Stop it!" but it was lost in the bedlam.

Tightening his hold on the two pizza boxes he was carrying, Twill glared at the three of them. "Shut the bejeezuz up!" he roared, "or I'll cuff a mackerel up the side of your heads!"

The shocked silence that followed was broken by Caden, whose brow was furrowed.

"A mack-a-what?"

Emma wasn't sure which was funnier, Twill's bemused expression or Caden's question, but she began to chuckle, and as the chuckle escalated to a belly laugh, the children joined in.

"Well, seeing as how I'm to be the laughing stock around here," Twill said, "I thinks I'll take these pizzas home and eat them myself!"

Julie sobered at once. "No, please! We'll be good!"

"We're really hungry!" added Skylar.

Emma took the pizzas from Twill. "I've got cold beer in the fridge," she said, leading the way into the kitchen.

When Caden lingered behind, Twill looked at him questioningly. "Surely, my son, you're as hungry as your sisters," he said.

"He doesn't like pizza," Julie told him. "It has more than one thing on it."

Twill laughed. "Well, now," he said, fetching one of the pizza boxes, "have a gander at this here," he said. Crouching, he opened the box so Caden could look inside. "This here's only got cheese, and since cheese is just one thing, there's naught wrong with it now. Am I right?"

Caden studied the pizza, solemnly surveyed Twill, and finally nodded. A few moments later Twill handed the boy a slice on a regular plate. Caden took it to the table and nibbled at the pointed edge, then grinned and took a larger bite. By the time the meal was over, he'd eaten two large slices and was demanding a third for his bedtime snack.

Twill finished his beer, and with his usual knee-slapping "Well that's that then," suggested that he and Emma retire to the roof to attach the tarp. When he saw the hole Emma had made, he shook his head. "I'm thinking you might want to get them roofers here a bit sooner than you were planning."

"First thing Monday morning," Emma said, "I'm going to the bank."

That evening, after dumping an armful of sodden towels into the washer and setting it to the fastest cycle, Emma made some final arrangements for the salmon release festival. Close to midnight, she dialled Kate's number.

"You couldn't have called earlier?" her friend answered sleepily.

Although Emma was in the kitchen, she kept her voice low.

"I only made up my mind a few minutes ago. I'm going to Campbell River first thing tomorrow morning."

"And this has to do with me, how?"

"I need someone to watch the kids."

She heard Kate sputtering on the other end of the line. "Emma! I'm catering the release party, remember? There's no way I can watch three kids."

"They can help you," Emma said. "And Sam can help, too." When Kate's protests continued, Emma's voice grew hard. "Listen, Kate. It was Sam who got me into this damned mess in the first place, and you're the one who said I should take an interest in these kids' welfare. Remember?"

"I said *you* should keep them," Kate said. "Not dump them on me. Anyway, what does this have to do with Campbell River?"

Emma carried the phone to the window and stared up at the stars that had replaced the storm clouds. "I'm going to talk to their aunt. Before she signs their lives away."

The line was silent for so long that Emma wondered if her friend had fallen back to sleep.

"Kate? Are you there?"

"I'm cogitating," Kate said, borrowing one of Twill's favourite words. She sighed. "All right. Sam and I will watch them. But you'd better not be late getting back."

"Twill will murder me if I am," Emma assured her.

Before retiring, she tiptoed into the girls' room. Skylar was asleep, snuggled in her newly washed jacket, but Julie's muffled sniffles revealed that she was still awake. Emma sat on the edge of the bed and gently patted her shoulder.

"I'm sorry about your angel, Julie," she whispered. "But you can make another one. I'll help you."

Julie shook her head. "We're going away on Monday," she sniffed. "Anyways, Skylar's right. That angel was just a stupid dream."

Emma tucked the covers closer around her shoulders. "It made you feel better," she said. "That's not so stupid."

Tears welled in Julie's eyes once more. "But the angel was going to talk to Daddy, and now there's no one who will." She whimpered. "An' I don't want Skylar to go away!"

Emma grabbed a tissue from the bedside table and wiped Julie's eyes.

"I don't want that either," she said. "Skylar told me your Aunty Glenda had a boyfriend.... She said she didn't like his kisses."

"Me neither!" Julie made a face. "But Aunty Glenda told him he couldn't come there no more." She looked at Emma closely. "Is that why Aunty Glenda doesn't want us?"

"No, no. I was just thinking about it." She smoothed Julie's forehead and carefully, staying well away from the "P" word, said, "I may have another trick or two for keeping you and Skylar and Caden together."

Julie's eyes widened. "So we don't gotta go away from here?"

"So you don't have to go to separate homes," Emma corrected. "But I'm not promising anything, Julie. Okay?"

"Okay." Julie smiled. "Thank you, Emma."

Emma sighed heavily as she got up from the bed. Somehow, even when she was trying so hard not to, she had made yet another promise that she probably wasn't going to be able to keep. She turned out the light and went to the bedroom across the hall. Caden was asleep, thumb half in his mouth, with Bear-Bear clutched close to his chest. When Emma pulled the covers over his shoulder, he began sucking his thumb in earnest. There was something so innocent yet so vulnerable about him that she had to fight the urge to pull him into her arms. Instead, she leaned over, gently kissed his forehead, and quietly left the room.

FOURTEEN

With a population of just over thirty-two thousand people, Campbell River was still big enough to get lost in. Emma gripped the slip of paper on which she had written Glenda Duncan's address and peered from it to the street signs she was passing, but none of them claimed to be Sapsucker Lane. After driving up and down the main street for the fourth time, she stopped at a 7-Eleven, purchased a map, and discovered the roadway was tucked between a bird sanctuary and a city park. Glenda's mobile home was located on a huge lot at the end of the lane.

Lots of room for kids to play, she thought.

Emma pulled up to the curb, turned off the ignition, and sat for several minutes reviewing the speech she'd rehearsed all the way from Shinglewood. Suddenly her list of reasons why Glenda had to take responsibility for the children seemed inappropriate. Maybe, beneath all the psychobabble, there was a really good reason why she had said no.

For all I know, she might be an axe-murderer trying to reform! She doubted that Wendy Grieves would have kept that kind of information quiet, but Emma was sorely tempted to turn her truck around and head back to Windrush. Only the thought of Julie's disappointment kept her hand away from the ignition.

"This thing has to be done," she said, and, squaring her shoulders, she stepped out of the truck.

As she walked up the wooden steps to the covered deck of the mobile, Emma eyed an assortment of purple tie-dyed paper lanterns that hung from the rafters. They weren't reassuring, and neither was the woman who answered the door. She was so frail a strong sea breeze could carry her away, and even the blonde curls wreathing her face were ethereal, a feature that was enhanced by her long-sleeved white blouse tucked into a flowing, flowered skirt. Beneath it, her feet were bare. Still, there was something oddly familiar about the way the woman was sizing her up.

"Glenda Duncan?" Emma asked, forcing her eyes away from the woman's purple toenails.

She nodded. "And you're Emma Phillips. I've been expecting you."

"You have?"

"I recognize you from your picture in the paper." Glenda opened the door wider and waved Emma into a room where heavy drapes blocked the light from the windows, but the soft glow of Tiffany lamps dispelled the darkness. The scent of orange, lemon and another aroma Emma couldn't identify emanated from a teardrop-shaped glass beaker that was hissing softly on a corner table.

"I thought Peace and Calming would be in order this morning," Glenda said, nodding toward the beaker. "Would you like to have a seat?"

Emma sank into the cushion of an overstuffed purple brocade couch. She had intended to be fierce with this woman, but it was difficult to generate anger when she was buried in brocade and smothered in peace. She bolstered herself by remembering Julie's despair the night before.

"Why can't you take the kids?" she demanded. "They'll be separated if you don't."

Glenda perched on the edge of her easy chair and carefully

arranged her skirt so it cascaded over her lap and down to the carpet. "You care very much for them, don't you?" she asked.

"Who wouldn't?" Emma said. "They're beautiful children."

"Yes, they are." A sadness passed fleetingly over Glenda's face. "Julie looks just like my little sister."

"And Skylar looks like you," Emma noted.

"Skylar's a drift child," Glenda said.

"A who?"

"A drift child. Her path isn't predictable." When Emma continued to look confused, Glenda explained, "All of us on this earthly plane are on a spiritual journey that will ultimately bring us to a place of pure energy." She paused, and her eyes glazed over as she stared at the ceiling, as if it were the threshold to some cosmic wonderland. "Many souls, such as Julie and Caden, choose to make this journey slowly. Sometimes it can take many lifetimes, and they always make sure in each incarnation that they have an abundant supply of spirit helpers to guide them through the lessons they've come to learn."

Emma shifted impatiently. "And how does this make Skylar a drifter?"

Glenda frowned. "A drift *child*," she corrected. "Skylar is a kind of free spirit. One of those souls who simply drift from one experience to another, hoping that at the end of their journey they will attain enlightenment. And because she has come unprepared, the quality of Skylar's passage into love and light will depend on whether those who've come to help her actually do."

"Meaning yourself," Emma said.

Glenda laughed shortly. "No. My work with Skylar is done. Now we'll only hurt each other. She'll fight my energy and I'll suppress hers. But Spirit has sent others who *can* help her...." She looked at Emma significantly. "... If they choose."

Emma glared back. "Yes, well, that's all very interesting, but what those three kids really need is a home. Together."

"And that's why you've been sent to them," Glenda said.

"Excuse me?"

Bestowing a Mother Mary smile upon her, Glenda fanned her hands, palms up. "Spirit has reunited you and the children."

"Reunited?" Emma struggled to the edge of the cushion and revisited her axe-murderer theory.

"Why, yes," the woman asserted. "You were a family in a previous life." She smiled at Emma. "I saw you in a Salish longhouse. You were the father and Julie was your wife. Caden and Skylar were your children."

Glancing uneasily at the door, Emma wondered if this woman had totally flipped out.

"Spirit often sends me such dreams," Glenda said, "and then I wait for the true meaning to come clear. Your appearance here this morning revealed the message. You were meant to be reunited. My sister and I have been your spiritual helpers, looking after them until Dennis could deliver them to your care."

"Ah… yes. Of course." Emma got to her feet and sidled toward the door. "I'll keep that in mind. And I'm really sorry I bothered you."

Glenda's tinkling laugh filled the room. "You needn't be frightened," she said as if the concept delighted her. She rose and followed Emma out to the deck. "I wish I could take the children. But it won't work. Mine is a spiritual calling, helping to connect lost souls and guiding them to where they're supposed to be."

"I'm sure that will be a great comfort to your nieces and nephew," Emma snapped, her boldness rising as her escape route expanded. "They have spirits, too, you know."

"Of course they do." Glenda flashed a benign smile. "Julie and Caden especially have been waiting a long time to reconnect with you."

"And it doesn't matter to you that I also have a life?"

Her scorn intensified the woman's mystic stance. "It matters," she said. "That's why you have a friend who is going to help you."

Emma shook her head. This lady was too much.

"Ri-i-ght.... Well, I won't waste any more of your time, Mrs. Duncan. Or mine."

Glenda pulled an envelope from a pocket in her skirt. "This is for you. It might help."

Emma tucked what she assumed was a pamphlet on psychic phenomena into her pocket.

"I'll read it later," she said, not wanting to engage Glenda any further. She walked down the steps and onto the drive, but just before she reached her truck, she turned back. The woman was standing on the top step, watching her.

Unable to stop herself, Emma asked, "So what happened to that family in the longhouse?"

"Smallpox," Glenda said. "You have a reminder of it on your forehead."

Emma climbed into the truck and inserted her key into the ignition. Absently, she reached up and touched an old chicken-pox scar next to her hairline. "That's just too weird," she muttered. She started the truck, shifted into gear and pulled away from the curb.

The clouds that had darkened the skies all morning dispersed shortly after lunch and by the time Emma left Campbell River, the sun was shining. Still, her journey home was delayed by construction crews repairing sections of the highway where parts of the roadbed had been washed away. Already late, she groaned when she saw more backhoes and men with shovels working on the approach to the Cold Creek Bridge. She stopped behind a sawhorse barricade and turned off her engine. An exhausted-looking traffic controller came to her window.

"Be at least half an hour before they get a lane cleared," he said. "Part of the approach has caved in."

Emma frowned. "It was okay when I crossed this morning."

"Probably before the transports started moving." He nodded toward a line of trucks waiting on the far side of the bridge. "Between the weight and vibrations, the road just gave way."

As the man moved on to the car behind her, Emma settled back and tried not to think of what Twill would say when she didn't show up to help with the final preparations for the release party. Absently she picked up the envelope Glenda had given her and pulled out a folded sheet of white paper. Her eyes widened as she read the short letter, written in large flowing script.

To Whom It May Concern,

I, Glenda Marie Duncan, do hereby assign guardianship of my nieces, Julie Andrea Warner, Skylar Marie Warner, and my nephew, Caden Dennis Warner, to Emma Phillips of Shinglewood, British Columbia.

Beside her signature ending the letter, Glenda had affixed the current day's date.

A coincidence? Emma wondered, staring at the paper. She shook her head and shoved the letter back in the envelope. It didn't matter. Psychic or not, the woman was obviously trying to ease her conscience by dumping the children onto Emma's lap. *Well, it's not going to work!*

She tossed the envelope aside. Why couldn't she dismiss the children as easily as Glenda Duncan was doing? Make up a bullshit story. Just as Emma's mother had done.

She closed her eyes. She didn't want to think about her mother and the ordeal that had caused their estrangement, but the memories came anyway. As clearly as if it were yesterday, she relived the night twenty-one years earlier when her bedroom door opened and her stepfather entered the room. With her eyes squeezed shut and her heart pounding, she had listened to the floor creaking beneath his feet as he crept toward her bed. The mattress sagged beneath his weight and every protective sense she had was awakened. She smelled his sweat, felt the air move above her head and his fingers in her hair. Afraid to cry out, she made an irritable sound, as if she was in a deep sleep and something had disturbed her, and then rolled on her side, away from him. But he moved with her, his breath grazing her cheek. His hand slid beneath her pajama top and she jerked away and began to scream and lash out with her fists.

"No! No! No!"

In an instant he was gone, but she kept screaming until her mother stumbled into the room.

"Another nightmare, Emma?" The words were thick and slurred from the sleeping pill she'd taken, as she did every night.

"Someone was in my room!"

Fiona turned on the light and looked around. "There's nobody here but you and me." She tottered across the room and sat beside Emma, who was clutching her blankets to her chest. "It was just a bad dream, honey."

"No, Mom! It was Peter. He was on my bed. He touched me...."

She felt her mother stiffen and inch away from her. "It couldn't have been, Emma. Your stepfather's in bed, asleep." She frowned. "And that's an awful thing to suggest about a man who has been so good to both us." The effect of the sleeping pill was wearing off and her speech was almost normal as she launched into the story of how Peter Friesen had saved her life, a story that Emma had not only lived through, but had also heard many times before.

"You know how bad it was for me after your father died, Emma. The hospitals. The drugs. I just wanted to die. And then I met Peter, and right away I began getting better. He's a good husband and a wonderful father, and he'd never, ever hurt you." She patted Emma's back, but there was no comfort in the gesture.

After her mother returned to her own room, Emma moved her dresser in front of the door.

The following night her stepfather started the first of seven shifts at the town's main sawmill, and Emma spent that week collecting as many empty tin cans as she could find in the recycling bins that lined the back alley. By Friday morning, when his final shift ended, she had gathered enough to make a small tower in front of her door, and a hammer was hidden under her covers. But no one visited her room that night and she had fallen asleep watching the door handle, waiting for it to turn.

It was three weeks before the tower came crashing down. Emma had awakened instantly, and her hands trembled as she grabbed the hammer and switched on the light. The door was ajar and the cans were scattered across the floor when her mother came into the room.

"Are you all right?" she cried, and this time there was no slurring of her words. When she had confirmed that Emma was safe, she fisted her hand to her throat. "My goodness! I almost jumped out of my skin! It's a good thing Peter hasn't returned from his poker game yet." She avoided looking at the hammer in Emma's hand. "What on earth happened?" There was an edge to the question and desperation in Fiona's eyes as she looked at her daughter, and with a feeling of shock, Emma realized that her mother was pleading with her.

She knows, Emma thought. *She knows it was him, but she doesn't care.*

A coldness swept through her, numbing the pain that wouldn't let her breathe. And in a voice she scarcely recognized as her own, she said, "My sculpture just fell over."

Relief flooded Fiona's face and she escaped back to her room to wait for the man who had saved her life. In a daze Emma stared at the closed door. Then she slipped out of bed and restacked the cans. The next morning she left for Shinglewood.

✦✦✦

Emma jumped as a horn blared behind her. She opened her eyes and saw that the barricade had been removed, but the traffic controller was still holding up the stop sign. In the rear-view mirror she saw that the man in the car behind her was shaking his fist at the workers.

"Suck it up," Emma muttered.

She looked back at the envelope and frowned. She was sure Wendy would find good placements for the children, but there was no guarantee they would last. Every month it seemed there was another announcement in the newspapers of funding cuts to Family Services, and the family care supervisors were notoriously overloaded with case files. And while Emma knew that most foster parents really cared about children, she also knew there were a few among them who were only in it for the benefits they received. And sometimes, those benefits weren't about money.

What would Julie or Skylar or even Caden do if an unwanted visitor came to their bedroom in the night? She shuddered at the thought and picked up the letter once more. She reread Glenda's statement and stared out the window. Then she thumped the steering wheel with her fist.

"Oh, what the hell!"

At that moment the men and the backhoes moved to one side and the traffic controller turned his sign so it now read "SLOW." Emma started the truck shifted into gear, and slowly drove over the bumpy approach and onto the bridge. Once she was across, she picked up speed.

Maybe I'll make it to the party after all.

She felt strangely light-hearted, and as she drove along she began whistling "The Entertainer," that old ragtime tune from *The Sting.*

229

The sound of fiddlers playing a catchy polka reached Emma long before she pulled into the hatchery parking lot. All evidence of the previous night's rain had vanished, and the dusky twilit sky was streaked with fiery clouds that were matched by the flames leaping from Sergeant George's barbecue grill, which was set up in front of the hatchery's education centre. As she threaded her way through the crowd, pausing to exchange greetings with the people she knew, Emma's stomach growled, reminding her that it had been hours since she'd eaten lunch. Before she reached the barbecue, however, Kate appeared, carrying a tray of buns and frozen burgers.

"So what happened to you?" she asked crossly.

"Not my fault," Emma said. "Road crews closed the Cold Creek Bridge. They were clearing a washout." She scanned the crowd. "Where are the kids?"

Kate shifted her load and slowed her pace toward the barbecue where Sergeant George, wearing a massive white apron, was flipping burgers. "In the lunch room," she said. "Twill sent Skylar in there for fighting with Danny Shuter."

Emma stomach tightened. "Oh, great," she groaned. "The last thing I need is for her to be acting up right now."

"She was good all day," Kate said. "They all were until folks started arriving. That's when the kids began asking how come you weren't back." They reached a long table near the barbecue, where people were coating their burgers with relish and ketchup. Balancing the tray on the edge of the table, she opened the bags of buns and dumped them into a bowl. "Skylar kept saying some magical trick you told them about hadn't worked, and you weren't coming back."

"It's about time," Sergeant George boomed, grabbing the tray from Kate and laying the burgers out on the empty grill. As they began to sizzle, he switched his attention to Emma.

"So how did it go?"

"Not the way I thought it would," she said, "but maybe better. I can tell you more after I find Sam."

Kate inclined her head to the base of the tower where a beverage table was set up. "He's tending bar," she said, glancing at a tub filled with ice and canned drinks. "Get him to send over another case of pop. The kids are draining this thing as fast as I fill it."

Kate began gathering up discarded paper plates and empty pop tins, and Emma walked over to the tower. She waited several minutes before the bar cleared and Sam noticed her.

"So Kate tells me you went on a mission today," he said, setting down a freshly opened wine bottle and untwisting the cork from the corkscrew.

Emma nodded. "Hopefully not a useless one." She pulled out the envelope Glenda had given her and handed it to him. "The children's aunt has signed custody of them over to me. I don't know if she can legally do that or not."

While Sam scanned the letter, Emma sold a beer to Joe Spangle and poured a glass of wine for his wife.

"The letter will certainly help, if that's what you want," Sam said when they were alone once more. He looked at her. "And is it?"

She leaned against the cement wall of the tower. "Yeah," she said, "it is. I had a lot of time to think about it on the way back from Campbell River. It sounds crazy, but since those kids have come into my life, I've felt different. Like there's a reason for me to be here."

He shook his head. "What reason is there for any of us to be here? It just *is*, Emma. We don't have to go around accepting other people's responsibilities to justify our existence."

"No, we don't." She dug at the gravel with the toe of her shoe. "Only it feels good, Sam. Having them around. Worrying about someone besides me for a change." She took a deep breath. "I really want to do this."

He folded the letter slowly and put it back into the envelope. "And what about your job?" he asked, handing it back to her. "If Kazinski sends us more work, we'll be too busy for you to be taking time off."

"Then we'll have to hire that secretary you've been promising me, Sam. And Kate says I should get a computer so I can work from home if I have to."

Twill stepped up to the bar and accepted the beer Sam handed him. "Now why would you be workin' from home, Emmie?" he asked, popping the tab and releasing a noisy fizz of air.

"I'm going to adopt the kids," she said, meeting his gaze and steeling herself to withstand his protest. She felt deflated when he simply shook his head.

"Well, I guess you gotta do what you gotta do," he said gravely. "So long as you understand you'll be doing it on your own."

Arriving at the bar in time to hear Twill's pronouncement, Kate shook her head. "Emma won't be alone," she corrected. "Folks in this town have always looked after each other. Like supporting this hatchery, Twill." She grinned. "I think it's a great idea. Those kids need a home and Emma needs a life. Perfect combo, if you ask me."

"No one did ask you," Twill said.

"Now, now, there's no need to be rude," Sam said. "Besides, as near as I can tell, I'm the biggest loser if she adopts them."

"Nonsense," Kate said. "Emma's the best legal assistant you've ever had. She could handle the work of three lawyers and still look after a pack of kids."

The group fell silent as Wendy walked up to the bar, dressed for the occasion in a plaid flannel shirt and denims, and sporting a derby hat decorated with an assortment of fishing flies.

"What's going on?" she asked.

"Emma wants to adopt the kids," Kate said, watching Sam pour a glass of red wine.

Sam said, "It's not quite so simple, dear. The adoption will still have to be approved by the Ministry."

"The child welfare system has been taking a beating in this province for years," Wendy said as she gently swirled the wine in her glass. "So everything has to be done by the book."

Emma held up the envelope. "So this letter from their aunt giving me custody won't make a difference?"

Conversations droned around them, interspersed with an occasional burst of laughter, but the group around the bar was silent as Wendy scanned the letter's contents.

"It might," she said at last. "Especially if you agree to take the foster parenting courses the Ministry has developed, and a few more on the treatment of ADHD."

"Skylar doesn't have any attention problems," Emma argued, shoving the letter into her jacket pocket.

Kate raised her hands. "For God's sake, Emma, work with the woman, will ya? It sure won't hurt to take the courses whether the kid's got problems or not."

Twill waved his beer bottle at Emma. "You're not thinking any of this through, Emmie. Three weeks ago you didn't even know them kids. You don't have a clue what kind of storms are brewin' inside of 'em after all the bad stuff they've been through."

"He's right about that," Wendy agreed. "Those children have suffered a lot of abuse in the past. And I can tell you, Emma, the heartbreak they'll experience if you take them on and then dump them later will be far worse than if you end it now."

Emma's eyes narrowed. "I tried to tell you that when you left them with me in the first place, Wendy. Now it's too late. Besides, when I commit to something, I don't walk away. And now if you people will excuse me, I have some children who badly need reassurance that their lives are not going to end tomorrow morning."

Turning on her heel, she stomped away, but not before hearing Twill say, "She's right about that, Wendy. There's nothing Emmie takes on that she don't finish."

The tables and most of the chairs had been removed from the lunchroom, accentuating its usual starkness. Julie was sitting on one of the remaining chairs, holding her dolls, while Caden, thumb in mouth, was curled up in the other with Bear-Bear clutched in his arms. Skylar sat cross-legged on the floor, bouncing her soccer ball against the wall. As soon as she saw Emma, she caught the ball and held it in front of her like a shield. The kids' expressions held a mixture of fear and yearning, and a need so visible Emma was overwhelmed by the enormity of the task she was undertaking. Wordlessly, she stepped all the way into the room and closed the door, leaning against it as she took a deep breath. Finally, she spoke.

"How would you lot like to stay with me permanently?"

They kept staring as if they didn't comprehend — or believe — her.

"You said we couldn't," Skylar said at last, her voice hostile, but hope clearly flickering in her eyes. "You said they wouldn't let you."

Emma nodded. "I did, but your Aunty Glenda has signed a letter saying she wants me to be your guardian. Mrs. Grieves says if I take some courses and we all go to counselling, they'll let it happen."

Julie put her dolls aside and got to her feet. "Will you?" Emma nodded, and the girl crossed the room, wrapped her arms around Emma's waist, and began to sob.

"Hey, I thought you'd be happy," Emma said, prompting a

choked laugh from the girl. "And how about you?" she asked Skylar, who was mulling over the announcement. "You willing to go to counselling with me?"

Skylar shrugged. "I guess so." She tossed the ball at the far corner of the room, jumped to her feet, and ran to catch it on the rebound.

Caden took his thumb from his mouth and stared, first at Skylar, who was dancing around the ball, and next at Julie, whose arms remained wrapped around Emma's waist.

"How come Jooolie's crying, Emma?"

"She's happy-crying, Caden!" Skylar shouted, bending over him and nuzzling her forehead on his. "'Cause we're all gonna live together with Emma. Forever and forever!"

Caden wriggled out from under her and went to stand in front of Emma.

"Is that true?"

Emma nodded.

With a loud whoop, he joined Skylar in a raucous dance. They both grabbed Emma's hand, pulling her and Julie into a circle. None of them heard the door open or saw Twill step into the room.

"I hate to break up the party," he said, "but there's some fish waiting to be released into the river."

A short time later, beneath a million stars and the sliver of a new moon, and surrounded by a hushed crowd of villagers, Twill stood beside Emma as they watched the tiny smolts flow out of a pipe leading from the containment pen to a small side stream that led down to the river. On the bank of the stream the children knelt with their faces almost touching the water.

"What if they get eaten by a seal or a big fish?" Julie asked.

Skylar snorted. "Fish are smart. They'll swim away and hide!"

Their interest in the fish lasted until the numbers coming

from the pipe dwindled to just a few wriggling smolts, at which point Caden got to his feet and slapped his knee. "Well, that's that, then," he said.

Emma looked at Twill, and they shared a smile.

EPILOGUE

The white-robed pastor finished his eulogy to Dennis Warner by inviting the crowd gathered around the coffin at the Shinglewood Cemetery to join in a moment of contemplation. The respectful silence that followed was shattered by the cry of a seagull, a sound that drew everyone's eyes skyward, where a ray of midmorning sun illuminated the underwings of the bird, turning them snowy white.

"It's like an angel!" Julie pointed with the red rose that Glenda Duncan had given her to lay upon the coffin. In her other hand Julie clutched a crudely shaped ceramic angel, its polished white finish resembling runny icing.

I should have helped her put on the glaze, Emma thought. But Julie had insisted she do it all herself. Feeling hot and sticky in her woollen suit jacket and skirt, which was the only black outfit she had in her closet, Emma had positioned herself behind the children and Glenda, ready to step in if needed, but respecting that this was their moment of closure.

Beside his older sister, clutching his own rose, Caden asked, "Does it know where Daddy's gone, Julie?"

Skylar hissed from his far side. "Daddy's in the box, Caden. I seen him when Aunty Glenda peeked inside." Several petals from Skylar's rose were scattered at her feet, after being thumped loose against her leg. Most of its lower stem was hidden by the sleeve of her denim jacket.

She's made a lot of progress in one week, Emma thought, studying the middle Warner. The two of them had already attended a joint counselling session, and she smiled, recalling the amused expression on the psychologist's face when Skylar asked if *he* had ever been in a fight as a child. After he foolishly admitted that he had, she asked if his doctor had made him take stupid pills as a consequence.

"She's always ten steps ahead of everybody," Twill had pointed out as they tore shingles off the roof in preparation for the contractor. "And there's never any telling what she's gonna say next."

That was why Emma braced herself now, as Glenda Duncan stepped into the children's argument.

Dressed in a purple cotton sari and sandals adorned with buttercup blossoms, Glenda assumed a mystical stance, arms raised as she gazed heavenward at the gull and said in an awed tone, "His *body* is in the coffin, Skylar. His *spirit* is all around us. I can feel him."

"Yeah, right," Skylar scoffed. "Our daddy's a seagull."

"No...." Glenda's words were slow and measured. "I think he's not any one thing. He's just... around us."

"I can feel him, too," Julie said.

Skylar's eyes narrowed. "So he can hear what we're saying?"

"I... suppose so," Glenda said, then, before the gleam in her niece's eye could be transformed into words, she added, "I think it's time to put our roses on the coffin."

Leading by example, Glenda stepped over to the polished cedar casket and placed her own red rose on the lid. Then she lifted Caden so he could do the same, along with a drawing he had made — surprisingly, Emma thought, not of tombstones but of a big yellow sun shining down on a dog and a cat. Julie came behind her aunt and, rising up on tiptoes, placed her rose and the ceramic angel between the first two flowers.

"Aunty Glenda says the angel will show you where to go, Daddy," she said softly.

When Julie stepped back, Glenda looked expectantly at her youngest niece, who had resumed thumping the rose against her leg. With a final scowl at her aunt, she marched forward and dropped what was left of the flower among the others, then pulled two crudely fashioned flies from her pocket and placed them between Julie and Caden's gifts with much greater care. As she stepped away from the coffin, she squinted up at the seagull.

"Tell him not to catch the fishes we set free," she shouted. With an abrupt turn, she stomped across the grass to Emma's side.

"Can we go home now?" she asked.

"Works for me," Emma said.

Ten minutes later, with the three Warners belted into their seats, she backed the truck from the cemetery, shifted gears, and started down the road to Windrush. There her grandmother's table was laid out with an array of potluck edibles provided by her neighbours — the same people who had attended the funeral service of a man they had never even met, but whose children were now in their care.

ROSELLA LESLIE was born in Alberta, but spent most of her life in British Columbia. She moved to the Sunshine Coast in 1980, residing for a time on a floathouse at Clowhom Falls. She has written feature articles and short fiction for local and national magazines, and has authored several nonfiction books. Her first novel, *The Goat Lady's Daughter,* was published by NeWest Press in 2006.

A past member of the Sunshine Coast Festival of the Written Arts and the SunCoast Writers Forge, Rosella (along with co-writers Stephen Hume, Alexander Morton, Betty C. Keller, Otto Langer, and Don Staniford) was a winner of the Roderick Haig-Brown Regional Prize for *A Stain Upon the Sea: West Coast Salmon Farming.*